Copy

Edited by P. J. Blakey-Novis, Red Cape Publishing

First Edition Published 2021 by Red Cape Publishing

The characters and events in this book are fictitious. Any similarities to real persons, living or dead, is coincidental and not intended by the author.

SWEET LITTLE CHITTERING

A HORROR ANTHOLOGY

CONTENTS

The Old Man's Truth at Foroferan's Walk by Rae Dixon

A Night Out from the Paradise Inn by Tony Sands

Helga's Crusty von Buns Bakery by Freddy Beans

The Spivey Lane Boot Strap by Damon Rickard

A Killing in the Local Butcher's by Bob Pipe

Hawthorn Lane by Matt Davies

A Break-In at St. Benedict's by P.J. Blakey-Novis

A Story on Baker Street by Jack Joseph

Dream Cottage by Richard Rowntree

Rare Editions at Mysterious Magpie Books by Tristan Sargent

Gingerbread Lane and its Vicious Cycle by MJ Dixon

Bryan vs The School Basement by Annie Knox

History Comes to Life at the Museum by Teige Reid

Epilogue

The Old Man's Truth at Foroferan Walk

Rae Dixon

The old man stared at me as he wheezed through his last breaths. For the first time his eyes showed fear, the normal steely, hateful look finally broken and transformed as he realised he's moments away from dying and facing whatever awaits him. I chose this time to speak the last words I'd ever speak to him.

"Bet you're wondering why I moved you back here from the care home?" His eyes continued to stare as he wasn't strong enough to respond. "I wanted to be the last face you saw. And to tell you how happy I am that you're finally going to die, you piece of shit. Only we knew the real you. That's why she left you, but I'll never understand why she left *me*. I may only have a couple of scars left that you can see, but I'll always have the ones inside. So look at me and know as you die that I hate you with every ounce of my being."

I looked down at the chain around his neck, a single key at the end of it that has been there for as long as I can remember. "And now I'll also finally be able to find out what you've hidden from me my entire life when I take that fucking key off your cold, dead neck."

He brought an old weak hand up to the key and held onto it, those fearful eyes never breaking from mine. Then with every ounce of strength he had, he managed to gasp the last words he would ever speak. "I'm sorry," wheezed from his dying lips.

I leaned towards him, placed my mouth by his ear and whispered back, "I don't care." I then watched the life drain from him, closed my eyes and sighed with a sense of relief as a lifelong weight was lifted from my shoulders. The room, his old room, fell silent, the belongings in there exactly as they were when I shipped him off to the care home. I always knew this day would come. The day I brought him home to die. I wanted to surround him with everything he missed whilst cooped up in that shitty place which really shouldn't have the word *care* in it. But I deliberately chose the cheapest and worst reviewed place I could find. Who knew Tripadvisor could help you find somewhere completely awful to live out the remainder of your life?

Of course, over time, I had gone through his things to see if I could find anything that would open up his secret world to me and maybe help me understand myself a little more. The world Mum left him because of, where he was out most nights and didn't attempt to come up with an excuse when he got home. I was only six when she walked out on us. That morning I left for school and instead of Mum picking me up it was him. Standing there, cigarette hanging out of his mouth, hands in his pockets, leaning against his beat-up blue car. I wish I could tell you what the car was but at six my knowledge of makes and models was limited, and he scrapped it fairly soon after that day.

There were letters to and from girlfriends, quite the variety of them and all whilst he was married to

Mum. I figured that's why she never bothered asking for reasons he wasn't home, because she already knew. I found trophies from when he was at school and he seemed to be quite the athlete, but his report cards suggested that was about all he was good at. His yearbooks showed he was neither loved nor hated but just someone who didn't really matter. Which is unusual as often those that excel at sports are popular by default, so I presumed his winning personality was the reason. There was little to nothing in the way of memories of him and Mum. Barely a photo to be found and no knickknacks that they had shared between them. All I really discovered going through his personal belongings, minus his clothes and some books as I at least let him keep those, was that his marriage to my mum was clearly loveless - and not just for her from the bruises he left on her, but for him as well. Either that or he actually thought he loved her and so keeping memories of her around was uncomfortable, however I doubted that was the reason. Sadly, I also found a letter to him from Mum telling him she was pregnant with me, and it seems like that was the reason they stayed together for as long as they did. I made peace with the fact I didn't choose to be grown inside her, so it wasn't my fault.

And so, all that is left to try and fill these voids of understanding is a largish safe hidden away in his wardrobe for which he keeps the key hanging round his neck. It was clear that whatever was in there was very important to him and I felt that this was finally the moment I might understand him a little more. All I know of him is that he was a drunk and he was abusive. I wanted to take the key off him immediately, but it had been a long day and I was feeling far too tired. I had waited this long so one more night wasn't going to hurt. Besides, tomorrow will be the day of the village fete and if whatever is in that safe is depressing then at least I can go and eat candy floss and some of Helga's baked goods to try to cheer myself up.

I closed the door to his room, leaving his lifeless body on its own as it should have been when it was alive, and walked into mine. When I moved back in to ship him off to care, he hadn't done a thing to my room and the moment I first walked back into it I was eighteen again. Posters of my favourite bands still adorned the walls as well as a few of the women I had a crush on as a horny teenager. The walls were still painted black and the few albums I had accidentally left behind on the shelves were covered in dust. As executor of my dad's estate, which was minimal to say the least, I took whatever wasn't going towards his care costs and had my room redecorated to remove all traces of that life and start it afresh. I undressed and climbed into bed, wearily puffing up the pillow and pulling the duvet over me. I laid my head down and drifted off to sleep, hoping the dreams wouldn't come.

My daily alarm went off, beeping at me to get up. I have tried using a gentler method, but I found it all too easy to snooze so went for the angry sounds to force me out of bed. I fell into my daily routine of shit, shave, shower, brush teeth, do hair. It was a weekend so I could wear more comfortable clothes and I picked out a clean pair of jeans and a t-shirt with the logo for the band *The Wildhearts*. On my bedside table was a Bluetooth speaker which I picked up and took into my father's room. The smell was distinctly worse that morning than on the previous night but not unbearable just yet. I was aware that awful odour wouldn't be far off, so I called the village coroner, explained what's happened and he let me know he'd be over by 11am as he wanted to get off to the fete by twelve. I hung up, connected my phone to the speaker and blasted heavy, angry music as the soundtrack to the opening of the safe.

I grabbed his hand and struggled to move it from where he had it clasped around his key before he died. Bloody rigor mortis had set in! The fingers creaked and cracked as I unfurled them from the key. As soon as it was loose enough, I yanked it from his neck and headed over to the wardrobe where the safe had waited patiently for me and I opened the door. And there it was, that little steel box of mystery and after all these years I could finally see what was in it. I placed the key in the lock and turned, hearing the satisfying sound of the metal teeth unclamping. Placing my hands on the handle to open it, I suddenly froze and realised that after this there could be no more stories I could make up to help me understand who I am. This could give me everything I need and have wanted, and you know what they say about getting what you wish for. My hand released from the safe handle and I sat back against the bed, my father's body above me, still managing to control me even in death. The fear of potentially knowing who he was stopped me dead in my tracks. Images of my mum flooded my mind's eye and the thought that this could be where he kept everything about her gave me the impetus I needed to see this through. I grasped that handle tight and yanked the safe door open. What I eventually set my eyes upon was both completely surprising yet at the same time, completely expected.

There were newspaper clippings of stories of women that went missing, some of which the bodies were eventually found but the majority not. Stapled to these were three polaroid pictures, all of the woman in the article they were attached to. The first was of one woman smiling, and some of the women were even laughing. The second was of a woman tied up and frightened. The third was of their bloody, beaten body with my father sat beside it, a look of pride adorning his face. The women were not just from Sweet Little Chittering but from the neighbouring towns and villages, as well as some further afield. As I looked through them, I saw faces I recognised, one being the mother of a friend from school. Someone I remembered in the multitude of names that ended the letters sent to my father. The internet clearly hadn't created this sort of monster, emails and instant messaging just made it easier for them. Letters must have taken a lot of effort to build up that trust and so patience was clearly one of his virtues. He saw his prize and was prepared to play the long game to get it and, who knows, maybe that was part of the thrill for him. The chase, as it were.

    I went through article after article until I stopped on one in particular. I saw the face of my mother staring back at me. The article dated two weeks after she had left us stating that the search for the missing woman was being called off and she had been presumed dead. Stapled in the top left corner were three polaroid pictures. I dropped it to the floor in shock and before I knew it floods of tears were streaming down my face. I couldn't believe he had done that to my mother and then casually picked me up from school that day. Oh God, the thought she might still have been alive but hidden somewhere just waiting for him to kill her. I never had children myself, mainly due to worrying I'd be as much of a failure at being a father as he was to me, but the one thing I knew is that I could never conceive of hurting the mother of my child. I guess having to raise me on his own was his punishment for that one. And I use *raise* in the loosest possible of terms.

    Having now found out who my father really was I decided what I needed was a drink. It may only have been 10am but sometimes the term too early for a drink is lost in a situation. I picked myself up, my body feeling unusually heavy, and headed downstairs to my drinks cabinet. In there was literally a bar's worth of liquor and then some. Towards the back sat a bottle of expensive Japanese whisky which I'd mainly bought as an investment but if ever there was a time to say fuck it, that was it. I grabbed it and cracked it open without a second thought, pouring it neat into one of my pretentious whiskey glasses I kept in the same cabinet. I knocked the shot back in one go and the sumptuous warmth ran down the back of my throat. Glass still in hand, I wiped my mouth with the back of my hand, closing my eyes to enjoy the sensation of the expensive liquid running through me. I poured a second glass and did the same. The third glass I sipped, I wanted to start savouring the taste, enjoying the delicacy of it, washing me away from the reality of the day.

 A bang at the door woke me. I didn't even realise I'd fallen asleep. Clearly the whiskey mixed with the emotional heavyweight of a morning tired me out. I picked my phone up from beside me and looked at the time. 10.30am. The coroner must be early. I forced myself up and headed to the door, wishing I hadn't arranged this but also knowing that it wouldn't be long before the smell became too much. Upon opening the door, I was greeted by a tall, very skinny man, dressed entirely in black, looking almost exactly as you would expect a stereotypical coroner to look. He held a hat in his hands, tightly clasped to his body and wore a smile on his face. The words he then said did not make a good bedfellow with that expression. "Apologies for being early sir. And may I say I am extremely sorry for your loss." He purred the words through his gleaming white toothy smile and so I thanked him and gestured him in. He was followed by two men, much larger in frame than he, and one was carrying a large black piece of plastic which I could only presume to be the bag to carry my father's corpse away in. I directed them upstairs and informed them that I wouldn't be watching as they zip him up. Just as they started to head to his bedroom, I suddenly remembered that I'd left all the newspaper clippings and photos all over the floor. I knew they were his killings but the sins of the father and all that.

I hurriedly barged past them on the stairs and made my excuses as I knocked into them.

"I completely forgot. He had a bowel movement as he passed."

"That's fine sir. It's perfectly normal for that to happen and something we have seen many times."

Shit! I needed to add more to this.

"Oh, well yes, I am sure you have, but this is my first time and I'd prefer not to have you go into a room in my house and the first thing you are greeted with is a pile of poo."

"I totally understand sir. You go ahead."

I thanked him again and headed into the room. I quickly picked up everything and put it back in the safe, closing the door but not locking it. Even quicker, I then ripped the duvet off the bed, pulled the sheet as far as I could, then rolled him off it which released the other side and allowed me to take it off. I rolled him back over, the smell of death penetrating my nose and making me gag. I bundled the sheet and duvet up to look like I was hiding something in it and made my way back past them.

"Thank you. He's all yours." I was fairly certain when they walked in they would be able to smell that there hadn't been, until a few seconds ago, a pile of shit in there.

It only took a few minutes for them to package him up and carry him out the front door. I waved them off, thanking them again, and checked the time on my phone. 10.45. I decided I needed to get out, so I grabbed my car keys and headed to the fete. A little fresh air would do me good so I chose to take the long way round, air con on full blast and window rolled down. It's something I do to make me feel like I am driving a convertible.

I headed out of Foroferan Walk and down towards the Paradise Inn, which would normally be the way to get to the green. Knowing I'd want to stop in for a quick drink if I went past it, I chose to turn right instead of left and took the scenic route down the wealthy Spivey Lane. The warm air through the open window and cold air con blew into my face and I let the moment take me away. My thoughts took me to simpler times, relaxing on a boat, owned by a wealthy woman I had met and had a short fling with. I was enjoying this moment of reminiscence until I heard a bang on the side of my car. Snapping back into reality I hit the brakes. I stared in the rear-view mirror and saw a man on the floor and a woman from the house across the street running out towards him. I got out of the car and stood there in stunned silence.

"You going to help or just stand there?" she yelled at me.

I realised I needed to go and help sort this poor man out. The woman asked the man if he was okay and thankfully he replied that he thinks so. He didn't seem to be too hurt and strangely hadn't said a single thing to me, almost like he didn't even care that I was there. I felt like I could have just got right back in my car and driven off and he'd have been fine with it. I was confused by how this was playing out. She told him that she was about to head to the fete with her family and then asked me to help get him up and inside. I was very unsure about all this; it was certainly a strange turn to the day. But, being the good citizen I am, I did what was needed and grabbed him under his arm and helped him hobble into the house. I took this opportunity to apologise to him and his odd reactions to this continued as he told me it was all his fault. I thanked him, I seemed to be doing a lot of that, and without thinking I told him that was very generous, which I realised was a strange response. He wouldn't know I'd had a few drinks already, so I started hoping I hadn't made him suspicious. Last thing I needed was them to call the police and they smell whiskey on my breath. After we laid him down, I looked at the woman and tried my best to express that I would prefer to leave at this point, to which she seemed to get the message and told me I could go. I headed out after apologising again and got back into my car which was still in the middle of the road.

I looked at myself in the mirror and took some deep breaths. "You're a mess today," I mumbled. Finding out what that bastard did to my mother had really messed my head up. I wondered if it was the best day to be out and about as I wasn't thinking straight, but ultimately decided that I needed to get on with some regular activities to get my mind off things and sort my head space out. So I started the car and continued on my way to the fete.

It was still early so there were plenty of parking spaces available which meant I could pick my spot wisely. After much consideration I went for one that was close but off to the side, making it easier to get out once it fills up. I made the short walk to the entrance and stopped to study the photos adorning it, finding one of myself with my father from when I was still in school. Without anyone noticing, I quickly snatched it down and ripped it up, placing the shards of the picture in my pocket and calmly entering the village green.

Plenty of people walk to this event so whilst the car park was currently quiet, there were enough people here for it to have atmosphere. When I would come to these as a child, you recognised everyone. Now I look through the faces and there are many I do know but also many I don't. Sweet Little Chittering grows in number each year and it has now become impossible to know everyone. The people in the centre of town still retain that value but it's those from the outskirts who can still be viewed as strangers, even if they've owned their house for years. Our house has always been on the outskirts, so we had to make that extra effort to feel part of the community. I say we, I mean I. My father didn't care about that side of things, which surprised me doing what he did as being the weird outsider type surely must have looked more suspicious. But it didn't seem to matter as he never got caught.

As I walked round, I spotted a woman on her own, who looked very high class from the way she presented herself. Well-tanned and nothing fake about it, so clearly had plenty of time to spend working on it. Her hair looked immaculate like she'd just come from a salon appointment and a fete didn't seem a good enough reason to get a style done specially for. Her outfit was well co-ordinated from style to colour, and she had flash looking jewellery. Importantly none of which was on her ring finger. So, either she had a partner elsewhere here, on their way, or she didn't have one. Just from her look she seemed interesting, so I was hoping it was the latter and that she had an interest in men. Although she did seem a bit too perfect to let herself be wasted on us, so I was fully prepared to be well knocked back here. Unlike my father, I am not in any sort of relationship and don't plan on being. It is not suitable to my way of life, but I am always up front about that.

She was standing by the game where you have a flimsy fishing pole with a hook on the end and try and capture a plastic duck with a ring attached to its head. I used my phone to check how I looked and realised it wasn't great but considering the day I'd had so far, it was better than I expected. I casually walked up behind her and said, "Going fishing?". I couldn't think of anything better in that moment.

She turned to me and replied, "Excuse me?", which seemed like the appropriate way to react to this situation from her perspective.

"The fishing game. Well, it's not fishing really is it. More like duck hunting."

"Oh, haha. I see. No, not really my thing."

I couldn't work out if that laugh was forced or not.

"Yeah, me neither," I replied. "I'm definitely more of a throw a ring over a bottle kind of guy."

She laughed again, this time it felt genuine which made me realise the last one was almost certainly false.

"So, you here with the family?" I asked.

"No. Just thought I'd get out of the house for a couple of hours."

"A little bit of me time. I get that. I'm kinda here for the same thing. Been quite the morning for me. But these things are always more fun when you have company."

She smiled warmly at me, so I mirrored her and returned it.

"You know what?" she asked. "You're right. Would you like to join me in finding a ring over a bottle game?"

"I would indeed."

We spent the next couple of hours walking round the fete, chatting about anything and everything. She used to be a teacher until one of the children in her class sadly passed away from cancer which hit her really hard and she felt she could no longer deal with those sort of emotional connections as part of work. So she now runs a successful jewellery business from her home. She also told me of a friend she lost recently that committed suicide by jumping off her building during a blackout. A place called Castle Heights she said. Personally, I'd never heard of it, but apparently the night of this blackout even ended with the army arriving. She explained that she no longer gives herself time for relationships and never really wanted children of her own so instead she has four cats. I lied and told her I love cats when the fact is I can't stand the things. But hating cats is not a popular stance these days, especially in the age of the viral cat video. I often wonder if cats have surpassed deities as the most worshipped of things. When I explained about also not wanting children this seemed to delight her. She told me that normally she is greeted with surprise and then dismay at the unconscionable decision of a woman to not want children.

I continued to tell her things about me, some that were true and some that were not, managing to make things fit to what I thought she'd like to hear. I wanted her to feel at ease with me so I made sure I put forward the person that would do that, even if it meant telling her that I used to volunteer at a cat sanctuary. As we walked, talked and played games, I saw the man I hit with my car as he grabbed one of Helga's baked goods. I may not live in the centre of the village, but Helga's legendary baking was known for miles along with her also legendary attitude problem. He was walking just fine, and I wondered if he had faked the whole thing. And if he did then why? I weighed up staying with this rather wonderful woman or following Mr Mysterious and confronting him about it. Ultimately, I decided I needed to carry on with what I was doing otherwise I wouldn't have put my needs to rest and my thinking would start to get confused.

So, I ran the next thirty minutes or so around my head. *I'll offer to take her somewhere else, and we'll go to my car parked in its less obvious space. I'll tell her about this spot near the local Henge that is wonderful, and we'll drive out there. In the boot of the car, I have everything I need for when we are in a quiet spot on our own. A pair of gloves, zip ties, some piano wire and sheets for lining the boot.* Finding what I found in that safe did help me get to understand who I was. I always thought that I became who I am because of childhood trauma and that I could maybe one day get better, but finding those clippings I realised that this was how I was made and there would be no changing it. I guess the most appropriate term would be like father, like son. Although as I said earlier, I would never hurt the mother of my child and I made the determination that there are varying degrees of monsters. And although the word monster is how society would deem me if they knew, I'd know that there is worse out there and take some comfort in the fact that I'm not the worst.

Knowing what I now know, there is one thing I'd like to still be able to ask my father, as I feel it would be incredibly useful information… over all that time, how did he manage to never get caught?

A Night Out From The Paradise Inn

Tony Sands

Darren Neville wasn't in the mood for work, so the fact the village fete had dragged virtually all the regular custom away suited him fine. 'Nev' as he was known to everyone, had lived in Sweet Little Chittering all of his fifty-six years and had worked at The Paradise Inn for twenty-two of them. He and the Inn's owner, Nicholas Eden, were close friends, so it hardly felt like actual work. Today he just wasn't always in the mood for it, especially when there were other things to tend to, other things which he felt more adept at. He wouldn't stay at the bar for long; Kerry, a twenty-two-year-old barmaid who was currently more engaged on her phone, texting in between long sighs, had turned up ten minutes ago. Although he wouldn't call hers safe hands, it wasn't like she could mess up much considering the custom they had.

The bar itself was empty apart from a guy in one corner wearing a colourful shirt and sandals. He wasn't someone he'd seen before, but he seemed harmless enough. He'd ordered a coffee and an egg sandwich, which he was now tucking into. Anybody who ate an egg sandwich dressed like that wasn't going to cause any trouble. Besides the shirt and sandals guy, Nev had two customers sitting at the bar, men in their late forties he guessed, casually dressed, pork pie hats perched upon both their heads. They were scanning the menu. Nev took a deep breath and strolled over to them.

"Hello, gents." The two men looked up, smiling. "What can I do you for?"

"What would you recommend?" said the one on the left.

"That you go to the fete," grinned Nev.

"I told you it wasn't a wedding, Freddy," said the man on the right, smugly.

"I didn't say it *was* a wedding, Frank-*ie*, I said it *looked* like a wedding," said Fred defensively.

"Well, I don't know what kind of weddings you have in Liverpool, but I've not seen any that look like that." Frank tipped his hat back victoriously.

Nev rubbed his greying temples, sorry he'd walked over.

"Liverpool, what have Liverpool weddings go to do with it?" Fred said, confused.

"That's where you're from," Frank said, then shrugged a shoulder at Nev as if his companion was an idiot.

"What?" exclaimed Fred. "I'm not from Liverpool."

"What?" Frank turned his attention back to Fred.

"Are you telling me that, in all these years we've known each other, you thought I was from Liverpool?"

"You are from Liverpool."

"I am not!"

"It's okay to be from Liverpool," said Frank.

"I know it's okay, but...I'm from Cheshire!"

Frank stared blankly at his long-time friend and business partner.

"Can I get you fellas any drinks?" Nev said, seeing an opening.

"So, is that near Liverpool?" asked Frank, oblivious to the question.

"Are you trying to wind me up?" Fred moaned.

Alan Clements, the guest at number twenty-two, appeared at the other end of the bar and signalled Nev, giving him the perfect exit.

"I mean, I've heard of Chester," Frank rubbed his head in thought. "Are you really not from Liverpool?"

"Sorry to bother you, Nev," Alan smiled. "It's just I thought I'd let you know that I heard some odd noises coming from the apartment below me last night."

"Ah, that'll be the ghost," said Nev, matter of factly.

"Ghost?" Alan croaked, his throat suddenly bone dry.

"Yeah, but I wouldn't worry, he's harmless."

"Right, okay," said Alan, in no way reassured.

"The one you have to worry about is the woman in grey, she's just plain vicious." Nev noticed the front door swinging shut and looked down the bar to see it was now empty, Frank and Fred having left in a hurry. Nev laughed loudly.

"Have I missed something?" Alan said through a forced smile.

"I'm only messing with ya," Nev beamed. "No ghosts, though don't tell the tourists." Alan breathed a sigh of relief. "It's probably the pipes, it's an old building. I'll take a look, thanks for letting me know."

"That's all right," said Alan. "Could I have some water?"

***

With Alan watered and directed to the fete to join the festivities, Nev left Kerry to look after the bar and went to the kitchen to make himself lunch. He threw a burger on the grill, prepared some salad, a slice of cheese and voila - a handsome hamburger to sit and enjoy, which he did. He sipped a beer in between bites whilst reclining on the comfy chair in the office. He could hear the festivities drifting in through the window from the village green. He'd join it soon enough, but first things first. He binned the empty bottle of beer, dropped the plate he'd used for the burger into the kitchen's dishwasher and set off to check on Room 12, the source of the night-time noise. The inn had few customers, but then it never was busy. Sweet Little Chittering was the type of place that usually went unnoticed. Nick Eden, who saw himself as the village's champion did like to make an effort to see it recognised, hence the podium finish that it had achieved in some 'pretty villages' magazine. He slotted the key in the lock, they liked to remain old school at the inn, no electronic swipe cards to enter, just good old-fashioned keys. He checked there was nobody around, turned the key and entered following the click acknowledging the door was now unlocked. He stepped in quickly and closed the door behind him.

The room was dark as the blind had been pulled down, fully covering the sole window, faint light pushing around it like a picture frame. Nev scanned the small, tidy room - which had been described by a recent guest as 'incredibly quaint' - and was satisfied that everything was as it should be. He pushed open the bathroom door.

"Now, what did I tell you about making a noise?" Nev shook his head and tutted at the man bound to the base of the sink with a pillow over his head. "Pretty certain I asked you to be quiet. Didn't I, Tom?"

Nev checked Tom's wrists and ankles, still all secured tightly by zip ties. There was a smell of urine and a drying damp patch on the groin of Tom's jeans.

"Couldn't hold it?" Nev pulled the pillowcase from the man's head revealing him to have a mop of sandy hair and two-day-old stubble. His brown eyes squinted up at Nev, a gag in his mouth prevented him from saying much, but his face was riddled with fear and confusion.

"I'm gonna remove the gag, all right? But, and listen good, if you even breathe loudly I will kill you. Understand?" said Nev calmly, as if relaying instructions to a new employee. The captive man, Tom, didn't respond as Nev unsheathed the knife attached to the back of his belt, from under his shirt.

Tom's eyes widened in terror at the sharp blade.

"Good, good," Nev removed the gag. Tom gulped in air as Nev observed him, ready to silence any shout or scream. But none came. Tom stayed quiet.

"Well done," said Nev after a minute sitting down on the floor opposite his terrified captive. "Now, do you know why you're here?"

Tom slowly turned his head to Nev but didn't look him in the eyes and he didn't speak.

"It's all right, you can talk. Just, not loudly," Nev chuckled gently.

Tom gave this some serious thought, Nev could almost hear the cogs whirring inside the scared chap's head. Then, finally, "no."

"You don't know where this is?" Nev leaned slightly forward, his voice still very calm.

Tom shook his head, no.

"Interesting," said Nev.

"I think…I think there's been a mistake," Tom's voice trembled.

"A mistake?" Nev raised an amused eyebrow. "How so?"

"I don't know you, sir," Tom said. "I don't know this place."

"Firstly, I like 'Sir', that's nice, thank you for that. I feel like a nobleman. I like that a lot. However, I am a little…concerned, that you don't actually know where you are." Tom held his breath, his heart thudding hard in his chest. "I mean, how can you not know where this is?"

Tom shook his head, "I'm sorry…I don't."

"You do not recognise this place, yet you somehow deemed it only worthy of third place in your magazine's 'Village of the Year' awards?"

The man shook so hard the chair rattled and Nev spun around to face him once more.

"Doesn't that seem a bit odd?" Nev frowned. Tom tried to talk, but his words were caught in his bone dry throat. "Doesn't it seem a bit odd?" Nev repeated, but with some venom in his voice this time.

"It's kinda difficult to see where I am…in a dark room…you know?" the man said helplessly.

"So, you're saying it's my fault?" Nav threw his arms out wide then let them flop back to his sides.

"No…no…no, that's not what I meant," the man's words tumbled out of his mouth and fell into the void of darkness before him.

"Do you even know the name of this village?"

"Little Chittering," spluttered Tom.

"Sweet!" snapped Nev, "*Sweet* Little Chittering. Sweet!"

"Yes, yes, that's what I meant," the man tied to the chair blurted.

"Yet that's not what you said, is it?" Nev leant forward so they were face to face.

"It's kinda hard to think straight here," Tom, for the first time, dared to look at Nev properly. Into his eyes.

"So, it *is* my fault?" Nev mocked.

"You've got me tied to a fucking sink," Tom leant as far forward as he could, straining at his bindings.

Nev glared at him, then smiled and shrugged. "Fair point."

"You've got me here because you got third

place?" Tom shook his head in disbelief. "What's wrong with third place?"

"It's not first!"

"It's still a great achievement. Do you know how many villages were involved?"

"I don't care."

"You got a trophy." Tom was calming his voice, trying hard to get the crazy man to see sense.

"A third-place trophy, second best loser. We should have been first."

"It wasn't just down to me, there was a panel," pleaded Tom.

"Do you have names and addresses?"

A double tap on the door followed by a high pitched "housekeeping", called their attention away. Nev opened the door to let a spindly, tall, scruffy haired man and a slim blonde of about average height in, closing it behind them. The man was in blue jeans and a short-sleeved sky blue shirt which was only buttoned half way up, revealing a bare chest. He couldn't stand still, constantly moving, his rangy neck twisting his head around the room as he bounced from one foot to the other. The blonde looked like she hadn't smiled in several years, her eyes were blue but dark and devoid of light. They brought with them a cleaner's trolley.

"Nice of you to turn up," said Nev, sarcastically, returning to the bathroom, stopping by the doorway.

"S'all right," said the man, oblivious to Nev's annoyance.

"You're late, Mark," growled Nev.

"It's not my fault," Mark's long, thin arms

stretched out, preaching innocence.

"Nobody is at fault today," Nev sighed. "Are they, Tom?"

"It was that fucking baker woman, what's her name? Heinrich?" Mark said.

"Helga," the woman, whose name was Lucy and Mark's wife of nine years, corrected him.

"Yeah, her. I'm trying to decide on what I'm getting, you know? Do I want a bun or a bagel or a sausage roll? Or a sandwich. I'm only fucking thinking it over and she tells me to fuck off. I mean, what the fuck, is that about?" said Mark, ambling around the room like a drunken spider.

"She actually said, 'fuck off'?" Nev said flatly.

"Well, no, she didn't say those words, but it's what she meant."

"What did she actually say?"

"No actual words, but they were in her fucking eyes," said Mark, two long fingers indicating his eyes.

"The words were in her eyes?"

"Fucking right they were," nodded Mark.

"Never trust a German baker," said Lucy firmly. Her father had passed that piece of wisdom onto her.

Nev sighed and looked at Tom and shrugged helplessly. Tom was finding it difficult to understand what exactly was going on.

"And did you know there are Morris dancers at the fete?" Mark pointed angrily out the window. "Did you know that? Mother fucking Morris dancers. I hate those bastards! What's their purpose, does anyone know? They jingle - fuckin' - jangle around, waving their fucking handkerchiefs in the air circling a large bastard totem pole. What the fucking fuck? It's fucking weird, man."

"A may pole," Tom muttered in a whisper.

"You what?" barked Mark.

"It's not a totem pole, it's a may pole," Tom said.

"What's the fucking difference? A pole is a fucking pole!" Mark said dismissively.

"Well, a totem pole represents the ancestral lineage of the indigenous people in the…" started Tom.

"The fucking what of the fucking what? Who is this cunt?" Mark wiped spittle from his chin.

"This is Tom, the guy from the magazine," said Nev.

"Let's not forget about the face paint and the burning of the stick men. Do they still burn the stick men, are they allowed? I fucking hope so, then we could stick the whole fucking lot of them in one and set them all alight. Yeah, let's have a Morris dancer barbecue!" Mark continued, not yet done with his rant. "Not that I'd eat a Morris dancer. Fuck that! I wouldn't eat another fucking person, man. That's fucking cannibalism!"

"It's not, is it?" Nev said, again, sarcastically.

"And that fucking Ian fella tried to sell me raffle tickets…"

"The sheer nerve of the man."

"…like, what the fuck do I want raffle tickets for? To stand the fucking chance to win a bastard fucking fluffy bunny rabbit? 'Give me a fucking break, man', I told him and the fucker rolls his fucking eyes at me and just walks the fuck off. What the fuck is that about?"

"I thought they had some whiskey as one of the prizes," said Nev.

"Whiskey, what the fuck? He didn't fucking well tell me that," groaned Mark.

"Must have slipped his mind."

"The bastard." Mark was genuinely peeved. "I might go and get some tickets."

"You have something else to do first, or have you forgotten?" Nev took a step toward Mark and Lucy. Nev would never refer to, or think of, Mark and Lucy King as friends. They served a purpose, and they were always rewarded for their efforts, but that's all they were. They weren't bright, but they were loyal, and loyalty was a rare quality. They also did a fine job of keeping The Paradise Inn clean, no matter what type of cleaning was needed.

"I ain't forgotten, fucking hell, Nev. Have I ever let you down?" Mark's pride was wounded and he didn't hide it.

"No, you have not," said Nev. "Don't start now."

Mark looked at Tom on the floor.

"And you know what you're to do, right?" Nev said.

Mark and Lucy nodded, eyes fixed on Tom who shifted nervously on the floor.

"We're good to go when you are, Nev," said Lucy.

Nev took three quick steps to Tom, bent down,

and before Tom could speak again Nev grabbed a clump of hair tight to hold his head firm. With his right hand he thrust the knife into Tom's left eye, bursting the eyeball with a sickening squelch and pushing the blade deeper into the brain. Tom's body spasmed uncontrollably as the knife jarred in all the way to its hilt. Blood squirted out, then after what felt like minutes, the body finally fell limp as life left it.

"I'm good," said Nev.

"Right, Nev." Lucy pulled out some rubber, yellow cleaning gloves.

"You sure you know what to do and when to do it?"

"The usual."

"Head out around eight, the Morris dancers like to waltz up and down the high street..."

"Fucking freaks," spat Mark.

"...they'll do that from eight 'til nine, ending with the fireworks. That's your window, attention should be on all that. Got it?"

"Abso-fucking-lutely, Nev. No fuckin' worries." Mark gave a salute.

"Good, let's get it done, I'm going to show my face at the fete."

"You couldn't pick up some raffle tickets for me, could ya?"

***

There was a good number of people at the fete, of course, and Nev recognised pretty much all the faces. He spotted Ian Stuart, a villager who was always happy to get involved in a good cause, in an animated conversation with a couple he didn't recognise, most likely passers-by who saw the fete and decided to give it a look. He smiled at the two idiots from the bar earlier, *a wedding indeed,* he thought. The couple walked away with a handful of raffle tickets and Nev gave Ian a wave as he walked up to him.

"Hello, Nev," smiled Ian. "Can I interest you in any raffle tickets?"

"Only the winning ones, fella," Nev returned the smile.

"I'll swap you for the winning lottery numbers," said Ian.

"If only, eh? Charlotte and William not around this weekend?"

"Visiting their nan in Sunderland," said Ian. "Nice to be kids free for a few days but can't say I don't miss them."

"Enjoy the peace whilst you can. Well, when all this is over. I will take some raffle tickets. Told Mark I'd get him some."

"That man needs to learn some manners. And if I had a pound, nay a penny, for every time I heard him swear, I wouldn't need a lottery win," Ian laughed. "How many do you want?"

"A tenner's worth, buddy," said Nev, pulling a crisp ten-pound note from his wallet and handing it to Ian. "I wouldn't give a second thought to Mark. He's dim-witted, but he means well. Most of the time. He does like to curse, though."

"He's positively potty mouthed," Ian said, as he pulled two strips of five tickets each from the raffle book and handed them to Nev. "Those Kings pull at the threads of my patience rug, but I can handle them."

"Your 'patience rug'?" Nev rubbed his temples, already regretting asking.

"In my mind I have a rug of patience, it's beautiful to look at, so when people annoy me, I picture it so I don't get angry. I imagine threads being pulled from it, but, because it's a big rug and because I keep rethreading it, I'll never let them get to me." Ian was very pleased with himself for having formulated this concept and had often thought of writing a paper or even a book on it. Nev wasn't as impressed.

"Right, Ian, that is fascinating. Thanks for the tickets. You haven't seen Nick around, have you?"

"Sorry, not for a while. He'll be around, somewhere, you know how much he loves days like this."

"That's an understatement, right, I'll see you around. Thanks again for the tickets, I'm guessing there's no money back if I don't win."

"Them's the rules," shrugged Ian with a grin, then a thought occurred to him, the grin dropped, and he leant into Nev with a whisper. "It's probably nothing, but I saw a chap roaming around the fete earlier. He didn't look right."

"How do you mean?"

"It was like he didn't want to be noticed, you know? Gave the impression he was looking for something, or someone. Like I said, it was probably nothing, my imagination going into overdrive, just thought I'd mention it. Neighbourhood watch!" Ian started to feel a bit silly for mentioning it, but Nev didn't dismiss it.

"What did he look like?" he said with genuine interest.

"Um, about six foot, broad shouldered. Blue baseball cap. Um...denim jacket and jeans, yeah, I remember thinking he was going double denim." Ian sucked his teeth and shook his head.

"Double denim, do we not go double denim?" Nev raised an eyebrow.

"You never go double denim. At least, there was a time when you didn't. Maybe now it's okay. Times change, I struggle to keep up," Ian adjusted his glasses.

"They certainly do," Nev nodded and walked away to look for Nick. "If you see that guy again, let me know."

"Will do," said Ian.

Many years ago, Nick and Nev had set up 'The Sweet Little Chittering Neighbourhood Watch', to ensure that residents remained safe. The police were not always readily available, being in the next town along and seemingly only working on a part time basis. Besides, Nick and Nev preferred to handle things themselves. So, whenever there was trouble or something suspicious Nick and Nev were notified, and the problem would soon be resolved. Their way.

Nev found Nick standing with a glass of red wine, proudly observing the festivities by the old oak tree. Nick greeted him with a smile and a hearty handshake.

"Isn't this lovely?" said Nick.

"Yeah, sure," Nev shrugged.

"How did it go?"

"So far, so good. All going to plan." The plan being the Kings crash Tom's car, with his body inside near Hartbridge Town and make it look like he was attacked there. They hated Hartbridge.

Nick patted his friend's shoulder. "Fancy a drink?"

"Thought you'd never ask."

They both nodded at David White who was as dapper as ever. He smiled and nodded in return, tipping a wine glass at them before pointing himself in another direction as if he had business to attend to.

"I don't like that guy," Nev said.

"I know, you keep telling me." Nick gently waved at a couple of the village children who were showing off their prizes from Hook-A-Duck.

"He'd have your head, if he could."

"He could try. Now, let's not waste our time on David. Let us drink!" Like two knights of the realm, they marched forth to the wine tent.

***

"You know what I love about this place?" Nick said as he and Nev walked through the smiling crowd, drinks in hand.

"That there's no other place like it?" Nev raised his plastic cup. He'd heard this more than once.

"Nowhere in the world." Nick stopped, his mind switching to other matters. "When will the cleaners be disposing of the waste?"

"Around eight."

"What will they do between now and then?"

"Not a clue."

***

With Tom's corpse crammed into the trolley and the cleaning done, Mark sat down on the bed surveying the room.

"You all right?" said Lucy as she pulled her rubber gloves off and stashed them into the plastic bag hanging from a hook on the trolley.

"Just admiring our fucking work, babe."

"Well, you got plenty of time to admire because it'll be a while before we can dump this bastard."

"Fuck, yeah," sighed Mark looking at his watch.

"We could find a way to pass the time," grinned Lucy, indicating the bed with her eyes.

Mark turned around and looked at it, before testing its springs with a small bounce. He turned back and smiled.

"Let's get naked, baby!" she trilled, pulling her top off and launching herself at her husband.

***

Nev found himself enjoying the fete. He probably ate and drank more than he needed to, but it was fun. Chatting, laughing, and even though he didn't win anything from the raffle, which took place at 6pm, he laughed more than he had in a long time. Time positively flew by, and he was surprised when 8pm came along and the Morris dancers set off on their march. He wasn't like Mark, he quite liked them, there was something reassuring about Morris dancers. Something that tied the world tightly to the past. He liked that.

"Jingle-jangle away ya fuckers," he smiled to himself.

***

Mark slammed the boot shut sealing Tom's body inside it. He walked around to the driver's side, looking over his shoulder at Lucy who sat in their car ready to go. It was a simple set up, he would drive Tom's car to their destination, she would follow. They'd roll Tom's car into a ditch and then head back to the village in their car. Simple yet brilliant. He blew his wife a kiss, she blew one back, he got in the car, turned the key in the ignition and heard the engine roar into life.

"I'm one smooth fucking criminal," he said as he put the car into gear and drove out of the courtyard.

Lucy followed. Nev was right, all the villagers' attention was centred on the march of Morris men. Lucy could imagine her husband swearing at them. He hated Morris men. He hated pretty much everyone, everyone except her. He loved her. She loved him. Life was good when they were together, and they were nearly always together. They drove fairly slowly, taking a long route out of the village to avoid being seen and because the high street was taken up by the parade. She tried the radio to keep her company, the first station that came up had some foreign guy talking about some film he'd made. Probably some pretentious shit, so she changed the station to find some jazz. She liked jazz and that saw her through for the rest of the drive. All in all, it took them over thirty minutes to get to their destination. Mark pulled over on the darkened country road, only the headlights of their cars breaching the darkness of nightfall.

"You all right?" said Lucy, walking up to her husband.

"Yeah, yeah. I thought I saw some fucking car lights ahead of us, but they're gone now. Let's get this done, eh?" He swiped a forearm across his face to ease an itch.

Lucy opened the boot and they hoisted the dead body into the driver's seat.

"Nev's a bit full on sometimes, ain't he?" Lucy observed the empty eye socket as Tom's head tipped back.

"You gonna fucking well tell him that?" Mark pulled the seat belt across and clicked it in.

"Fuck no. Why you putting his seat belt on?" She looked quizzically at her husband. "He's dead."

"*I* know he's dead, *you* know he's dead, but when they find his body, won't it look a bit fucking suspicious when they find he hasn't got his seatbelt on?" Mark tapped a finger on the side of his head to accentuate his point.

"Won't they find it a bit fucking suspicious when they find one of his eyes missing?" said Lucy, tapping the same spot on Mark's head.

"Fuck," said Mark, looking at the corpse, rubbing his chin.

"Like I said, Nev is full on sometimes."

"Yeah, yeah," Mark paced around in his drunken spider routine. "Okay...okay...I got it."

"Wanna share it?"

"We burn the fucker," grinned Mark.

"Burn it?"

"Yeah, it'll work out even better. It'll look like those bastards from Hartbridge burnt him alive. Yeah, fuck yeah." Mark was very pleased with himself.

"Okay, let's burn it." Lucy wasn't against arson, she enjoyed it. She'd once burnt a whole barn down; it had been exhilarating. She was twelve years old at the time, still got a buzz thinking about it.

Lucy opened the cap to the petrol tank and slid an old rag, as cleaners they tended to have plenty of rags in their car, into the slot.

Mark took the handbrake off Tom's car and steered it slowly so it was facing over the verge at the side of the road. It was a steep slope and dropped for a few feet, so the car would easily gather pace and end up a good distance from the road. He looked at his wife.

"Ready?" she asked.

"Ready."

She flicked a match and lit the rag. Flames fanned out. He closed the driver's door and they pushed the car over the edge, the weight pulled it forward and down and they quickly stepped away to avoid being caught by it.

They watched, arm in arm, as the car vaulted faster and faster down the hill before bursting into flames with a loud bang and what sounded like a scream. The car continued forward for a little more before twitching a veering left, then tipping over and sliding to a halt.

"Let's get the fuck out of here," said Mark.

"Did you hear a scream?" Lucy continued looking down the verge.

"Yeah, but it was probably an owl having a heart attack," Mark shrugged.

"An owl having a heart attack?"

"Wouldn't you if a burning car flew at ya?"

Lucy returned the shrug, they got in their car and headed back to Sweet Little Chittering.

***

When they got back, there were still villagers around enjoying the final flickering moments of the fete.

"Do you think there'll be any sausage rolls left?" Mark wondered. There weren't.

They found Nev relaxing on a plastic chair. "How's it looking?" said Nev, sipping his umpteenth cup of wine.

"Clean as a fucking whistle," said Mark.

"And cleaner than your mouth, I hope," smiled Nev.

Mark was puzzled by that remark and looked at Lucy who was giggling.

"Great," said Nev. "Great work."

"Thanks," said Lucy.

"Got just one more thing for you to do," Nev smiled.

"Eh?" said Mark.

"Room 14," Nev chugged the last of his wine down.

"Room 14?" said Lucy.

"What's in room fucking 14?" asked Mark.

"The magazine's photographer."

"Why didn't we deal with him earlier?" Lucy gasped.

"Well, he cycled in from the train station this afternoon, we figured we'd let him take some photos first. Took some beauties." Nev walked away humming an indistinct tune to himself.

Forked lightning slashed across the sky not too far away, followed by a sudden downfall of rain and a loud rumble of thunder. Lucy and her husband looked up at the dark sky forlornly.

"I fucking hate cyclists," said Mark. And he did.

Helga's Crusty von Buns Bakery

Freddy Beans

Helga startled awake to an empty bed, the sheets entangled tightly around every limb.

Henrik had given her shit about her sheet-tugging. No longer. Her wonderful husband had passed to the other side a few weeks back.

A headache from the sudden wakening was forming in her temples. She held it at bay by laying down for a bit longer.

When the clock hit 6:15 she was forced to move. Raising her creaking seventy-six-year-old frame off the also creaking mattress.

On a normal day, she'd call in and let Lelia run things at the bakery. Lelia had been amazing at taking up the slack since Henrik's passing. Always doing extra without question. Helga thanked her lucky stars for Lelia. A friend when she needed one. Wonderful to her bones. Perfect to run the shop while Helga caught up. On a normal day.

Today wasn't a normal day. It was the big to-do village fete.

Helga much preferred sitting at home, reading a book or tending her garden, to catering to a bunch of pompous pricks dancing together. Pricks that don't even get along on a 'normal' day. Then again, she'd chosen this life. Left the states to open her bakery here in Sweet Little Chittering. She and Henrik had fallen in love with the Snow White'esque cottages on sight. Without any children, there was nothing holding them back and they went for it.

Baking for pleasure was very different to baking for profit. Plus, now she has to get up so early every day. It wasn't all it was cracked up to be, but once all the kinks were worked out and her old body acclimated to the different hours, she kind of loved it. It gave her purpose. The bakery certainly gave her something to live for now that Henrik was gone. To Helga he wasn't gone; he was just up the street at the cemetery. A new address. She saw him regularly.

Henrik had been such a hard worker and soft and understanding in nature. He was everything she needed in a partner, which he'd dutifully been for the last thirty years. Waking her on days she didn't want to get up, but needed to, and letting her sleep in as long as she liked on other days. He was a true godsend. With him gone, she could no longer afford to sleep in.

Helga started the shower, knowing it wouldn't warm for minutes. The showerhead vibrated and knocked somewhere behind the tiles before the water flowed. She took the time to walk into the kitchen to get the coffee going before returning to the bathroom, undressing, and getting under the barely tepid stream.

Crusty von Buns bakery needed her full attention today. Henrik had snuck the 'von' into the title, promising her it would add pizazz. None of his words changed her mind. None of his actions worked either but those deep baby blues did. She always had a hard time telling those beautiful eyes no. Crusty Buns became Crusty von Buns that night and the rest, as they say, is history.

The bakery started on rocky ground. On opening day, they didn't have a single visitor. The second day they sold one croissant. One fucking croissant. Helga had cried in her husband's arms that entire night, ready to give up. Of course, he didn't let her give up, and instead encouraged her to be ready for some imaginary big order tomorrow. The make-believe version he made up settled nicely in her hurt heart, though she knew it couldn't be true. How wrong she was. The man knew his stuff. The next morning, they were bustling. None of it made sense. They were busy morning to afternoon. Word got around quickly in such a small village. This one time, she had been grateful for that truth.

The shower finished the job of waking her old body. She went to the kitchen to grab her coffee and keep herself awake. Sitting down in her seat of the last eight years, Helga's eyes settled on the empty seat across from her in sadness. The emptiness made her miss him more. She didn't miss the pain he had been inflicted with.

Henrik had put up a hell of a battle against his declining colon for nearly two full years. Helga was happy he was no longer in pain. Glad she didn't have to pretend she didn't see the pain he was swallowing down to spare her. Nothing hurt more than seeing those beautiful blue eyes grey out in undeniable pain while the stubborn man insisted everything was okay.

"*Alles ist Liebe.*" All is love. A line he repeated every time she had worried about him in their lifetime together.

Helga missed speaking German with him too. No one here in Chittering seemed to speak it. Lelia had picked up a few words here and there but otherwise the only German she heard spoken was an occasional *Gesundheit*.

Enough. She gulped her sorrows down with a last of her coffee. She rose from her seat and grabbed the notepad, with all the orders on it, off the counter and left without locking her front door. No one locks their doors around there.

Exiting the stale air of her home awakened her further. The fresh air taking gentle swipes at her wrinkled skin. The streets were bare. Not another soul around as she started her walk to the bakery a few blocks away. Helga loved living here. Every place was littered with a bunch of brickwork. Yet, the smallest *hauschen* in the entire village belonged to the mason. Nothing made much sense to Helga anymore.

After getting a couple blocks of fresh air in her lungs she felt strong, her awareness beating back the weakening headache she had awoken with. It was a blessing. If she felt this good after the work was done, she might head up the hill to the cemetery and end her day talking with Henrik.

She arrived at her second home and opened up shop, lifting the blinds and filling the till with smaller bills and change, before heading out back to start the oven and mop the floor. When she was done, all that movement rudely reminded her of her age, and she took a mini rest. Finally, she looked up at the clock once she felt rested enough; 7:15.

She'd have customers soon. Without much time left, she moved the mop and the bucket of filthy water to the back door to dump later.

The first cracks of dawn chased after the shadows, reeling on their heels into their safe crevices.

Helga removed last night's hard work from the refrigerator. Baking sheets full of goodies ready for the oven. She placed the first sheet of jalapeno and cheese, onion and garlic, and plain bagels on the far right of the island behind the oven. The bacon and cheese, cheese and ham, and sausage rolls filled sheet slid in next to the bagels. A sheet of bread loaves was next. She'd bake that soon and later turn it into slices for her homemade sandwiches. First, she had to get the cinnamon buns going. She pulled them out of the fridge and slid them into first place alongside the other competitors.

The cheese filled items were thrown into the oven first, along with the cinnamon buns. Then she removed the bowls of prepped dough from the fridge and tossed them behind the sheets. The dough would need to thaw some before it would be of much use to her. A few minutes to catch her breath again and she was back at it.

"No rest for the wicked, Miss Helga," she reminded herself in her best imitation of her mom.

At 7:30 Lelia arrived right on the dot, like she always did. It was like clockwork. Helga had no idea how she did it. Lelia waved without a word and started brewing the coffee. Her usual start to a work shift. When she finally stopped moving and looked in Helga's direction, Helga asked the same question she's asked every day since they started working together.

"Ready?"

Lelia looked back at Helga with a confused look plastered on her face before responding, after a long pause.

"I'm bloody ready!"

They both laughed. It felt good to laugh. Helga loved how easily Lelia made her feel light inside. She was pretty sure she could use more lightness in her life.

Lelia was much younger than Helga but still an elderly woman at sixty-two. The woman was also more dependable than the teenage help she'd used. Lelia knew her stuff too. They'd had many conversations and soft arguments about everything. The woman was tied into the rest of the world in ways that Helga had purposely escaped. Of course, Helga found she didn't mind revisiting via her friend. It kept the mind fresh. That's what she told herself.

Where Helga was seen as standoffish and hard to connect with, Lelia was amicable and as approachable as they came. It was an easy choice to have her largely run the front counter. Today, it was different. Too much to do. They'd have to share their duties. She directed Lelia on when she threw the last sheets in the oven and what was next in line when she heard the first tinkle of the bell.

Working hard to get her most unapproachable face on, she waddled out to meet the first customer of the day. She opened the door and saw the big bald head dip in her direction.

"Hello Ian." She spoke to the smooth dome nicely enough, while wondering how his stupid glasses don't fall down his stupid face as he started to speak.

"Well, hello beautiful."

Helga stared back stone-faced. Lowering her eyelids halfway, the only response he got.

"One of those amazing bacon and cheese croissants and a coffee, please." Ian handed her his large white mug labelling him *SUPERDAD*. Helga had no doubt he was a good enough dad, but she felt he was a pompous prick otherwise.

Without a word, she grabbed the mug from Ian and placed it on the counter. Then grabbed a wax napkin and removed a bacon and cheese croissant that Lelia had just thrown through the pass through. Her old, wrinkled fingers expertly wrapped around the croissant and removed it delicately, even as it stuck to the sheet a little. A quick final flick of the wrist and it was freed. She handed the croissant over to Ian who greedily took a bite of the too-hot morsel.

His enjoyable, "mmmmmmm," turned quickly into "Ah. Oh. Hoo. Hah. Whooo."

The croissants are definitely best eaten warm out of the oven, Helga thought, *but not right out of the oven, you moron.* She decided on nicer words before speaking. "Should wait."

It's all she gave him before turning around and filling the *SUPERDAD* mug.

"Yikes. That's gonna blister. But...It's sooooooo gooooood." Ian exaggerated her talents in a way she didn't mind. She did, however, mind the open-mouthed way he persisted in chewing the still too hot croissant.

"4.25, please."

The money changed hands and she opened the till. She dropped the money inside and removed his change before closing it shut and turning back to Ian.

"You want any raffle tickets?" Helga didn't show any response at all. "Welp. See you at the fete. Isn't it exciting?"

Helga also didn't respond to that. She'd just remembered the bucket and mop out back and her legs carried her there, ignoring Ian every step of the way. Before the door closed, she asked Lelia to man the front for a bit. Lelia nodded, pulled the loaves of bread out of the oven and added the rolls, then walked to the front of the shop.

"*Beeil dich!*" Lelia looked back in feigned shock and then the women both smiled at Helga's joke.

The bucket was heavy, and it took Helga a while to get a good enough grip to get it outside. It was more a case of sliding it across the floor than lifting it. Once outside, the putrid water, and whatever else sat on her floor overnight, was tossed into the weeds to her right.

Helga knew she should get someone to tend this

back area. Everywhere she looked, there were nothing but weeds. They were huge too. Some went well past her knees. There were weird bulbous plants peeking through the weeds too. They looked like the caps of enormous mushrooms. She could barely see to the gate not twenty feet behind the weeds. They'd grown that tall. It made her feel a bit like one of those shitty neighbors everyone gossips about. Not that she'd ever let any of her nosy neighbors know she cared. What happened behind the fence stayed behind the fence!

With no time to worry about the forest out back, she closed the door and laid down. Maybe it was the smell of the mop water but Helga didn't feel so good. Dizziness overcame her. She closed her eyes until Lelia came in and asked what she was paying Helga for.

Helga missed when she threw the rag at Lelia in response, both of them laughing. Helga had to bat her eyes a bit to keep them fully open, before she rising to remove the trays from the oven and throwing the last of the prepped items in.

Then Helga did what she does best; using the now thawed dough to create more of her baked masterpieces. Knowing fingers slowly kneaded the tough dough, splashing a special concoction that was mostly water here and there until it was literal putty in her hands. Fingers expertly danced with the falling dough. In and around, twisting and twirling, dipping and eventually tearing. Until what started as a mound of dough, was a mix of creations waiting for the oven's loving. Finally finished, she had lost count of how many times the front door had chimed. The fete was proving to be a very good day for Crusty von Buns.

Still, a part of Helga worried. She'd gone gung-ho and doubled her usual daily order. If she didn't sell half of her stock by noon, she'd be heading to the fete with a basket full of goodies in hand. Hopefully, it wouldn't come to that. Helga wasn't one to let anything stand in her way for long but being resourceful had its limits too. Right now though, she needed to sit down again. Exhausted but resisting the urge to close her eyes this time.

The next few hours flew by. Her and Lelia switched between manning the oven and dealing with the front counter. By the time Helga bothered to look at the clock again it read 11:17AM. Taking stock of the remaining inventory she realized quickly that while it was a good day, she was going to have to lug that basket. She felt tired already.

Helga updated Lelia with the new plan, and they got to work in unison. Helga lined the inside of the basket with her whitest cloth napkin. Lelia grabbed a plethora of croissants, bagels and rolls and placed them carefully on their own wax napkins inside the basket. When the basket was three quarters full, the ladies nodded at one another, and Lelia looked at Helga with true worry in her eyes.

"You sure you're okay? I'm honestly a bit worried about you."

"You just worry for the store, lady!" They both laughed at that.

"Okay. I'll hold shop. I got it. But...Please take

it easy. It's been a good day. It will be fine."

"Thanks, lady." Helga smiled in her friend's direction. Lelia reciprocated with a smile and a shake of her head.

"You. You're crazy woman." It sounded serious but she was smiling. Always smiling. Helga loved the woman and her endless smiles.

Lelia turned to man the oven and Helga took it as her cue to head out, placing the basket on the chair by the front counter to get change out of the till for her adventure. Then, the bell rang.

Helga raised her eyes without raising her head. It was a guy with an impossibly long neck. The giraffe must have been proud of it because it was even more apparent with his blue shirt only buttoned halfway.

"Yes?"

The man didn't really respond with anything she could work with. Something about how hungry he was and so many options. Helga was patient for as long as she could handle. So, after thirty seconds of the guy hemming and hawing, she yelled to Lelia to come up front. The man gawked at her, obviously hurt. *Weakling*, she thought, grabbing her basket and leaving his indecisions to Lelia.

Reaching the bicycle out front, she wished she'd asked Lelia to help her load the basket. It was much heavier than she thought it would be. With some effort, she loaded it in the bicycle basket and pushed the bike along to get enough momentum to pedal. The white cruiser bicycle obeyed her commands, bouncing down the street in no time. The uneven street shook her headache back into the open. The sun was out, beating hot upon her skin. Helga wished she had grabbed a bottle of water and kept pedaling. She was suddenly very thirsty.

Helga dismounted the bicycle outside the village green. There was no worry if it would be there when she returned. Another reason she enjoyed the country. She leaned it on the first building to her right, under a nice shady tree. The basket took more effort to lift it out of the bicycle basket than it took to get it in. After, she needed a few minutes to catch her breath. Finally able to move again, she slid the basket down to the crook of her elbow, using her left arm to support her right one. Helga stood straight and the basket rested a bit easier with her leaning it on her tummy. She didn't like that she had a belly now. She'd spent her younger years working hard to fight the gaining weight. The fight was one she lost long ago, trying to find ways to appreciate her changing shape along the way. Resting the basket on her belly soon became more bearable. Helga moved forward to try and lighten her load as quickly as possible.

It seemed like she knew everyone she ran into. Most bought something from her too. Though the basket persisted in staying heavy in her arms, no matter how much lighter it was getting. The baked goods were selling like hotcakes and Helga was proud her creations could sell themselves. It also kept her from conversing in that annoying small talk she never enjoyed. It wasn't that Helga hated her neighbors, she really just hated hearing the same questions over and over. And over again.

"How are you dear?" "I'm so sorry to hear about your husband." And then her personal favorite empty promise, "If you need anything at all. Please let me know."

Helga was pretty sure they'd disappear if she went crawling around asking for help. To their dismay, she didn't need any of them. They were all nice enough, but she only needed Henrik in this lifetime. And he had decided to leave her earlier than she intended.

Then something happened that let her know Henrik was watching. A man in what looked like a Hawaiian tourist shirt, sandals and jeans loomed over her and asked for a cinnamon roll. He seemed so tall but then everyone was tall to Helga.

"Not from here?"

"Sounds like I'm not the only one."

Helga didn't like the tone of the man and tried to convey that with her eyes.

"What do you mean? I live here!"

The man was nonplussed and mentioned her accent before saving himself further by biting into the bun.

Embarrassed, a surprised "Oh," escaped Helga's lips before she continued. "I was born in Germany."

"*Das war lecker.*"

It filled her heart with so much joy to hear those words. Not being told that her work was delicious, she knew that already. That he had spoken to her in German. She thanked him, making sure to tell him it was very nice of him. He nodded and walked off, her eyes following him a bit before lowering to an almost empty basket. It made her feel happy to see it empty and feel a newfound heaviness in her pocket. She decided to head back to the bakery. Maybe she'd meet enough hungry folks to have an empty basket by the time she got there. Helga was already excited about lifting the much lighter basket into the bicycle.

Turning around in what felt like an amazing mood, everything changed. She ran into bald Ian again, who looked down at her like he hadn't seen her before. She felt vindicated in assuming he was a pompous prick. He was staring at her with a confused look on his face, not saying a word, when finally he moved. Something behind her shoulder grabbing his attention, Ian walked off in a rush without looking back and Helga went in the opposite direction. It felt creepy. That loudmouth was never quiet. It was very unsettling.

It took longer than she wanted to get to her bike. She was out of breath when she did arrive and leaned on the shady tree. Slowly, her breath returned to her. The headache was thumping hard inside her head now. A constant thump she'd given up on fighting.

Helga flipped the kickstand back with a swipe of her foot and noticed the mug on the ground. It was sitting next to one of those weird bulbous plants that was out the back of the bakery. She'd never seen them before. Her old eyes squinted at the mug and plant. Her head went to work.

What was Ian's mug dropped in the dirt for? If I

can carry a basket full of baked goods, he can carry a mug. What a weak and pompous prick. Something was wrong. She just couldn't put her finger on it.

Then the plant shuddered slightly.

That was all Helga needed. She was beyond scared and on the bike, bouncing back down the street to the bakery in no time. Racing past the first few houses before she dared to look back. Maybe she was losing it. She was getting old and she'd felt dizzy all day. The headache smacked at her temple, a not-so-subtle reminder to not be forgotten.

Homes she had appreciated hours ago raced by as a fear grew inside her. Everything still has that 'picture perfect' quality under the beating sun, but Helga couldn't help noticing a lot of people were screaming and pointing at one another. Everything felt weird and disorienting. Plus, the damn headache.

The bulbous plants had sprouted up everywhere she looked. Polka-dotting each lawn with their obesely round base. She pedaled the rest of the way, panic growing in her heart, refusing to see any more of her surroundings. Calming a little as everything blurred on her way to the bakery.

Helga dropped her bike, the basket still within it, to the soft grass outside her shop. Her heart was racing and the two bulbous plants out front weren't helping her any. She stopped to catch her breath and stared directly at her new guests. They weren't shifting this time. It made her feel a tiny bit silly, which helped settle her a bit.

Calm yourself, you old dingbat. What's gotten

into you? The questions sat unanswered.

She entered the bakery to Lelia taking care of a customer. Lelia acknowledged she was back with a nod in Helga's direction.

Everything was normal there. She was regretting her 'old lady' panic and feeling stupid for being so fearful. It made her angry to be so susceptible to her fears. She'd spent many years living as a strong businesswoman and maturing into a successful business owner. That alone should be enough to build her confidences. It wasn't that easy though. The old unsure Helga found a way to rear her ugly head whenever she pleased.

Shaking her head at herself, she walked into the back and tended to the oven. She tossed the warmed sheets through the pass through. There was no time for her to act like a scared old lady. Too much work to do. It was clear she was the only one with any issues. Hell, she wasn't even sure what she was afraid of at this point.

The used wax sheets pushing out of the garbage called for her attention. Time to empty the trash. She grabbed a new bag and pulled the full one out of the receptacle, holding the full one by the pink strings to keep it closed while she maneuvered the new bag into place.

Then, Helga took another rest, taking the time to catch her breath and calm her heart a little. Once she felt calm enough, she tossed the full bag over her shoulder, and walked out the back door. She regretted her decision before the door had even closed shut behind her.

The two bulbous plants had turned to four.

She dropped the plastic bag to the concrete and ran inside, slamming the door behind her. A long tremor began in her stomach and worked its way out of her limbs violently. Helga sat after the involuntary spasm, trying hard to catch her breath when Lelia walked into the back.

"Are you okay?"

Helga hated being placated.

"Are you?"

"Yes, I'm okay."

There was no smile on Lelia's lips. Something was wrong. Helga felt silly. She was fretting over nothing again.

"Almost rush hour. Ready?"

Lelia responded immediately. That alone set off alarms in Helga's head. But the words she used were the most upsetting. They were not Lelia at all, though her smile was back.

"Yes. I'm ready."

Helga was frozen to the spot. The person in front of her wasn't Lelia. She knew it. She didn't know how she knew it, but she was fucking certain. No answers appeared in the air for her. She was left to make her own choices. Not knowing what to do, she continued in silence.

Helga didn't want her voice to betray her.

She missed Henrik terribly each of the last twenty-six days, but right now she missed him more than usual. He'd always been so quick with solutions. She appreciated that about him. Just maybe not his inability at times to hear other ideas.

Helga did the only thing that came to mind. She pointed up front, hoping Lelia would turn and leave the back area.

It worked. Lelia did as she was directed, walking to the front of the building. Helga didn't move until the door stopped swinging. Her entire body shook uncontrollably. She felt a mess.

What was she supposed to do?

Helga had no answers. The only thing she was sure of was the plants had something to do with her confusion. Whatever was going on, it started with them. She worked her way to the back door again, very slowly, opening it a crack and peering outside. The four bulbous plants beckoned her. Helga obliged but not before reaching for the spade leaning just inside the back door. Only then did she feel ready to move forward.

The closest plant looked bigger the closer she got to it. As she neared it, the thing clearly shifted. Helga stopped, holding the spade as strong as her two hands could grip it before approaching any further. A foot away from the thing, she leaned down to get a closer look.

Up close it looked harmless. Dark green in color, like freshly grown pine needles, with large bulging mauve veins littering its exterior. The thing was so large she thought she could scoop its contents out and curl up in it. Then the contents moved again. She realized the plant wasn't really moving. It was whatever was inside. She shivered and shook before touching the plant with the tip of the spade.

A face pressed into view. Lelia's unmistakable

face, pressing up from the interior of the plant. Her eyes looking at Helga unnaturally.

Helga gasped and tripped backward, falling on her butt hard. She tried to keep her torso in a sitting position, but she flopped hard onto the cement, with her hands protecting her face. Her face was now nose to nose with another of the plants. Its contents shifted when her nose touched it.

Helga jerked back in absolute fear. The thing inside this plant pressed up from within.

She couldn't believe her eyes. Helga rose with a scream. The Helga inside the plant opened her eyes and looked back up at the now standing Helga. The imposter Helga's mouth opened but no noise came out, making Helga wonder if the plant was suffocating her imposter. It didn't make any sense. None of this did.

The spade was lifted, pausing slightly at the top of her extended arms, before slamming down into the imposter Helga's face. Her head split into two halves, just like a cracked coconut. A dark green liquid squirted out of both halves loudly. She raised the spade again and again, hurling it down into the plant's innards. Helga was a true mess by now. The gelatinous green insides dripped off every inch of her.

That was when Lelia walked out back. Instead of seeing if Helga was okay, Lelia began screaming something at her and pointing. It was too much for Helga's persistent headache.

Helga swung the spade at the face of her best friend of the last few years without a thought. It stuck in the side of Lelia's head and Helga was unable to remove it. Red and green liquids sprayed from Lelia's new wounds. *At least her screaming stopped*, Helga figured.

Then the gurgling started. She almost missed the screaming. Helga stood staring and watched all of it - Lelia flailing a bit before fully falling down, the spade hitting the pavement first, spooning out Lelia's inner thoughts and dishing them cruelly onto the warm pavement. Having seen enough, Helga ran as fast as her legs would carry her to the back gate.

Large weeds whipped at her face as she ran in sheer terror, barely noticing the few tendrils that snatched at her, trying to keep her home. Nothing managed to stop her, and she reached the gate. Flipping the wooden lock, then pushing the gate open, she ran northwest down the road. In the opposite direction of the fete.

After a while, her lungs demanded she stop. Her running slowed to a jog and then a slow walk. Finally, she dropped to her knees, trying hard to catch her lost breath. A slight sweat glistened on her brow.

"Henrik. Please. Help. Me." Each word was gasped after a long-winded inhale. There was no magic in the sky. No Henrik to help in the clouds above.

"I always knew that place wasn't for you," she giggled.

She needed to get her bearings. Helga had no idea where she'd run off to. The important thing was she didn't see any of those bastard plants around. She looked behind her and saw the Needful Things roof cresting over the first hill. It seemed like a weird sign. She was close to Henrik, even if by accident.

Helga was headed to the cemetery. And she knew the exact spot she would end up at. She was glad there wasn't anyone else on the streets. That wasn't necessarily unusual in her small town, especially with the fete taking place in the opposite direction. A soft chill rose up her spine anyway.

Helga walked off the road behind St. Benedict's church. She looked up, maybe searching for Father Harris. Maybe for a sign. Neither show. And besides, Father Harris wasn't very friendly.

She took a path she'd used before, one that led directly to the cemetery. The air was cooler there in the shadows. She welcomed that. Henrik felt so far away as she moved down her well-trodden path to him.

The landscape was littered with tombstones, crosses, and sporadic flowers. Everything was spinning and it confused her further. Every few steps, she reached out to steady herself. It was a frustrating walk, but Helga wasn't a quitter.

Finally, she saw him, like an oasis after a long dry trek through the desert. Her eyes lit up at the temptation.

A larger headstone announced Henrik von Scholz's last resting place. A much younger man's picture was framed within the cement. She had picked that picture because it showed him at his best. Long, young and trim. Ready to take on the world.

The last few steps to the headstone were the easiest. Curling up next to the cool cement like she used to snuggle up to his warm welcoming body at night.

"My herr. Oh, Henrik. I miss you." The words were barely whispers. Helga was tired. Her eyes betrayed her raging emotions. Closing against her will. Soon her mind shut down and she slept.

Waking, Helga felt much better. Her headache was barely there. Something to be thankful for. The rest had done her good. She didn't feel so confused after resting next to her lover. The picture she'd placed within the tombstone had held up despite the sun beating down on it. Helga kissed the Henrik in the picture on the lips and stood to catch her bearings.

Rising, she saw them. They were everywhere. There were so many of the plants around her she couldn't possibly leave the area without touching one of the damned things. Helga was no quitter. She grabbed the nearest rock and dug it out of the soft earth at her feet.

She lugged it over to the closest plant, raised it to smash it down. Below her were not one but two of the large round plants. The face staring back at her from the right is Henrik's. His blue eyes looking up at her. The rock almost exploded his face, to her surprise. Happy, she kept her grip on it.

The plant to the left shuddered suddenly. Helga took her eyes off Henrik's baby blues begrudgingly.

She stared down at the Helga staring up at her.

There was no emotion on imposter Helga's face. It made everything that happened next not feel as bad.

The rock smashed down. Imposter Helga's face exploded in a shower of different shades of blues, greens and runny reds. The rock disappeared with a 'floomp' into the plant's depths. Imposter Helga's face now a soupy mess.

Helga didn't have the strength to lift her arms. They hung loose at her sides as she waited. Standing there motionless and emotionally defeated, Helga waited for her husband.

It took a lot longer than she thought it would. Roughly an hour later, Henrik birthed from the plant, spilling out of the sides sloppily in a gelatinous cocoon. They both tore at the membrane containing him and when the liquids inside leaked out below his mouth he coughed. A wreck of coughs that wouldn't stop. Helga wanted to wrap her arms around her husband. Instead, she waited.

Henrik rose, naked as the day he was born. Helga watched him stand. She had missed him so much. There was no more confusion for her. If she was sure of anything in this world, it was Henrik.

Helga walked into his arms right as he opened them for her. He tried to say something to her but only a weird croaky grunt came out. No bother. She wrapped her arms around his wet skin, Helga happy beyond words to hold her *herr* once more.

She didn't notice the plant tendrils that wrapped around her ankles and climbed her legs, reaching her calves and trying to pull her down to the earth Henrik just rose from. Helga knew she wasn't a quitter. She considered her options. Then Henrik, looking at her with his baby blues, lowered with her. There was no resistance on her part. Unsure if she was in a dream or reality, and not really caring either way, she simply held him tighter.

Helga was never very good at saying no to that man.

The Spivey Lane Boot Strap

Damon Rickard

Sunlight has been breaking through the almost transparent curtains of the dank hotel room the man has found himself in for hours now. He knows because he has laid awake for most of the night, unable to sleep on a mattress which feels like all the springs have been replaced with rocks. Lying there, mulling over what brought him here, he realises it all feels strangely familiar, as though he'd woken up to this day a hundred times before but not knowing how all the events of the day will transpire but at the same time knowing how they will end.

The warmth of the sun has been slowly heating the room, bringing out all the musty smells to their nasal bothering worst. The man continues to stare at the ceiling, yesterday's meeting running through his mind over and over again, knowing what it means for this day. He sits himself up and tiredly swings his legs over the edge of the bed, delicately placing his toes on the carpet, imagining how long it's been since it was cleaned and of all the skin particles and bodily fluids from countless strangers before him that now inhabit it. *It's likely more human than carpet now,* he thinks to himself and allows a small chuckle to escape. He can't see that many more reasons to laugh are lying in wait for him today.

A banging starts on the wall, that his headboard backs onto, which he soon realises is very rhythmic in its nature. Standing on the bed, he leans himself against the wall and gently presses his ear to it, the coarse wallpaper providing an uncomfortable rest. In time with the banging, he hears the moans of a couple in the throws of a steamy morning sex session and slowly his focus on his surroundings dissipates and he loses himself to the intimate sounds of strangers. In his line of work, this is as close as he gets to any sort of meaningful relationship. The passion doesn't last for too long and once done, the man presses his hand against the wall. This was not a sexual experience for him but more of a reminder to the things he's lost and the ability to still experience them vicariously through others, even if it means doing so without their knowledge. *Thank you,* he thinks to himself.

Refocussing himself, he picks up his watch, laid purposefully next to a neatly folded newspaper, off the bedside table and sees that it is now 8.45am. He needs to be on Spivey Lane by 11am for things to proceed as planned. You could almost say his entire life has led to this moment but only in the last year has he understood why. Raised by his mum after the death of his father whilst he was still in his formative years, he was a difficult child and left for a new life as soon as he was legally able to. Whilst trying to find himself, he ended up joining the army to gain a direction in his life that he never felt he'd had. Somewhere he could channel the anger at the loss of his father more productively. After easily completing basic training, he was soon showing he had skills for removing enemy targets before anyone knew he'd even been there. His aptitude for war time assassination was only matched by his intellect and thirst for knowledge. This meant that when the tech companies came calling for soldiers to use in their sometimes wild experiments, he would nearly always put himself forward. Often the army hesitated as they were unsure about risking damage to one of their primary killing machines. The most recent experiment turned out to be his last as the company won a contract with the government and ended up recruiting the man to be one of their leading lights.

Pulling himself off the bed with little enthusiasm, he slowly makes his way across the human carpet and towards the bathroom. He certainly needs to overcome this tiredness but it happens with every assignment so he knows he can cope. Each trip consists of a sleepless night, even without the addition of a piece of shit mattress, followed by a difficult morning. But after a coffee and some food he finds the energy he needs. Every time.

Opening the door to the bathroom he realises this is going to be as unpleasant an experience as feeling that carpet under his feet. He looks around for the small but wrapped bar of soap you'd expect in a hotel bathroom but there isn't one to be found. Without having any toiletries with him, he reconciles with himself that today will be a smelly day, especially given the heat. He pulls back the flimsy shower curtain, knowing full well as soon as he steps in, it will come to life, demanding long, plastic hugs. From behind his soon to be hugging partner he spots in the dirty soap tray a small, already used bar of soap. He stares at it, sighing to himself. *Of course it's used soap. What else would I expect from here?* It feels like the soap is staring back at him, mocking him, knowing that if he wants to be clean there is no alternative to what lay in front of him with a random stranger's body all over it. Or even many strangers! Who knows how many times that soap has been used? *Why are crappy shower curtains and bars of soap still things? Well, at least here anyway.*

He reaches in, turning the hot water for the shower onto full then places a hand under the weak stream of water emanating from a filthy shower head, waiting for the water to warm up. After what seems an age of standing there naked, arm raised, head pointed to the ceiling as though in deep thought, the water finally begins to show signs of actual heat permeating its way through. The heat intensifies slower than a snail with no rush to be anywhere and so adding the cold water into the mix is a painful process of continuous readjusting. He steps into the shower and places his head into the water, letting it wash over him as he closes his eyes and masturbates. Time has taught him that what lay ahead needs as low a level of testosterone as possible, a mind free of any unfocused thoughts. And where he doesn't get to enjoy the company of other women or men, and it's been so long he now can't remember which was his preference so either would suffice, he has to perform this lonely ritual as part of his mental preparations. He decides to avoid the soap and just hopes he can find somewhere with deodorant on the last part of his journey.

After drying himself with what could only be described as sandpaper pretending to be a towel, he rustles through his bag to find the clothes he needs for the day. There is a fete in the village, so he wants to make sure he looks like that is why he is there. He pulls out a pair of blue jeans, a bright and summery casual t-shirt, and a pair of sandals. He doesn't remember this being a thing for fetes, but the researchers said they'd studied it. He pulls the clothes on and studies himself in the grimy mirror. *Well, with this hell hole, they certainly found a safe place which you could guarantee no one from Sweet Little Chittering would ever contemplate staying at.* He needs to not be seen before he's supposed to be. Overall, he feels he just about looks the part and shouldn't stand out in the village. He then picks up the trousers, shirt and shoes that he was wearing yesterday, spends time folding them and very carefully puts them in the bag. He starts zipping the bag up and realises he forgot to grab something. He unzips it again, reaches back in and ruffles around a bit, undoing all the careful work he'd put in to avoid his smart clothes getting creased. The folding was more out of habit than necessity as he won't be wearing them again. His hand finally rests upon the cold metal of what it was searching for and pulls it out. He slips the gun into the back of his jeans and covers it with his t-shirt. He then zips up the bag, throws it over his shoulder and heads to the door, stopping as he remembers to grab the newspaper from the bedside table. With his free hand he scoops it up, stands briefly in front of the ridiculously thin curtains and takes in the musty smell for one last time with a deep breath.

"See you next time, you fucking smelly piece of shit," he says to no one, but hoping the room heard him. He slips the paper under his chin, grabs the door handle with purpose and whips it open, stepping outside and bravely heading into the last day of his life.

The cars are parked directly outside the rooms as the whole building has been designed to look like an American motel, the thinking being that it would give the place some charm and bring in the people passing through that hadn't booked anywhere. As it turns out, it mostly got used by residents of Chittering's neighbouring village of Hartbridge for romantic liaisons, just without the actual romance, even though it was a fair drive. Maybe the distance between town and hotel was the winning feature, providing a certain level of anonymity. The ground outside was dusty and the wind, as gentle as it was, had caused a light covering of his car. The man decides a wet towel from the room would be enough to wipe the windscreen as he knew there was no fluid left in the car to do it with. He places his bag on the dusty floor, rolls up the paper and slips it into the handles of the bag. Once the paper no longer has the man's grip on it, it releases itself to fill the same size as the handle holes and therefore keeping itself safe from being blown away. He takes the few steps back to the room heavily, longing for his coffee and food only to find that, of course, the door was now locked with the keys still inside. *SHIT!* He steps heavily back to his bag, unzips a pocket on the front and pulls out the car keys. The button no longer works to unlock it, so he has to put the key in the door and turn. The door creaks open, gasping for a drink of oil, and the man reaches in, places the key in the ignition, his foot on the accelerator and turns. After some chugging the car eventually splutters into life and he clicks down the windscreen wiper lever. The wipers smudge the dust all over the windscreen, potentially making the visibility even worse than it was. *DOUBLE SHIT!* He unzips the bag and pulls out the good shirt that was no longer nicely folded. Looking at it apologetically, knowing what he was about to do to it, he slowly places it against the glass and presses. He sighs to himself then begins to wipe. After five minutes of elbow grease and determination he makes the driver's side clear enough to be able to see through. He drops the shirt to the ground, a puff of dust billowing up as it lands sadly and no longer wanted, picks up the bag, throws it onto the passenger seat and steps into the car. Putting it into gear, he pulls out of the hotel grounds, sticks his hand out the window and gives the finger to the hell hole he leaves behind. *Fuck you and I'll see you again.*

After a short time on the road the man checks his watch. He has forty-five minutes to get to Spivey Lane in Sweet Little Chittering (*who the fuck names a place that?* – he always hated it) and get this assignment properly started. The scenery blurs past him as he speeds by way above the limit. The lush greens of the fields and various colours of the full trees' leaves unnoticed by the man who is deep in thought and concentration. He knows he will get this right as there is no other option, though he still needs to ensure he is correctly focused. But his rumbling stomach and caffeine deprived body was making that difficult and, so far, there had been nothing on the way that could help him with this particular issue. Or provide him with deodorant. Without warning, his mind slips and pushes forward a memory that hasn't surfaced in some time. The day his father died. The day that changed the direction of his life forever, leading him to this very moment. This car, this road, this, fucking, rumbling stomach. *Fuck it, I'll just have to eat after I meet them.*

Thirty minutes later he has driven through Hartbridge and is heading past the cemetery onto Cumberbatch Lane. The names of the streets in this place have always made him laugh. In a few minutes he'll be in Spivey Lane and knocking on the door of number 11 for a conversation he has been dreading. He passes by many sights he recognises, including the village shop and of course The Paradise Inn. Even though he'll be passing by the latter at a distance and can't see it from the road he is on, he knows he is passing it. He also knows he'll be heading there shortly to sort out this hunger problem.

The man pulls onto Spivey Lane, stopping

opposite number 11. The road is full of picturesque houses, all with their own character. This was clearly the rich side of town. The gardens all neatly maintained with their own individual fencing keeping them penned into their own private lives. The man sits and stares at the house through the driver's side's dirty window, the grey red of the dust changing the house's charming whites and blues into something entirely more sinister. He looks over to the passenger seat and pulls the paper from out of the bag handles and stares at the front page. A day filled with some sensational stories, the overall headline reads "Sweet Little Chittering Devastated by Murder". Underneath the headline is a picture of his dad. A single tear escapes his eye and slowly glides down his unshaven cheek. Checking himself, he wipes away the tear and slaps himself around the face. *Pull it together you pathetic excuse of a man.* Words he remembers from his early army days. Whilst he was good at it, the first few kills were far from easy to deal with, exacerbated by the childhood trauma of having killed the man that killed his father. For a year he had to undergo court ordered psychotherapy to undo the damage that day did, although he's fairly sure it didn't work. He shakes off the emotion, pulls the door handle, the door once again groaning at having to be a door, and climbs out of the car.

He checks his watch which reads 10.56 and leans back against the car as this needs to happen at 11am. In the distance he hears the faint sound of an engine and across the road he can see movement in the open curtained windows of number 11, a young boy being part of it. The boy turns to the window and sees him standing there in the street, leaning against a dusty car. The man smiles and waves and the boy waves back as the man notices the sound of the engine getting quite close. 10.59. The door of number 11 opens, and a woman starts to walk out. She calls back into the house and the man sees the boy disappear from the window and moments later reappear at the front door. A figure, presumably the boy's father, appears behind them. The man stands up and starts making his move towards the house when a car comes past so close to him that it touches the crease in his jeans. The man punches the side of the car as hard as he can and then falls back yelling in pain. The driver slams on his brakes and the woman from number 11 comes running toward him.

"Oh my God, are you okay?" she yells. The driver has now gotten out of the car, staring on in stunned silence. She turns to him. "You going to help or just stand there?" The driver snaps into action and paces over. The woman turns back to the man. "You haven't answered. Are you okay?"

"I think so," replies the man grimacing.

"Let's get you into the house and take a look. My husband is a doctor so you're quite lucky. Doubly so in fact as we're just leaving for the fete. A minute later we'd have been briskly walking down the road and probably not heard you."

"Well, I shall count myself as most fortunate. Thank you."

The driver, now standing over the man, looks lost and unsure.

"Help me pick him up and walk him inside," the woman says curtly. The driver grabs him under one arm and the woman under the other. They help him hobble inside, the man feeling very pleased with his acting ability.

"I'm so sorry dude. You just stepped out in front of me!" says the driver

"I know. It was entirely my fault. So, no need to worry about me claiming against you."

"Thanks man, very generous of you."

Generous? What a strange way to respond to not having a claim of hitting a pedestrian filed against you.

Walking him into the lounge, they rest him on the sofa and the father follows closely behind. The driver stands up and looks at the woman, his expression suggesting that he just wants to get out of there.

"You can go," she says.

"Gracious of you miss. Sorry again dude."

The man just nods at the driver who quickly sidles past the family on his way out of the house and back to his car which is currently sat in the middle of the road. The woman looks at him.

"I'm Sarah, by the way." She takes a moment and before he can respond she carries on. "You look oddly familiar but I'm fairly sure I've not seen you round here before."

"I grew up here. But haven't been back in years. Maybe my face as a child has been in some of the fete pictures which get brought back out each year to decorate the entrance with. If they still do that, of course."

"They do. They love a bit of history here. Anyway, if you don't mind, I'll be getting my son off to the fete so he can enjoy the games they have before the crowds get too big."

The man wonders what a big crowd is at the village fete. Maybe it's a queue of more than two people for an activity. "Of course," he replies.

"I'll leave you in the very capable hands of my husband then." With that she stands up and leaves. The man hears the footsteps of her and the boy leave the house and the door shut gently behind them. He looks around the room, a large television sits opposite, the centrepiece of the seating arrangement. Shelves entirely devoid of dust but filled with trinkets flank the television. And at the other end of the room, the family dining table, glistening from the sun that reflects off its glossy surface which has clearly been varnished to within an inch of its life. The father pulls up the footstool which matches the sofa and sits himself down on it. He stares at the man intently.

"What do you want?" he asks.

"Why do you think I want something? I mean other than medical attention?"

"The way you limped in here. You're not hurt. You may have fooled the driver of the car that hit you," the father uses air quotes as he says the word 'hit', "and my wife, but not me. Which I can only assume means you wanted to get in here to me. So, you clearly want something. Shall we stop beating around the bush?"

"Okay, you're right. I need to talk to you about the work you're doing with the Hartbridge Henge."

"I don't know what you're talking about. I'm a medical doctor and have no interest in the Henge."

"Thought you said you didn't want to beat around the bush? But, okay, I'll lay out some facts and then you can decide how you want to continue. For years in dear Sweet Little Chittering there's been the old rumours of the Henge having some unknown power. The type of rumour that gets sprinkled around at school, sounds amazing, then as you grow up you realise how stupid it is. Only someone in Hartbridge grew up and didn't realise that. No, no. They grew up and became a scientist and started experimenting with it. And discovered something. Something that only a handful of people between here and there know about. You being one of them. I'm not here to get into the how's and why's of you finding out and becoming part of the secret team. Just here to say that you, not the team, but you, are onto something and you don't know the size or danger of it. And that you need to stop."

The father has sat quietly through the man's speech, and the more the man spoke the more the father's panic grew. *How did he know this?*

"Well, that was a nice flight of fancy to be taken through this morning. I hope almost getting yourself hit by a car was worth it. Now, if you don't mind, I'd like to join my family at the fete. So, as you aren't hurt, you can see yourself out and I'll look forward to not talking to you again."

The father stands up and holds out his arm, gesturing to the lounge door and ultimately out of his home.

"Please," says the man, "you don't know what you're tapping into."

"I don't want to have to ask again."

The man runs his tongue round the inside of his mouth trying to generate saliva, the nerves knowing what the outcome of this conversation not going to plan means. The man slowly reaches his hand behind him, feeling the shape of the gun under his t-shirt. He looks up at the father in his eyes and sees the fear in them. Maybe, if he gets his food and coffee, he can re-engage at the fete and perhaps do this better. At least the father will now know they need to talk alone so getting him away from the wife and kid will definitely be easier. And then if he still won't listen, well, his death will be his own fault. The man brings his hand back out from behind him and stands up.

"Okay, I'll leave. But you need to think about what I've said. So, I'll give you some time and I'll see you later. Not going to say when or where so you can't try and avoid me, but I strongly suggest using this time to think about the consequences of your actions." With that, the man gets up and walks out.

He doesn't look back at the house as he crosses the road to his dusty car and climbs back in. He runs his hands over his face as he thinks about what would have to happen later. Why did he delay it? Is he really giving this guy another chance, or did he chicken out of his mission and what had to be done? *This fucking empty stomach! I always make shit decisions on an empty stomach.* He starts the car up and makes The Paradise Inn his next stop.

The entrance of the place is a rickety wooden door, not having been changed since the pub opened. The man pushes on it, careful not to push too hard in case it comes off its hinges. That would be a perfect way to make sure his not being noticed came to a very quick end as the man who finally broke The Paradise Inn's door. The inside was very bland and free of colour, with faded browns and greens all over the place. Brown tables and chairs, green carpet and wallpaper, this place was long overdue a makeover. It would get one eventually but one which would turn it into nothing more than rubble. Two hundred years of history gone in an instant along with all the people inside it. The man spots a table in a dark corner which looks perfect for remaining away from prying eyes and having to have conversations. He walks over and sits himself down.

He was expecting the bar to be completely empty, it is only 12pm after all and the fete is on. The other people in there are two men sitting at the far end of the bar, an older gent behind the bar, perhaps in his fifties the man guesses, and the young barmaid who has her face buried in her phone. He figures the two men here either have no family, have a drinking problem, or have family but need a little Dutch courage to cope with a full day of fete'ing with them. He picks up the menu off the table and is surprised to see a variety of dishes on there that actually sound quite delicious. Although all he wants is protein and coffee so once he spots an egg and cress sandwich on there, he heads over to the bar to order.

He looks over at the two men and sees they are deep in conversation. He doesn't listen to what they are saying but could clearly hear one of them has a thick northern accent which he places as Cheshire. The barmaid looks up from her phone and smiles at him warmly as he places his hands on the brown bar and just before he can order she gets the first word in.

"Don't get too many strangers in here on fete day. Not that we get many in here on other days neither." She starts laughing, clearly having found herself quite amusing. The man fake chuckles back. "What can I get ya, love?" she asks.

"Just the egg sandwich and a cup of black coffee please."

"Coming right up. Just point to where you're sitting and I'll bring it over to you when it's ready". The man points at his table in the dark corner. "The quiet type then, eh?"

"Sorry?" he questions.

"People who pick that one are generally people who don't like to be disturbed. Been here for years and you just get a feel for these things."

"I guess so."

"Full of words you are, aren't you? Don't worry I won't stand here yapping at you and I'll let you go sit back down." The man turns to walk away. "But after you've paid of course." She laughs again.

"Of course," he says, this time not even bothering to raise a fake chuckle. "How much is it?"

"Four seventy-five."

The man reaches into his pocket and pulls out some notes. He plucks the five-pound note from the selection he has and hands it over. The barmaid swiftly takes it from him and rings it through the till, returning him 25p. "Now don't go spending that all at once," she jokes, the man just wondering when this tiresome brand of humour will stop. He smiles at her, turns and heads back to his table. She rolls her eyes as he walks away.

After almost thirty minutes of waiting, the sandwich and coffee finally arrive. The barmaid puts them down in front of him with little care, the plate with his food on clattering against the table. "Enjoy," she says with little inflection in her voice to suggest she meant it. His charm clearly won her over. He shovels the sandwich down, barely even tasting it, and then catches his breath. He could spend time with the coffee and savour it now that he had temporarily satisfied his hunger. Besides, he now has quite a wait ahead of him as attempt two will need to take place later in the evening. He'd read there was a thunderstorm due at 10pm and if he still needed to take the more severe route then the thunderclaps would potentially cover any gunfire.

As he's eating, the two men sitting at the bar begin to raise their voices. It's now very hard not to be attentive to what they're saying and the man groans in frustration at the mundanity of their conversation. "It's okay to be from Liverpool," one of them says. *Liverpool?* From all his travelling around he had become very adept at recognising accents, both regional UK dialect and international ones. "I know it's okay," began the other one, "but I'm from Cheshire". *Ah there we go. I'm not losing it.* He tries to block out the sound of their tedium and concentrate back on his coffee.

After what seems like an eternity of staring out the window at the blandness that is Sweet Little Chittering, the man decides to take himself off to the fete and partake in some normal fete activities. He decides it a lot less conspicuous than being the loner sat in the bar that didn't talk to anyone. Those are the people that get remembered as they stick out as different. He pushes the empty plate and cup away from him, slides his chair back and stands up. The barmaid sees him and so he flashes her a forced smile, hoping it looks genuine and not just creepy. She smiles back warmly, as she did when he first came into the bar, so the man decides he pulled off the fake smile and heads back out.

He stands and stares at his car, looking up to the sky. The hot sun beats down on him, the glare causing him to squint so he shades his eyes with his hand and continues to stare blankly into the cloudless blue. He wonders how things would have turned out for him had fate not interfered in such a devastating way. Would he still find himself here? Is everything pre-ordained and so no matter what he had done this day would always have been where he ends up? The silhouette of a goose gliding through the sky between the sun and his eyes breaks his thoughts and brings him back into the here and now. The man decides to make the most of the moments he has and so walks to the fete instead of sitting in his shitty car in such nice weather. Besides, if he remembers right, it's only a few minutes away.

He heads off down the high street towards the village green. So many different lives all coming together in this one place. People all heading in the same direction, some meandering on their own, some families rushing as they feel that they're late, some couples walking hand in hand soaking in the sunshine and unaware of anything outside their own sickly romantic bubble. The man reflects on all the potential lives he could have had, wondering if he'd have wanted any of them. Did he want to have to come home to the same person every day or have the responsibility of looking after children needing to be taught how to navigate the world. Did he want to be alone, being served repetitive day after repetitive day in this green, dull and annoyingly friendly part of the world? Given the choice he'd probably burn this place to the ground, taking everyone in it and offering them all the sweet release of death. He feels he may be projecting his own desires onto the entire community of Sweet Little Chittering but that doesn't change his mind. It certainly wasn't sweet to him. *I'd love to know what's been happening in all of their todays,* he thinks. He bets there are some pretty juicy stories in there full of miscreants and mayhem. Then remembers where he is and realises that, in reality, they're probably some of the dullest stories you'll find. Maybe someone had run out of milk and so couldn't have their usual cup of coffee that morning or there was a house with an overdone egg and so no runny yolk. Although here they probably have their eggs with fully cooked yolks anyway and their steaks well done. Sweet Little Chittering was not a place of refinement.

The sound of the fete slowly grows louder as he nears the entrance, the giggles of children, the whirring of machines, from small candy floss makers to large rides spinning their guests round at vomit inducing speeds. He could never understand the appeal of these things. He walks through the photo laden entrance and the buzz of the fete was exactly as he remembered it and it actually makes him happy. As a child this was one of his favourite days of the year and even though it wouldn't take long for him to come to hate it, the memory was a happy one. He walks through the village green among the crowds without anyone paying him a second look, just as he wants. He sees a man winning a bottle of wine on the tombola and handing it over to the woman he is with, who's clearly older than him. She looks suitably pleased with this chivalrous gesture. He sees children dragging their parents to each stall with games that offer up stuffed animals as prizes. He hears a speech being given which starts with intense feedback and talks about councillor Thomas being absent. The man wonders what happened to Thomas and invents a story of his disappearance in his head to help pass the time. It even helped block out the sound of the fucking Morris Dancers. He can't believe they still have those jangling cunts here.

He mindlessly wanders for a while and as he people watches he sees a lot of them sitting at benches feasting on the delights offered up by the food vans which provide an assortment of burgers, breaded things, fried stuff and pizza. It was at this point the man realises his hunger has returned with an all too sudden vengeance. Clearly the calories in the sandwich didn't handle slowly walking round a village green too well. He looks around and sees a slightly plump, sour faced woman with a basket that was quickly emptying. Understanding that the locals knew where to get the best food from, he heads in her direction. The woman greets him with a furrowed and questioning brow. He peruses what is left in the basket and his eyes rest upon a perfectly golden cinnamon bun which he points to.

"I'll take that one thanks," he says without offering a greeting.

"Not from here?" responds the woman with a distinct German accent. The man picks up on this easily, but from past mistakes he always knows to double check he'd clocked the right accent before trying to converse in their language. People can often travel and pick up accents different from their native tongue.

"Sounds like I'm not the only one."

The woman hands him the bun. "What you mean?" she says curtly. "I live here!"

"The accent." He takes a bite out of the bun in case he's stuck in this conversation he didn't mean to start.

"Oh," she says. "I was born in Germany."

"*Das war lecker.*"

The woman takes a moment and lets a smile creep across her lips. "*Danke. Sehr nett von dir.*"

The man nods at her and walks off. He likes her as, similarly to him, she seems one to not mince her words and not say more than she needs to. He snaffles down the rest of the bun, smiling to himself as he does so. It really was delicious - he didn't lie about that when he told her in German, which she seemed to appreciate.

To ensure he seems like he is supposed to be there, the man plays a few of the games, handing off any toys he wins to excited kids and thankful parents. He shares some words with the people he comes into contact with, as painful as it is to generate enough energy to do small talk with deeply uninteresting people. After a few hours of this he realises the sun is starting to set, retiring from a hard day of ensuring fete day is another successful one. No fete day has been rained off. He remembers the village used to think it was the henge that looked over them and kept the town dry for this day. *This fucking place was always drowned in insanity. If only they knew the truth.*

A woman suddenly bumps into him and she seems very disoriented. It turns out her name is Sarah, and she is looking for her husband, Julian. She's concerned as, apparently, he is quite drunk.

The man finds this encounter amusing as he considers it is probably the most exciting thing that is happening today. Even the fireworks which follow soon after are just as lifeless and dull as the village that is hosting them. As he watches the tiny explosions in the sky, he realises the clouds are gathering and that the storm must be getting close. *Time to finish this.*

He walks around far more focused than he'd been in hours, carefully looking over the all the people until his eyes eventually rest on the family he'd paid an earlier visit to. The boy is busy throwing rings around jars as the mother cheerleads him on. The father is, thankfully, a few steps back and completely uninterested. The man walks over with purpose and when he reaches the father he puts a deceptively friendly arm around his shoulder and, with his free hand, pulls the gun from his jeans and holds it close to him so as not to be seen.

"Fancy seeing you here," the man says casually. The father turns his head and sighs.

"I thought this was dealt with," he replies.

"Unfortunately, not to a satisfactory conclusion. I told you I'd find you again. Let's take a walk, shall we?"

"Absolutely not. I have nothing more to say to you. Now, if you don't mind, I am enjoying this time with my family."

"Actually, I do mind as it happens. Now, let's take that walk." The man puts the gun into the ribs of the father and whispers firmly into his ear, "I insist".

With those two sinister words, the father realises what is happening and decides the safest course of action is to comply. The boy turns around just as the two men head away. They leave the sounds of the fete behind them, slowly getting fainter but never being lost completely. With each step they take the man knows the father is coming closer to his fate, whatever that may be. The village has pockets of trees scattered all over it and so the man chooses a nearby one for them to finish their conversation in. The light from the fete still manages to provide some illuminance for them as they cross from village green to the mini wood.

The man pushes the father up against one of the trees and presses the barrel up against his head.

"You still want to tell me I'm wrong then go ahead. And I'll just have to risk killing the wrong man. Or we can talk, and you can live."

Terrified, the father replies, "No. No you're not wrong. But we're nowhere with anything. It's little more than theory at the moment."

"It's certainly more than theory. You need to stop. You have no idea of the damage the power contained in there is capable of."

"If we're still theorising, how do *you* know what it can do?"

"I've seen it. Over and over again. This needs to be different. You need to listen and trust me. Destroy your findings. Walk away from the project and lives will be saved. There is work in your theories which unearths the terrible things that wreak havoc that is wider ranging than just this village. The alternative is I shoot you tonight, burn down your house and destroy the work myself. I don't want to do that; you'll never understand just how much I don't want to. But this is more important than you and far more important than me."

"I'm sorry, I can't just flush away what could be the source of energy that saves the planet."

"It's the exact opposite of what you think. This isn't an infinitely renewable energy that you can just tap into. It's an unstable energy from a time and place you don't understand and nor do I. And we never will."

"I guess you'll just have to shoot me."

The man raises the gun, loads the chamber and is just about to pull the trigger when he hears a rustling from behind him. The man swings round and from the shadows the boy appears.

"Dad?"

"Go home kid," says the man forcibly. Whilst he is turned and his gun slightly lowered, the father sees his chance. He charges at the man, knocking him to the floor, the gun flying from his hand as he hits the ground hard but it only slightly winds him. The man ignores the discomfort of his struggle for breath and quickly stands back up. *Looks like this is a fist fight now.* He punches the father hard in the face and then quickly and harder he lands a blow on the father's throat, smashing his windpipe. The father grasps at his neck, wheezing, unable to breathe as he falls to his knees and the man gently pushes him over.

"It didn't have to go this way," the man says as he stands by his victim's head, raising his foot. Just as he is about to stamp down, extinguishing what little life was left as the father struggles to breathe, he briefly hears the sound of a gunshot. After that he neither hears nor sees anything. The man's limp body flops to the ground, blood spraying from his face as he falls. The boy is left standing with the gun in his hand and smoke emanating from the barrel. What seems like a lifetime passing, the boy just stands there, staring until the sound of his wheezing father refocuses him. He runs over and falls to the ground next to his father as his raspy breathing slows and eventually stops.

The boy will walk back to the village and find his mum and explain what happened. The next day the local paper will carry the story on its front page. A paper which he will keep with him for the rest of his life. The people working with his father will search the house and take all papers pertaining to his work on the henge and use it to further and complete their research. Research that would have stalled were the events of that night not to have happened as the boy's father would eventually realise what he stumbled onto and destroy his paperwork himself without intervention. But that is not to be, as these events *did* happen. The boy will go before a court and be given a year's mandatory psychotherapy which wouldn't really work. He will be a troubled child and difficult to manage, eventually leaving home and joining the army, where he will learn to become a skilled assassin. He will find a company that hires him to use their new technology to assassinate people who are a danger to their current way of life. And after a mass explosion near his hometown of Sweet Little Chittering, caused by a new source of renewable energy, he is given his final mission. A mission destined to fail over and over again. And he will die, the final memory passing through his mind being that of when he was a boy waving at a stranger who was leaning against a dusty car across the road on fete day.

A Killing in the Local Butcher's

Bob Pipe

Zack hated the annual village fete. Once a year his hometown was invaded by an army of pink-faced, obese white folk, trampling about, getting horrendously drunk and being sick in the flowerbeds.

His father was the local butcher and supplied the meat for the fete, including the famous hog roast and the pig's head for the Morris Men parade.

His father's shop, J.M. Cockcroft & Son Family Butchers, had been in the village for three generations - his great-grandfather opened it in 1931. Zack wished his great-grandfather had opened a bakers or a florists instead and often wondered what it was that runs in his family that meant they enjoyed cutting up dead animals so much.

It made him sick. He was vegan and could no longer stand the sight and smell of meat... or the smell of death, as he saw it.

Zack was a huge disappointment to his father and ridiculed by his brother, Adrian. When Zack turned vegetarian a few years ago no-one understood or even tried to. In fact, his father and brother would call him mental and tease him endlessly for being soft; "What's the matter with you?! Come on, eat up - it will put hairs on your chest!"

He had to put up with no end of stupid

hypotheses like; "if we didn't eat cows, you'd have no end of them roaming about the land, have you thought about that? You haven't, have you?!"

He was sick of the questions too; "but what if you were stranded on desert island, would you eat meat then?" He'd patiently tried to say the chances of being stranded on a desert island were very slim, but they'd just laughed in his face; "ha-ha, you would! You know it!" He couldn't work out if the meat made them thick or if they were just thick to begin with.

Zack had grown to loathe his father, and his brother for that matter, who was lined up to take over the business when his father croaked - which probably wouldn't be long considering how bloated he was. A heart attack couldn't be far off. His father didn't even eat vegetables. "Don't believe in them," is what he'd say, or just screw his nose up and say "yuck, no thanks," like a child.

And without question, they'd always find a way to wipe their greasy hands on him after devouring meat with their fingers; "oh, give over!" is all they'd say if Zack flinched or ask them not to do it. "For Christ's sake boy, it's just a bit of meat, you bloomin' snowflake!" Snowflake being a new insult his father had learnt and was now using constantly, along with "woke".

Zack wasn't exactly making it easy on himself though. He had recently dyed his hair purple, got a nose ring, and was now a vegan after watching a documentary on the dairy industry and learning about the anguish that cows are put through for their milk... which of course, caused even more anguish back at home.

He had turned vegetarian when he was about ten. In school his teacher had set the class a project about their parent's professions. That night over dinner he asked his dad if he could watch him at work. He could see how happy it had made his father; he was close to tears as he patted him on the back.

Young Zack had dressed like his father for the occasion, and he was wearing a special apron which his family had been saving for him. He watched wide-eyed as the animal carcasses were chopped up into smaller pieces, he noticed the blood... the eyeballs... and the ears. He asked where the meat came from, and when it was explained to him, he went white. The experience had scarred him for life. He would never forget the sound of laughter from his father's customers as he ran out of the shop crying.

But he couldn't change who he was, even if he wanted to. There was no going back now. The older he got and the more he read, the more militant his view became. He had seen the horrors, the pain, and the torture the animals went through - why couldn't anyone else?

He'd given up trying to reason with his friends and family, or anyone in his village for that matter. No-one understood him and it was time to get out. Living above the butcher's had become untenable and some would say damn right ridiculous considering the person he'd become.

Zack fantasised about escaping Sweet Little Chittering and moving to a big city, London being the obvious choice. He wanted to embrace multiculturalism and alternative ways of living. Village life had crushed Zack's spirit. The people of his hometown were all so simple-minded and stuck in their ways. He had to get out of Sweet Little Chittering before it killed him. He felt like a shaken-up bottle of cola that was about to explode.

Just when he'd sunken to his lowest and almost given up all hope of ever finding anyone he could relate to, he discovered new friends online through gaming... and a means of escape.

His new friends were from all over the world, but they understood him and got what he was about. It was ironic that he felt closer to people on the other side of the world than to the people he was physically close to... and through a friend of a friend he'd met someone, though not in real life yet.

Her name was Rachel, and by some sheer stroke of luck she lived in Hartbridge, the next village over. Whilst playing *Fortnite* online, a gamer friend had said he knew someone who lived in the UK and she lived in place called Hartbridge, "did he know it?" He couldn't believe it. Yes, he knew Hartbridge! And so, that night Rachel had joined their squad and they met for the first time virtually. It was a little awkward at first - trying to flirt over headset with other people listening in - but a few weeks later, when his other regular Fortnite buddies unexpectedly didn't turn up for a planned game, Rachel and Zack decided to go on without them and it turned out to be the best night of his life. They immediately hit it off and bonded over their shared passions for saving the planet and being kind to animals. He honestly couldn't believe his luck - they were so alike! She had recently turned vegan, hated the Tories, and was desperate to escape the small-town mentality of where she lived.

Zack was desperate to live in London and it turned out so was Rachel. Her brother, Mike, lived in a factory in Hackney with his artist friends - musicians, filmmakers, photographers, and modern artists all living under one roof. And all vegan too, of course! Rachel said that Mike and his friends were very welcoming and that he could come and stay a while too; "Come and see what it will be like, you can always go back. What harm is there?" He was hesitant, it was very unlike him to do anything so drastic regardless of how much he wanted to escape. He was quiet and kept himself to himself. The London life sounded so alien to him, yet he knew it was his destiny. Zack was bursting with nervous excitement for the possibility of a new life. It was scary... but exciting. He was finally getting out of Stupid Little Chittering, as he called his hometown. His life was about to change - he knew it. He just had to keep his nerve.

Zack and Rachel had planned to finally meet at the village fete. The plan was to pick him up outside Mysterious Magpie Books and Mike was going to drive them to London that evening. They chose that location as it was their favourite shop in the Chittering area. Zack would spend hours in there, getting lost in fantasy worlds or reading up on conservation issues. It was surprising that Judy, the owner, hadn't kicked him out, but she'd always been really accommodating and he'd try to buy at least one or two books a month.

That morning he'd packed his rucksack with just the essentials, not to give too much away. His dad and brother didn't take much notice of him anyway as they were distracted by the preparations for the fete. Mostly they seemed to be stuffing dead animals into the carcasses of other dead animals. He wanted to tell them he was leaving for London, but his dad would probably flip out and not allow it. It was best not to risk it. He decided to just go and face the consequences after. He would tell his dad eventually... maybe after a couple of days.

He wished his mother was still here. They had been so close. Zack secretly knew his mother had hated what his father had become since marrying him, but she would never say anything, she was too kind. Too mild-mannered. She died last year of cancer. It had been tough. His mother slowly dying in her bedroom whilst the smell of death from the butcher's permeated the air. That had been the final straw for Zack, and he had decided to get out of Sweet Little Shittering the first opportunity he got. And surprisingly that opportunity hadn't taken long to arise.

His friend Mr. Burroughs had said, "If you put it out there, it will come," and sure enough, it did. To be fair, he pretty much told anyone he encountered that he wanted to escape Sweaty Little Chitbag.

It was nearly midday and Zack had decided to take one last look around the village and, in his own way, say goodbye to the past. It seemed appropriate that he was leaving on this day - a day that had caused so much misery in his life.

They planned to meet at two o'clock whilst the famous Morris Dance on the green was in progress, when his father and brother would be most distracted and on their way to full intoxication. He literally had never been so excited to be missing the annual Morris Dance.

But in the meantime, he had to pretend everything was normal. Zack put on a smile for his neighbours and the tourists alike. "It won't be long till I'm out of here," he kept repeating to himself as he watched his father joyfully turn the hog roast over the fire. The fete was beginning to get busy.

"Sorry mate," a man in a floral shirt and sandals said, as he bumped into Zack, knocking him off balance.

"That's…" Zack began but the smell of burning flesh suddenly made his stomach turn. He put his hand over his mouth and quickly walked away in the direction of the vegetable display.

"Hi Mr. Burroughs. I definitely think you're in for a chance to win this year," Zack said to his friend, trying to hide his emotions. "That's one of the biggest marrows I've ever seen."

"Thank you, sonny boy, you can have a hold if you like? But don't drop it!"

"I daren't!" Zack said, trying to fight back a laugh. "I can't take that sort of responsibility!"

Mr. Burroughs was a sweet old man and probably wasn't aware of the double entendre he was making. Zack had on occasion helped Mr. Burroughs on his allotment and he'd regaled him with stories of the war. Though secretly Zack doubted that he was even alive then; he'd have to be in his nineties. He certainly didn't act that old, he was very springy on his feet. But he wouldn't even think of contradicting Mr. Burroughs, and he'd given up a long time ago trying to marry up the dates.

Mr. Burroughs was also a painter. He had an easel set up at the allotment and, after the vegetable planting and weeding, they would sit for an hour or two attempting to "capture the beauty of nature on our doorstep", as Mr. Burroughs would put it. The rolling fields up to the old windmill were a particularly pleasant sight, which many local artists over the years had tried to capture.

Mr. Burroughs was also an expert in village history. He had once told Zack the village was named Sweet Little Chittering after the scoundrel Sweet Douglas Banks who won the town in a bet in the 1660s, though Zack doubted this and guessed it was just another one of Mr. Burroughs' stories. For hundreds of years, as he told it, the village was called Little Chittering, probably since Saxon times. Apparently Sweet Douglas had bet the town folk that if he could cross the stream at Fairy Creek without the use of a boat or his feet, he would take possession of all the land within twenty miles and all the women under twenty… but sure enough, it was a trick (the means of his trickery being lost in the annals of time). And the town was renamed Sweet Douglas's Little Chittering. After he was burnt alive for witchcraft, the town elders dropped the Sweet Douglas part of the name, but it was later readopted, in part due to some unexplained grisly murders.

He'd heard people from outside Sweet Little Chittering say that most of the inhabitants of the village share a similarity with Sweet Douglas. He looked in the library and sure enough, they do. It was the Sweet Douglas long chin, essentially.

Zack's great-grandfather had come over form Eastern Europe in the 1930s so thankfully he didn't have the Little Chittering Chin, as the people in Great Chittering and Hartbridge called it.

Mr. Burroughs had gone back to polishing his oversized vegetables, concentrating on getting a good shine, when Zack felt a tap on his shoulder.

He turned around to see Adrian, his rugby playing older brother, looming over him.

"Dad wants you to go and get more lard for the hog roast."

"Why can't you do it?"

"I'm doing the tug-of-war in an hour."

"So? It will only take you five minutes. Dad asked you to do it, didn't he?" Zack said suspiciously.

"Just go and get the lard for Dad you little shit, or I'll tell everyone about you and the paper boy. I've seen the way you look at him."

"Fuck off, dickbrain."

"So tetchy! I must have touched a nerve!"

Before Zack could think of a comeback, Adrian turned his back on him, laughing as he walked away. Zack unthinkingly stamped his foot.

He turned back to Mr. Burroughs, who he could tell was trying to pretend he hadn't heard their exchange and felt dreadful immediately. He wanted to crawl into a hole and die. Zack felt so ashamed that kind Mr. Burroughs had seen him like that.

Just then he felt his phone ping in his back pocket.

It was a message from Rachel. *Hey, sorry. I'm running late. I should be with you by 5 though. Meet you by the Paradise Inn. Stay safe.*

Oh damn. This was becoming even scarier than he thought. He was nervous and had butterflies now. A man in double denim was staring at him, eating a Mr. Whippy. He took a big lick of his ice cream.

"What are you doing Zachery?!" Zack jumped around to see Rob, a guy he used to go to school with, standing in front of him with two plastic pint glasses of warm ale.

"SHIT! What the fuck, Rob?"

"Want one of these? I got it for Paul, but he just disappeared."

"I'm fine thanks," Zack said leaning on his knees and panting.

"You going somewhere?" Rob said, noticing Zack's rucksack.

"What? No."

"Sure you won't have one of these? There's

nothing wrong with it."

"Honestly, I'm fine. I'm not really into ale."

Zack and Rob used to hang out together in real life a few years ago when they were the villages only goths, but Rob had turned his back on the Lord of Darkness (and Zack) and was now very much into rugby, fishing and sports in general, since leaving school with a totally new group of friends. Zack had felt betrayed, but he never said anything to Rob. In fact, he hadn't spoken to him in a couple of years. "People just grow apart," his mum had reassured him, but the rejection had really stung.

"Fair enough," Rob was saying. "Hey, wanna come smoke some doob with us by the windmill?"

He was about to say he couldn't when Lee, another old school mate (school acquaintance really), put his arm around him. "Come on Zack, don't be shy. We haven't seen you in ages, you never come out anymore." Lee was short and bouncy with an intense stare. He was known around the village for being a bit off the rails, but Zack had known him since they were in infant school together. He was harmless if you didn't say the wrong thing to him or bring up his family.

"Yeah, what happened to you?" Rob interjected. "We thought something bad had happened in the butchers."

"Oh, you know, I've just had other stuff on."

"Like what?"

"Oh er... looking for work... playing Fortnite."

"You need to get out more. Live a little!" Lee said whilst putting an arm around Zack's shoulders.

"Yeah, I guess…"

"Come on, let's go!"

Rob and Lee began to lead Zack off to the windmill. He would have complained but he knew he had at least four hours to kill now. He tuned to say goodbye to Mr. Burroughs (and was secretly praying he hadn't heard the weed talk) but he was nowhere to be seen.

It was a blisteringly hot day and by the time they reached the windmill they were all dripping with sweat.

Paul was there, his brother's best mate. Another rugby playing meathead.

"Little Zachary! What are you doing here?"

"Just mooching."

"Mooching! Haha!"

Zack didn't know what was so funny, but everyone was rolling around in fits of giggles.

"Little Mooching Zachery!"

"Anyway, I should go now." Zack turned to walk back into the village, but Lee and Rob grabbed him by the shoulders and spun him round.

"No, you can't go!" Rob said, holding onto Zack. "You have to try this dynamite weed we got off the Hartbridge boys."

"Come on, don't be a pussy Zack," Lee said with a glint in his eye that was almost threatening.

Zack wished he had the will power to say no but he found himself lying on his back looking up at the clouds as they swirled above him, two dragons fighting an epic battle, one consuming the other whole… as he saw it.

An hour or so passed when Zack suddenly snapped out of his reverie and stood up. "I gotta go," he said and began marching unsteadily back into the village.

"Pussy!" he heard Lee say behind his back.

"Hey! Wait up! I'll come with you," Rob was saying, a little out of breath, as he tried to catch up with Zack. "I've got to buy some raffle tickets for my mum."

They walked down the hill in silence from the windmill, back to the fete, stoned out of their minds. There was lots they could have talked about, but the paranoia was kicking in, making them both monosyllabic. The awkward silence was broken when a car pulled up behind them and started beeping its horn for an annoyingly long time. Zack decided not to look but Rob was tugging his shirt.

"Look Zack! What's going on in there?" He reluctantly turned to see what Rob was looking at. It was unclear at first what was going on, he could only see movement, but soon it became obvious that there was a fight in progress inside the car. "Should we do something?" Rob asked.

"Don't be daft! Come on, let's go, it's not our business." Just as Zack was turning away, the car door suddenly swung open, and a body-shaped object was thrown out of the car. The tyres screeched and the car sped off past them. Zack and Rob quickly turned their heads away so as not to be seen by the driver.

"Come on!" Rob beckoned as he ran over to see what had been thrown out of the car. It was Julie, a girl from the village, another ex-goth. She had got a bad reputation since leaving school and drinking in the pubs.

"Are you okay?" Rob was asking as Zack approached.

Her eyes were spinning, and she was drooling.

"She doesn't look okay," Zack offered.

"That was Paul's brother, wasn't it?" Rob appeared to be saying to Julie but then he turned to Zack. "That was Grant. I'm certain of it."

Zack felt the hairs on the back of his neck stand up. He knew Grant. He was a massive dick. He'd had a few run-ins with Grant over the years, including a time he nicked Zack's cap and posted it in a letterbox. On another occasion he had stuffed fried chicken down Zack's shirt. Zack had purposely stayed out of his way since then. That was a few years ago and was probably one of the reasons Zack had retreated to his bedroom and no longer wanted to hang out with his old friends anymore. Though he wouldn't like to admit it.

"We should get her help," Rob said, helping Julie off the ground. "Help me take her to my dad's. He'll be blind drunk at the Paradise Inn by now."

They put their arms around Julie's shoulders and led her to Rob's dad's house which was close by.

"He hides the key under the mat. He kept losing them," Rob explained as they arrived.

Entering, Zack noticed what a mess the place was, take-away boxes everywhere and the smell of cat poop lingering in the air. Rob's parents had divorced a couple of years ago and his dad had taken it badly, falling quite far off the rails.

"Dad! Are you in?!"

They waited a moment for an answer, and when it didn't come they dragged Julie to the sofa. They stood silently looking at Julie, stoned and out of breath.

"I'll get some water," Rob wheezed, wandering off to the kitchen.

Zack plonked himself down on the sofa next to Julie. Her eyelids began to flicker. "Shit. Sorry. Are you okay?" Suddenly Julie lurched forward and was sick on Zack's jeans.

"Aw no!"

"Sorry, sorry," Julie spluttered.

"Rob!" Zack shouted into the kitchen, but no reply came.

"Rob?!" Still no answer. Zack went into the kitchen. No Rob. He'd gone. Disappeared.

"You bastard," Zack muttered.

He went to the cupboards to find a glass, but the cupboards were bare. He eventually found an old, stained mug with lumps of mould festering on the bottom, under some rubbish, by the sink. He turned the taps, and they made a gurgling noise but no water came out. "Awww, for fuck's sake."

Zack went back to Julie. "Rob's gone and there appears to be no water coming from the taps - we should go."

"Take me to Paul's."

"What? No. What if Grant is there?"

"Please, I beg you. I need to get my things."

"Are you sure? Wasn't that Grant who threw you

out the car? He seems angry."

"I need to get my stuff, please. It's important," she said quietly.

Zack didn't know what to do, he couldn't leave her here. He was starting to think Rob had set him up. What the fuck happened to him?

"Please take me to Paul's. I have to get my stuff, I'll be quick - in and out."

He didn't know what else to do so he called a taxi. He expected it would be hard to get one with the fete in full swing, but surprisingly one was available.

"He'll be there in five minutes Zack." This flummoxed him.

"Oh sorry," Zack stammered to the operator, trying to guess the voice he was talking to. "I didn't know you knew me…"

"Course I do. I've known your family my whole life, your grandad was a great man. As is your father."

Everyone knows everyone in this damn town, he thought to himself. *No secrets.*

"Thanks…"

Zack was about to ask who he was talking to when the operator said, "and your brother." Zack lost all politeness and hung up.

The taxi pulled up within minutes and sure enough it was someone he knew, sort of. This was going to be awkward. "Zack!" It was Brian, the local art dealer slash taxi driver. "Hop in."

Zack opened the door for Julie and helped her into the cab, pushing her head down so as not to bang it on the way in.

"Where to then?"

Julie slurred the address and they set off to the destination.

"Got lucky did you, young Zachery?"

"What? NO! I'm just helping Julie home."

"Alright! Calm down fella." Then to Julie he said, "That ale isn't half strong this year, ay love?"

They pulled up outside Paul and Grant's house. Zack paid, a little begrudgingly, then helped Julie out of the cab and to the front door. She had slightly sobered up now.

"Well, this was fun," Zack said, trying to conceal the sarcasm. "I've got to go now. You be careful Julie."

"Please wait for me," Julie begged, holding onto Zack's jacket as he tried to walk away.

"I can't… I've got to go. I'm meeting someone."

"He's dangerous," Julie said, now staring intently into Zack's eyes. "Please wait outside and call the police if anything happens." She now appeared to be completely sober and deadly serious. He suddenly saw the old Julie he knew when they were kids.

Zack looked at his phone, he still had time but his battery was on its last bar.

"Fine. I'll wait over there. Behind that wall."

Zack went over the road and crouched down behind the bin collection area of the adjacent block of flats as Julie knocked on the door. Sure enough, Grant answered the door, said something angrily through gritted teeth, then pulled her into the house by her hair. The door slammed behind her.

Zack didn't know what to do. Should he call the police? But what if Grant found out he had called the police on him. He'd be dead for sure. Maybe he should call Adrian? Or Rob... what happened to him?!

Suddenly the front door swung open and Grant stormed out onto the driveway, still clutching Julie's hair. Zack ducked down behind the wall as he heard Grant snarl "Where?!" Foolishly, Zack took a peek round the wall as he saw Julie point in his direction.

"Fuck," he said to himself as Grant spotted him. "Oi! You little shit! Come here!" Grant began to run towards Zack at speed. Zack ran as fast as he could in the other direction, through the estates, through fields, jumping over hedges and fences, never looking back.

Somehow, he found himself by the old Henge. He stopped and lay down in the middle of the stone circle, making sure Grant was nowhere to be seen. He'd lost him.

He was now dripping with sweat for the second time today. He took his phone out: 4:32. Did he have time to go home and get changed?

He was trying to think what to message Rachel and panicking his phone was about to run out of battery, when a message came through. *Hey! I'm sorry we got held up again, meet you at 8 by the parade. I'm really sorry x*

The parade! Damn it. Everyone will be there. He'll be seen for sure. But at least he had time to go home and change first, he realised. His head was a fuzzy mess but the kiss at the end of the message made him forget his ordeal for a moment.

Zack was carefully making his way back into the village centre when Lee and Rob jumped out of the bushes in front of him. "Hey! Where do you think you're going?"

"Home. I need to change," Zack said without looking at them. Lee suddenly lurched at him and put him in a head lock. "You're not going anywhere, little man," he was saying as a car pulled up alongside them.

"I got him!" Lee shouted as Grant jumped out of the car.

"Why you running little Zachary? What did you do to Julie?"

"Nothing. I didn't do anything!" he spluttered whilst Lee held onto his neck.

"Get him in the car," Grant ordered.

Zack was bundled in the back of the car between Grant and Lee. Rob got in the passenger seat. Paul was driving. "I didn't do anything! Rob! Tell Grant I was with you!"

"This is between you and Grant," Rob said as Paul turned the engine and pulled away.

"You think I'm going to let you fuck around with my girlfriend and get away with it?" Lee shouted in Zack's ear.

"I didn't..." he began, when he noticed the four robed figures watching him from across the road.

"What the fuck?! Did you see that?"

"What?"

"There were four guys... in robes.... watching us... I swear."

Suddenly a bag was put over Zack's head. Grant held tightly onto the opening around Zack's neck. "Let go of me!" Zack struggled. His hands were free though, they hadn't thought to tie him up as well. With all his might, he elbowed Grant and Lee in their faces, leaned back then booted Paul in the back of the head. He kicked Rob in the face as he turned to see what was going on. The car swerved.

"You fuck!" was the last thing he heard as the car plowed into a tree.

***

Zack awoke to find he was now on the dashboard of the car; the four other passengers were either dead or unconscious - it was too early to say. Through a daze, he pulled himself out the passenger window, clambering over Rob in the process. As he fell to the ground, he kicked Rob in the face which brought him round. "What the fuck?" he mumbled.

Zack tried to stand up. He was unsteady on his feet at first but he managed it and brushed himself down feeling his body for any breakages. Miraculously, apart from a few scratches and bruises, he was unhurt.

"Grant, are you okay man?" he heard Rob saying. "Grant?"

"What's going on? What happened?" Lee and Paul were coming round too. Lee leant forward and blood gushed from a wound on his head.

"Fuck dude, you're bleeding," Rob said to him.

"Get me out here," Lee responded. "Rob, move your seat forward!"

"Grant doesn't look well. I think he's dead," Rob was saying as Zack started sprinting away from the scene of the accident.

***

His head was pounding, his legs were aching, and his eyesight was blurred. He fell down face first in the grass - was he back at the Henge? He couldn't be sure. He lay still for a moment trying to gather his thoughts.

He rolled over. The world was spinning. The clouds above were swirling and making strange shapes in the sky again. "I've got to get home," he said to himself.

Zack took his phone out of his pocket. He sighed as he discovered his battery was well and truly dead now.

"Damn it! Just my luck. Fuck it, I'll charge it at home. There's still time to get cleaned up and meet Rachel at the parade," he reassured himself.

"What have you done Zachery?" said one of the four robed figures as they approached him. He knew that voice, but he couldn't quite put his finger on it. He began propping himself up on his elbows.

"This was not part of the plan," said another of the robed figures gruffly.

"Grant is dead Zack, you killed him," said a female voice delicately.

"They were going to kill me! It wasn't my fault - we crashed!"

"Hold him down," said the first figure.

The others pounced on him and Zack screamed. Two held an arm each, one grabbed his head, squeezing his nose and forcing his mouth open, as Zack tried to scream and wriggle his way out of their grip. The first figure, whose voice Zack recognised, produced a bottle from under his robe. "Hold him still," he commanded, as he began to pour a green potion down Zack's throat. Zack tried to fight his way out of the robed assailant's grip, but it didn't take long for his body to go limp. "That'll doooooooooo...." he heard as his eyes rolled to the back of his head and he fell into the abyss.

***

The world was out of focus and there was music pounding in his head. Zack awoke and found himself naked in a crowd of dancing people, people from the town he half knew - his dad's friends and customers, all laughing hysterically in his face. He was dizzy and felt as if he was about to throw up. He was being pushed and pulled and twirled in all directions. His body was wet and sticky. Warm ale was being poured over him in celebration and the mob were feasting on hog with their bare hands. "Get the grease boys, let's lather him up!" he heard someone shout. He could see the meat grease around their mouths and on their fingers.

"Please, don't touch me," he cried, but the mob

laughed and took hold of him, taking pleasure in wiping their fingers on him, lathering him up whilst holding him aloft. He tried to scream but fingers were stuck into his mouth, prising it open. Bits of bone and dead animal flesh were being dropped into him as if he was a dustbin or a basketball net, and grease was being massaged into his body by the excited crowd. "Pleaseeeeee," he begged. His body was convulsing, and he couldn't stop gagging. He felt disgusted to the core. "Let go of me!" But the mania continued.

In the distance the Morris Men were marching through the village centre, singing and chanting as they approached Zack and the frenzied mob. He could see the pig's head now, mounted on a stick, held aloft by the head Morris Man, and they all cheered.

Suddenly the crowd parted and Zack was dropped to the ground. A hush permeated through the mob and he looked up to see a girl in a yellow dress swirling towards Zack. Her long blonde wavy hair concealing her face. "Rachel? Is that you?"

"Rachel, Rachel, Rachel," the crowd began to chant. The girl slowly lifted her head, her hair parting to reveal her face - it was Julie in a wig. "Julie, I don't understand. What's going on?" Julie began to laugh and the other town folk joined in.

"Rachel! Rachel! Rachel! Rachel!" The chant grew louder.

Soon, other *Rachels* appeared, all dressed the same with the same blonde hair. They danced around Zack and formed a circle. The circle became tight around him and one of the other Rachels moved in close to his face and parted her hair. It was Lee, his eyes were wide and he had a crazed look on his face. "Zacheryyyyyyyy!" Zack stumbled backwards but the mob caught him and threw him forward into another Rachel, she looked up and parted her hair, it was Rob. He too laughed in Zack's face, then other Rachels approached him, one by one, parting their hair and laughing in his face, the next up was Paul... then Grant... he was alive. Before he had time to reflect on what had happened, the crowd parted again and a figure moved in from behind the Rachels...

"Rachel, Rachel." they continued to chant.

Mr. Burroughs stepped forward. "You are one little wriggly piglet, sonny boy. You've caused us a lot of trouble," he said, rubbing his hands.

"Mr. Burroughs, I don't understand," Zack heard himself say, although it was at that moment he realised that he did understand everything after all. Mr. Burroughs was an evil bastard all along He knew there was something not right about him.

"Let's cut the piglet open," Mr. Burroughs said to the mob with an insane grin twisting on his face and then held aloft an ornate Nazi dagger. It was all too much for Zack, he felt his body double over and he threw up everywhere - projectile vomiting on the people dancing around him. There was screaming and a lot of confusion.

"You disgusting little pig," Mr. Burroughs said to Zack, as he coughed up his guts on one of the village's award winning flower beds. "Grab him!"

It was at that moment a huge crack of thunder boomed above the mob - to Zack it was as if a nuclear bomb had gone off - and everyone's eyes were averted towards the heavens for a moment. Spotting his chance to escape, Zack fell to the ground and rolled down the ditch.

The mob looked down and laughed, pointing at Zack. "Look at the little piglet," he heard someone say.

"Go on then! Run!" he heard Mr. Burroughs cackle.

Zack didn't hesitate - he sprung to feet and started clambering up the other side of the ditch.

"You can do it! Haha!" Mr. Burroughs chuckled.

Suddenly the sky was lit up by a bolt of fork lightning, distracting the angry mob for a moment. And then the heavens opened up and rain poured down on them all.

Zack began to run like he'd never run before. "Let's see if the piglet can run!" he heard another voice cry, possibly one of his old schoolteachers.

***

Zack was soaked and could barely see, he found himself running naked through Sweet Little Chittering in a blind panic, jumping hedges again and hiding behind trees - was this a nightmare? He'd had these dreams before. He was staggering, running, falling over, running some more, bumping into things but always moving, almost like he was on autopilot, a drunk pilot - and somehow, someway, he made it home. A thought had kept swirling round his head this whole time - *I just need to make it home... to my own bed... perhaps Dad and Adrian would forgive me.... perhaps they would protect me.*

It wasn't long before he found himself scrambling up the back fence of his house and creeping through the garden to the backdoor.

Behind him a twig snapped.

"Where do you think you're going?" As he turned around, he was hit over the head with a butcher's mallet.

***

Waking up in intense pain, Zack's world was upside down and moving. He recognised the white tiled room he was in. His body was on fire yet freezing. In the mirror a skinned, limbless animal swung into view... but that was no animal. It suddenly came to him... he was hanging upside down in his father's shop, skinned alive on a hook but still breathing. He tried to scream but his tongue had been removed.

"If only you could have tried to fit in, Zack. Sweet Little Chittering isn't so bad." Adrian approached him with a bolt gun. "Rachel," he snorted. "So gullible."

Zack wriggled and tried to make a noise but nothing would come out but air. "You didn't really think we were going to let you leave, did you Zachery?" Adrian said as he stuffed an apple into Zack's mouth.

"Hackney warehouse?! Classic," he snorted again.

"All right, that's enough Adrian," his dad said as he approached him from behind. "I wish we could have worked it out Zack. I had high hopes for you. But still, never mind, you'll make tasty meat for the hog roast next year." That was the last thing Zack heard before the sound of the bolt gun penetrated his skull.

Hawthorn Lane

Matt Davies

The bus wound its way along the country lanes. It was crowded with too many people who, Veronica thought to herself, paid too little attention to their personal hygiene. She'd been unable to get a seat and was now awkwardly wedged between a fat woman and her awful children and an older man who seemed to lean into her a little more than was necessary as the bus rounded the corners of the narrow lanes. They'd had to stop multiple times for tractors crossing between the fields or sheep being herded from one place to another.

During one of these stops Veronica had spied the henge in the distance. The standing stones jutted out of the land like nails haphazardly hammered into a piece of wood by a child. As she peered at the henge, she thought she could see movement around the stones. Probably day trippers lured there by the gaudy advertising she'd seen online for the 'Hartbridge Henge', that the nearby town of Hartbridge splashed across the ad space of any website mentioning the area. However, Veronica, like any good journalist, had dug deeper and found that the henge had an older name, ancient even: The Chittering.

The bus pulled away and continued its journey. As The Chittering passed out of sight, Veronica slipped her hand into her bag and felt the leather cover of the journal. She ran her fingers over its worn surface, an act she found oddly comforting. A tablet or a laptop was, she knew, a far better way to keep notes, but there was something about the writing and drawing by hand and pasting clippings into the journal that allowed her to engage with her research, and the story that research revealed, on a far deeper level than she'd ever been able to before.

The heat in the bus had grown stifling and the passengers, Veronica included, breathed a collective sigh of relief as the bus finally pulled into the village of Sweet Little Chittering. As the passengers piled off the bus, Veronica paused to speak with the driver.

"What time is the last bus back to Hartbridge?" she asked.

The driver seemed to ponder his answer in the way that country folk sometimes do despite knowing the answer off the top of their head.

"We lay on extra services the day of the fete," the driver said, somewhat unhelpfully.

"Okay, but what actual time is the last bus leaving?" Veronica politely pressed.

"Oh, nine, half nine, something like that." The driver was clearly clueless.

"Thanks," Veronica replied with a slight air of exasperation. She took her phone out of her bag and checked the time - 17:45. She'd have plenty of time to track down who she was looking for and still get the last bus back.

The rest of the passengers hurried towards the village green, from where Veronica could already hear the village fete in full swing. Veronica had no interest in the fete, so walked at a slower, but deliberate, pace.

As she walked, she took in her surrounds. Sweet Little Chittering was like the twee drawings on the lids of a biscuit tins brought to life. Quaint, neatly kept little houses packed along the sides of narrow streets, well-trimmed hedges and a row of small shops, including a family butcher's and even a candle maker. Surely these people had electricity? A hint of a smile crossed Veronica's face as she amused herself with the sarcastic observation.

As Veronica approached the village green, the crowd began to get a little denser and she had to weave amongst the people. Many clutched raffle tickets and Veronica wondered what prize could be so great, as to make people buy quite so many tickets.

An old lady stepped out and blocked Veronica's path. "You've still time to buy a ticket, deary. The draw isn't for another ten minutes!" The old lady held up a book of raffle tickets and stared at Veronica with a toothless grin.

"No, thank you," Veronica replied politely and old the lady looked almost shocked. "Could you tell me the best way to get to Hawthorn Lane?" Veronica went on.

"Hawthorn Lane?" the old lady replied, a look of complete confusion spreading across her face.

"Yes. Hawthorn Lane." Veronica pulled the journal from her bag and thumbed through it. "I believe it should be not far from here." She held up the journal, open at the page of her hand drawn map of the village.

"Well, deary, I've lived here my whole life and I've never heard of no Hawthorn Lane. You must have the wrong village." The old lady turned and shuffled back into the crowd, waving her book of tickets at anyone who wasn't quick enough to dodge out of her way.

Veronica stood and looked at her map. The crowd swirled around her, as she tried to orient herself to the map and her surroundings. As she was doing so, she noticed an information board on the wall between the 'Crusty Von Buns Bakers' shop and 'J.M. Cockcroft & Son Family Butchers'. She made a beeline for the board.

Veronica stopped in front of the board and saw, to her delight, there was a map of the village. It was badly faded and curled at the edges. The rusty drawing pins holding it in place testified to how long it had been there. She studied the map and compared it to the one she had drawn in her journal as she'd researched the village and the area.

"Looking for something? Or somewhere?" a man's voice said from behind her.

Veronica turned to see an older man with a vacant smile staring at her.

"I'm looking for Hawthorn Lane," Veronica said matter of factly and turned back to the board.

"Well, I hate to say it Miss. But I think you might have the wrong village. I've lived here most of my life and I've never heard of a Hawthor…"

"Here!" Veronica cut him off. "It's here, on the map, look."

The man peered at the map and then leant in closer. He wiped at the glass door of the notice board, as if this would change the map within.

"But…that doesn't make any sense. I mean, that shouldn't be there," the old man turned and looked Veronica directly in the eye. "I mean, I've lived here for years and…and… that's not been there."

Yet, on the map, very faded, but definitely there, was written Hawthorn Lane. Indicting that it could be found in what looked like a relatively short walk from the village green.

Veronica left the man still staring at the map in disbelief. *Perhaps he has dementia,* she thought to herself. *Why else would he have claimed to have lived in the village most of his life and then not know of a lane that was perhaps a few minutes' walk from the heart of the village*? She headed past the village school and away from the green and the festivities.

As Veronica walked, the noise of the fete faded away and the only sound was her footsteps on the pavement. As the houses began to thin out, the pavement did as well, until Veronica was walking on the edge of the road. As she walked, she looked at her hand drawn map and wrote in the location of Hawthorn Lane as it had been indicated on the map in the village. Yet still she walked and there was no sign of the lane.

Veronica checked the time on her phone; 18:20. She'd walked for twenty minutes! This could not be right. Certainly, there was no scale on the map in the village, but this was ridiculous. She tapped the screen of her phone to open the maps app. A blank screen opened with white text: *No Signal*. She held up the phone and saw that she had no data. Useless.

She decided to walk on but to turn back and head into the village if she'd still not found Hawthorn Lane after another ten minutes.

As Veronica walked, the landscape began to change. Overgrown hedgerows rose along the sides of the winding road, giving the feeling of walking through a maze. The sky turned from the bright spring day to a featureless milky grey. The air grew cold, there was a damp smell, and a bitter taste began to linger at the back of Veronica's throat. She shivered.

Just as she was about to turn back, she noticed a street sign partially obscured by the hedgerows. Gingerly she pulled aside the foliage. Most of the paint had flaked off the sign leaving the bare metal, but the name was unmistakable: Hawthorn Lane.

Veronica took a step back and realised that the entrance to the lane was set slightly back so had been obscured by the hedgerows until now. She glanced back in the direction of the village. She stopped dead.

Looking back the way she'd come, things looked completely different. She could see the village green, but it looked much closer. How could she have walked for so long and yet looking back the route looked like it should have taken no more than a few minutes to walk. Also, the road had been narrow and winding, but she was now looking back in a straight line towards the village. The village that was bathed in spring sunshine, yet she stood shivering in the gloom, beneath a milky and overcast sky.

An optical illusion, perhaps? Like not being able to see the entrance to Hawthorn Lane until she was right on top of it. Veronica dismissed the whole thing. She was now wasting time and needed to press on with the reason for her visit to Sweet Little Chittering and the resident who she had come to speak with: Diana Drake. Veronica stepped through the hedgerow and into Hawthorn Lane.

She stopped abruptly as her eyes adjusted to the light, looking about Hawthorn Lane. The sky above was still the flat milky grey, but things were somehow brighter here, like a light shining through frosted glass. Hawthorn Lane resembled the other streets of the village Veronica had walked down but here things were fundamentally different.

The houses looked ramshackle. Roofs were missing slates. Paint work peeled and wooden frames rotted. The windows were grey from what looked like years of not being cleaned. Some had broken panes with filthy curtains barely visible behind. Gardens were choked with weeds that stippled out onto the lane itself. The dilapidation continued onto the surface of the lane that was pockmarked with holes and the asphalt was cracked like a dry lakebed. There was no sign of life. The lane was silent.

At the end of the lane stood a house that was larger than the rest and must have been somewhat grand in its day. However, in the same way that it was larger than the rest of the houses, its level of disrepair was also more pronounced. The structure seemed to be sagging and twisted. Held together by the climbing plants that spread from the ground up across the outer walls, obscuring many of the building's features. Windows, of a similarly filthy state, were visible here and there.

Veronica flipped open the journal and pulled out an old photograph that was tucked between the pages. She held the photograph up, so it was in line with the house. The faded black and white image of a grand house bore the same outline as the building ahead of her. Veronica turned the photograph over - written on the back in pencil was: The Hawthorns. She tucked the photograph back into the journal and began to head towards the house.

As she walked, the crunching of her footsteps on the broken road surface was the only sound. Veronica wondered if the houses, perhaps the whole lane, was abandoned? Maybe her journey had been in vain?

Then she saw it. As she passed the second house, barely visible through the filthy window, a curtain twitched. Veronica saw the faint outline of a figure looking out through the gap. Looking out through the filthy glass, but unmistakably looking at her.

Veronica pressed on. Same at the third and fourth houses. Looming shapes at the windows.

As Vernonia drew level with the fifth house, she started at the sight in the window. The glass had been wiped from the inside and an old man's face leered out at her. His heavily lined sallow skin, sunken eyes, and almost grey lips gave him a ghoulish appearance. Veronica made a small motion, not quite a wave, to acknowledge the man. A thin smile, more a grimace, spread across his face to revealing yellowed tombstone-like teeth. Veronica walked on.

As she drew level with the last but one house, the front door swung open. A man and woman stared at her. They were old, no, ancient in appearance. Bent backs, white wisps of hair and skin like rice paper. They stared at Veronica as they stood wavering and gripping the doorframe for support.

"Hello," Veronica said awkwardly.

The woman made a hoarse noise, somewhere between a gasp and a groan, by way of acknowledgement. The man remained silent.

As Veronica walked past, their heads moved as they kept their eyes locked on her. As Veronica reached the gate of The Hawthorns she turned to look back. The woman peered around the doorway of the house, still looking at her. Then Veronica saw them. At every house along the lane, faces peered out from windows and doors that were barely ajar. The whole lane was looking at her.

Veronica paused. A feeling of unease swept over her. She wanted to flee. To run out of the lane, out of this strange, decayed place, and back towards the village.

No. She had come too far to be put off by some backward locals. She lifted the gate and pushed, the rusted hinges groaning in protest. Pushing past overgrown plants, Veronica reached the front door and knocked. She looked back up the lane. Still, they stared.

The front door jerked open causing Veronica to jump. Another ancient face moved into the light. The man was similarly stooped and frail, like the man and woman Veronica had seen in the other house.

"Yes?" a rasp of a voice escaped the man's lips.

"I...erm...I'm looking for a Diana Drake? I believe she lives, or lived here?" Veronica smiled, more to try to put herself at ease than anything else.

Without taking his eyes off Veronica, the old man let out what was almost a cry, "Diana! Visitor!"

Veronica heard movement from within the house. An old woman lurched into view behind the man. She limped heavily but stood erect and held her head up to look Veronica in the face. Long grey hair framed her lined face and piercing blue eyes met Veronica's gaze. There was clearly quite an age gap between her and the man.

The woman pushed past the man who shrank back into the house.

"Hello?" the old woman's voice was clear and firm.

"Diana Drake?" Veronica enquired.

"Yes. I'm Diana, what can I do for you?"

"My name is Veronica Jones. I'm a journalist. I was wondering if I might be able to ask you some questions? About something I've been researching?" Veronica held out her press card.

Diana's eyes flicked from Veronica's face to the

card, and then fell upon the journal Veronica still held in her other hand.

"You'd better come in then," Diana smiled, then her gaze moved past Veronica and her brow furrowed.

Veronica looked back over her shoulder, and she just caught sight of the other residents of the lane darting back behind their doors and curtains. She turned back to Diana, who still smiled.

"Don't mind them," Diana reassured her. "We don't get many visitors down here. Come in."

Diana turned back into the house and Veronica stepped after her. The old man was now nowhere to be seen. Veronica paused for one last look down the now deserted lane and closed the front door behind her. She followed Diana into a large sitting room.

The room was dated and dusty, a musty smell hung heavy in the air. Diana moved to an armchair and lowered herself, stiffly, into the seat. A slight grimace of pain crossed her face. *She must have been very beautiful in her youth*, Veronica thought as she sat down in the chair opposite.

"I'd like to ask about…" Veronica began but was cut off.

"A drink?" Diana asked.

"Oh, erm, no I'm fine. Thank you," replied Veronica.

"Tea?" There was an odd edge to Diana's voice.

"Well, yes, thank you. If it's not too much trouble?" Veronica didn't want to waste time but equally needed to engage with Diana.

"No trouble, dear," Diana's gaze was fixed on

Veronica. "Terry? Tea for two!" Diana called out.

"Yes dear," came the muffled reply from another room.

Diana settled back in her chair. "What did you say your name was again?" she asked.

"Veronica Jones. I'm a freelance journalist," Veronica replied, "I've been researching this area and wanted to ask you some questions, if that's okay?"

"Well, I'm not sure what I could tell you that would be very interesting, dear?" She couldn't put her finger on exactly why, but Diana's words didn't ring true to Veronica.

Diana motioned towards the journal. "I thought all you young people used your technical gadgets now? No more writing things down?"

"Oh, this?" Veronica held up the journal.

"Yes. That," said Diana.

"Well, this is part of the reason I'm here." Veronica opened the journal to its front page and held it up for Diana to see. "I found this journal in an old bookshop. A journalist named Murray seems to have started writing this in the 1950s but the dates get progressively muddled." Veronica turned the first few pages revealing handwritten notes in fountain pen ink.

"Murray's mother was originally from Sweet Little Chittering," Veronica continued, "and as a child he would come back with her to visit. Over the years it seems he got to know a lot of the children in the village. Later, when he was older and working as a teacher, he came back to visit again. What he found was very odd."

Veronica looked at Diana for some sign of a reaction, but the old woman sat attentively yet without giving away a hint of emotion. Veronica continued.

"He found that some of the children he knew from growing up, who would at the time have been young adults, were missing…"

"Missing…" Diana seemed to be affirming the statement rather than asking a question.

"Yes, missing. They'd disappeared and seemingly without a trace," Veronica explained.

Diana showed no sign of a reaction and silence filled the room.

"Ah, Terry." Diana looked towards the doorway.

The old man, Terry, was shuffling in with a tray. Precariously balanced on the tray was a tea pot along with two cups and saucers. Terry was so frail that it looked as if he could barely hold up the tray and walk.

"Let me help you…" Veronica began to rise from her chair.

"He can manage." Diana's words cut through the air like a knife.

Veronica looked at Diana and then back to Terry who continued to shuffle through the room. All the time the tray looked like it would fall from his grasp at any moment. Finally, and seemingly with great relief, Terry set the tray down on a side table. He turned to Diana and motioned towards the tray.

"Leave it. I'll serve." Diana's tone sounded like it would be better suited for a command to a dog, than to a human companion.

Terry shuffled out of the room. Diana watched him go and began to rise from her chair. Again, a grimace of pain crossed her face.

"Would you like me to..." Veronica began but Diana silenced her with a raised finger.

"I can still manage," Diana said bitterly. "It's not old age itself that will do you in. It's giving into old age that seals your fate."

Diana crossed to the tray and began to pour with her back to Veronica.

"Murray, you say, that was his name?" Diana asked, not turning.

"Yes. Murray. I think he'd have been about my age, mid-twenties, when he began the journal," Veronica replied.

"I don't remember anyone called Murray. Why have you come to talk to me?" Diana turned to Veronica and held out the cup and saucer. Steam curled into the air from the freshly poured tea.

"Because he mentions you, by name, in the journal." Veronica let the words hang in the air and noticed, just for a moment, Diana's jaw tighten and her outstretched hand twitch, causing the cup to shift slightly on the saucer.

Veronica took the cup and saucer, resetting the cup as she took it. Diana seemed lost in thought and then headed back to her chair.

Settling herself back into the chair Diana asked, "And what did this... Murray, have to say about me?"

"It's not just about you," Veronica set the cup

and saucer to one side and leafed through the journal. "Your family, the Drakes, have been in this area since medieval times. Correct?"

"Some say maybe even before that," Diana replied with a slight smile.

"Murray had researched back and found fragmented records of the Drake family holding a sort of 'spring festival' here. Over time I believe that's evolved into the village fete that's being held today." Veronica continued, "Murray was starting to draw a link between some of the elements of the old 'spring festival' and the disappearances in the 1950s."

Veronica looked at Diana, who stared back.

"What has this to do with me? You said I was mentioned by name," Diana asked firmly.

"Yes, but this is where Murray's dates seem to get muddled. Murray writes," Veronica thumbed on a few pages in the journal and continued, "that he spoke with Diana Drake, and she told him that as part of the spring festival families in the area would be obliged to send young family members to work on the Drake's estate. However, not all the family members would return. This bit is still unclear to me, but he writes that the families forgot their loved ones had even existed."

"Forgot?" Diana questioned.

"It doesn't really make sense and oddly this is where Murray's part of the journal ends," said Veronica.

"Murray's part?" Diana asked.

"Yes, you see, I was so interested in this story

that I carried on his research and his journal." Veronica turned a page and held the journal out to Diana. The flowing handwriting in fountain pen ink gave way to a modern handwriting in ballpoint pen. "It's been difficult to piece together as there are very few records, but I've been able to map out what look like regular disappearances in and around Sweet Little Chittering, going back hundreds of years. Mentions of the Drake family persist throughout but drop off in the early twentieth century. In fact, almost all references to your family seem to stop around then. Do you know why that is?" Veronica looked at Diana.

"Times change. The importance of landowning families dwindled as people moved to the towns," Diana mused. "In a way, we're a relic of a forgotten age."

"Do you know anything about the spring festival or the history of the village that you think might be relevant? Do you remember any disappearances?" Veronica started to press.

"Wouldn't there be police records of disappearances that you could check?" asked Diana.

"I've checked, there's no record of disappearances, but there are a few scattered reports of the police following up on claims made by people outside the village. Murray included," replied Veronica.

"And what do those reports say?" Diana asked.

"That when the police followed up, there was no record of the people who'd been reported missing. Nothing at all. Murray pushed for them to do house to house enquires and no one in the village remembered them. But Murray did," Veronica said.

"Sounds like your Mr Murray was a bit of a crackpot, dear," Diana replied with a smile.

"No. I don't think so. There are records before Murray that have the same pattern. Not many, but enough. Someone from outside the village reports a disappearance but no one from the village recalls the person even existed! Murray claims he spoke to you, Mrs Drake…" Veronica was cut short

"*Ms* Drake," Diana corrected with a steely gaze.

"Sorry, *Ms* Drake." Veronica held Diana's gaze. "Murray claims he spoke to you, and you gave him information about the spring festival. Do you know anything that might help me?"

"Why do you say Murray's dates were muddled?" Diana asked

"It's less his dates and more his timeline because he describes you as being in your fifties when he spoke to you, and I can't find a record of another Diana Drake. Here or anywhere else."

"I'm old, but not that old," Diana chuckled. "I'm sorry I don't remember any Murray. As for the spring festival, you seem to know more than me. Yes, the Drakes have been in this area for a long time, but as for disappearances, I really don't know." Diana started to get up. "If you'll excuse me, I must go and powder my nose."

As Diana limped from the room she called back, "Drink your tea, it will get cold."

Veronica picked up the teacup and drank. Perhaps this was a wasted journey. Diana didn't seem to know anything. But Veronica still had a nagging feeling that there was more to this. She stood up and stretched, the armchair was more uncomfortable than she'd realised.

Veronica looked around the room, a layer of dust covered everything. She walked over to some framed photos on the wall. One caught her eye because it had a handwritten note across the top. She looked closer.

The photograph was black and white, it showed the village green looking pretty much exactly the same as when Veronica had walked through it earlier, but the clothes of the people showed that it was taken in the 1940s or 50s. Clearly the day of the village fete. A woman stood in the middle of the photo but, oddly, she was out of focus, or rather, her face was. Veronica read the handwritten note and froze:

Ms Drake, thank you for all your help, Terry Murray.

Veronica held up the first page of the journal. It was the same handwriting, perhaps even written with the same pen! She stared at the woman in the photo, out of focus, but slowly the image became sharper. It was Diana Drake. Younger than today, but still maybe in her late forties.

Veronica stepped back and stumbled. The room began to spin as if she were drunk. She dropped the journal and steadied herself on the arm of the chair. Her legs gave way, and she shrank to her knees. She put her hand on the side table to stop herself falling further and noticed that Diana's teacup was empty.

"I was worried you hadn't drunk enough," Diana stood in the doorway looking down at Veronica.

"What...?" Veronica tried to get the words out, but her speech slurred into nothing.

Diana walked across the room and picked up the journal, fanning the pages with her fingers. She sighed.

"What a palaver! Was a time when a tribute was just offered up. Now we have to lure you in," Diana said, as if to herself.

"I didn't think Terry's idea would work, but here you are." Diana drummed her fingers on the cover of the journal. "An enquiring mind will come, he said, and come you did." Diana turned to look at Veronica.

"People will..." Veronica slurred.

"People will come? People know you're here?" Diana laughed. "Oh, I've heard it all before, dear. From many tongues, *in* many tongues, over many, many years." Diana allowed herself a moment for her mind to wander.

"If I can keep those weak-minded villagers from even knowing we're here, I can certainly make them forget about you," Diana snarled.

Veronica rolled onto the floor and lay on her back, unable to move.

Diana knelt next to her and took her hand. Raising it to her lips, she bit down hard, breaking the skin. The pain was excruciating but Veronica couldn't even make a noise. Diana let Veronica's bloody hand drop from her mouth. Diana was panting.

"It renews the body, as it will renew the land," Diana exclaimed with a note of ecstasy in her voice.

Veronica's vison grew dark.

***

Terry Murray busied himself arranging the glasses on the table in the garden, careful not to spill a drop of the precious liquid. He looked about him. He was sure he was alone in the darkness. He lifted a glass to his lips, letting the iron rich smell fill his nostrils. He drank hungrily.

"Greedy!" Diana's voice cut through the night air. Murray turned to face his mistress, terrified.

Diana stalked from the shadows of the house like a panther. Her jet-black hair making her blend into the night. She stopped and ran her hands down her tight, lithe body.

"Still, I can't blame you." Diana looked out into the night.

"Thank you, Mistress. Sorry, Mistress," Murray hissed.

Terry's hair darkened and his skin tightened on his face as the blood was absorbed into his system.

"Have the others done as they were commanded? Spread this upon the land," Diana asked.

"Yes. Mistress! It has begun!" Murray motioned to the house and the garden.

The structure of the house sagged no more, and the overgrown foliage had shrunk back.

"It renews the body, as it will renew the land," Diana said to herself and turned to Murray.

"You did well, the journal worked. It lured a good tribute. Drink your fill and then fetch the others." Diana walked away as Murray gulped down the rest of his glass and then grabbed another.

Diana Drake looked out into the night sky. She heard Murry scurry away to fetch the other. It had been a long time since they'd fed. She walked towards the pyre in the middle of the garden. The reporter's remains laid upon the top.

A firework rose into the night sky and illuminated the macabre scene. The villagers were celebrating the end of their fete. Diana smiled - if only they knew its true meaning. Diana turned back towards the house. More fireworks rose and burst; the flashes highlighted the shambling mass of the ghoulish inhabitants of Hawthorn Lane entering the garden. They shuffled to a halt and bowed their heads as they saw Diana.

"A tribute has come and been taken. It renews the body, as it will renew the land," intoned Diana.

"It renews the body, as it will renew the land," wailed the assembled mob.

"DRINK! Drink and be renewed!" commanded Diana.

Aged, claw-like hands grabbed at the glasses as the feeding frenzy began.

The now youthful Murray stood beside Diana and surveyed the scene.

"What now, Mistress?" Murray asked.

Diana smiled.

Break-In at St. Benedict's

P.J. Blakey-Novis

The day of the village fete was not Father Harris's favourite day of the year. In fact, any day that involved having to make small talk with the residents of Sweet Little Chittering was a day he could do without. Sundays were the worst, although he did like to see that the number of parishioners who would attend his weekly service was dwindling. For a village, or more accurately a *hamlet*, of less than five hundred residents, only having the same twenty to thirty worshippers to endure on a Sunday morning wasn't too trying. And almost all of those were so ancient they couldn't really hear him anyway. He could have been reciting the Satanic Verses at the pulpit and they would have nodded along regardless.

It was an odd attitude for a vicar to have, of this he was well aware. Aware, but couldn't care less. He had been placed in this church for almost thirty years with one particular task. The powers above didn't care about the congregation size, or how much loose change was sprinkled onto the donation plates. They just needed him to make sure their secrets were safe. Taking the reins at St Benedict's was a far higher position than anyone (outside of a select few) knew. Having gone into the ministry at the tender age of twenty, Father Harris had an eagerness for the spiritual fight. He had no interest in merely steering his flock on the right path, he wanted exorcisms, miracles, and all the drama that came with a life of battling evil. Now, alone in his office on the morning of the village fete, he found himself longing for some excitement of the spiritual kind.

***

Stirring a sugar cube into his tea, Father Harris glanced at the clock hanging a little off centre above his desk. 9.45am. The fete was due to open officially at ten and he spent the next few minutes wondering if his absence would be noticed before deciding that he had little option but to show his face. *But when?* he deliberated. *If I go now, I could end up stuck there until this evening. I'd rather not have to sit through those bastard Morris Dancers. Perhaps I can greet everyone and then disappear. Return later for the fireworks.*

Harris decided to go by soon, before it became busy, say a few hellos, and then disappear on 'important Church business'. He'd no doubt have to return at some point, but that could wait until much later in the day when it was dark and easier to remain out of sight. Getting up from his chair with a groan, he picked up the white collar and slipped it into place. The sun was streaming through the stained-glass around him and so he left his jacket draped across the desk. To the right of the small office was a semi-hidden door behind a filing cabinet. It blended into the wall, but the outline could be seen if you were really looking. Harris glanced at the door before leaving the office and making his way out of the church. The heavy double doors that made up the main entrance were left open, as was often the case should any lost soul be seeking a place of refuge.

Father Harris took the stroll slowly, enjoying the warmth of the sun and the relative quiet of the area. Fifteen minutes later, the sounds of children (both laughing and screaming), as well as some awful music, filled his ears. He let out a groan but kept walking, mentally preparing a route around the fete and already thinking about lunch. Harris patted the rear pocket in his trousers to confirm his wallet was where it should be as his stomach grumbled. *Could get some food from one of the stallholders,* he mused. *As long as it isn't rock cakes like last year. Tasted like actual bloody rocks.* Harris caught a whiff of food as he stepped onto the village green and it turned his stomach – a greasy, fried onion stench that had to be coming from an out-of-town burger van.

Father Harris glanced about, trying to ascertain who was where so he could plan a route which involved the least conversation. Cautiously, he made his way to the first stall and offered a cheery 'Morning!'. It looked like someone was just trying to shift their old junk so he moved on, greeting each trader while wondering if anyone would actually sell anything. *It's all a load of crap,* he thought. Having made his way around the entire fete, Father Harris had only parted with a few pounds which had gone on two cheese scones and a slice of homemade fudge cake.

It wasn't quite eleven and Harris had intended to take the food back to the quiet of his office, but his stomach suggested otherwise. Taking a seat at a bench to the far end of the green, he hoped for a few solitary moments to enjoy his food. He had taken one bite of a scone when the scent hit his nostrils. *Cannabis,* he decided, his eyes flitting along the edge of the field. He took a second bite as he continued scanning for the culprits and then he saw them, just behind a thick oak tree. Father Harris couldn't tell how many *they* were, but there was faint laughter coming from at least two voices and a feminine leg was visible, stretching out on the grass.

Sweet Little Chittering had a pretty low population of teenagers, so Father Harris could place a fairly safe bet on who that leg belonged to. And if that really was Leanne, then her headmaster father would not be happy with her drug use. *Just teenagers,* Harris thought. *Not hurting anyone.* For a brief moment he considered going over and doing his duty, attempting to steer the youngsters onto the right path. *Futile,* he decided. *Especially at that age.* Halfway through his second scone, however, he found himself forced to engage with the kids.

"I think the priest is enjoying the view!"

Father Harris looked up to see a seventeen-year-old couple approaching. He glanced back to the leg and, realising he had been staring in that direction, found himself becoming flustered. "Don't be so ridiculous, Tommy," he said, brushing crumbs from his shirt as he stood.

"Hey, Leanne! Old man Harris has been checking you out. I think he might want to take you to church for a baptism. You'll need your bikini." The girl on Tommy's arm, Lizzy, faked a sound like she was about to vomit.

Father Harris felt his face flush red with a mix of anger and embarrassment. *Prick,* he thought, but dared not utter aloud. "Here to enjoy the fete?" he asked instead. "Hope you're all going to be on your best behaviour today."

"Not sure yet," Tommy replied with a grin. "What do you guys think?" he yelled over to Leanne and her younger brother, Jonah, who were approaching from their position behind the tree.

"About what?" Leanne asked.

"Father Harris was asking if we're going to be on our best behaviour today."

"Oh Father, I'm *always* on my best behaviour," Leanne told him. "I've never done anything…*naughty.*"

Harris felt his face redden a little more. "Well, I hope you all enjoy the day. I need to get back to the church, but I'll be around again later, if any of you wish to talk about anything."

"Thank you, Father," Leanne replied sweetly as she watched him leave the village green and make his way back towards the church.

***

Tommy spent the next hour or so leading the group around the fete, looking at stalls and making rude comments to the other villagers. Lizzy laughed as Tommy placed a hand-knitted tea cosy on her head, much to the disapproval of the elderly lady who had created the masterpiece. Leanne and Jonah both felt a twinge of embarrassment at their friends' behaviour but not to the point they would actually leave. Everyone in Sweet Little Chittering knew what Tommy was like, and all secretly waited for the day he would undoubtedly end up in jail. All the villagers could hope was that it wouldn't be for any crime that impacted on them.

"It must be gin o' clock by now," Lizzy decided, looking at Tommy, eyebrows raised. She was putting in an order, that much was clear, and despite his bravado Tommy knew who was really in charge.

"What do you want me to do about it?" he asked. "I can't get served in this shithole. Everyone knows how old I am."

"I didn't say *buy* any," Lizzy replied, waiting for Tommy to catch up with her train of thought.

"Right…" he said slowly. For a moment he looked nervous at the prospect of stealing but quickly buried the feeling, marching towards the local store.

"Tommy!" she called, catching up with him.

"What?"

"Are you just going to walk in and grab a bottle? We'll need tonic water too…" Lizzy said, now in a whisper. "Take my bag."

Grabbing the cotton tote bag from his girlfriend, Tommy glanced through the store window. Only the clerk could be seen, and Tommy knew he'd be closely watched from the moment he entered. "I know, you two distract him," he suggested, nodding at Lizzy's breasts. "While he's gazing at them, I'll get what I can. Just ask him about something behind the counter."

"Aw, Tommy, you're so sweet. I'm glad my only use is my tits," Lizzy huffed. The desire for alcohol to fuel the day however meant more than a little self-respect and she entered the shop, followed a moment later by Tommy. The clerk was no fool, and while shoplifting in such a small village was rare, Tommy and Lizzy were famously a couple and certainly bad news. For Lizzy to be rather awkwardly thrusting her cleavage in the clerk's face whilst Tommy skulked about with an empty bag wasn't going to fool anyone.

"Out," the clerk ordered, sounding almost bored. Neither teenager felt it was worth protesting innocence and left with a huff.

"No luck?" Leanne asked as the pair joined them outside the shop.

"Nah," Tommy said. "Didn't think it'd work anyway. Guess it'll be a dry one."

"We can't get any gin," Leanne said, "but how about red wine?"

"Yuck," Jonah added.

"Obviously not for you, you're far too young," Leanne added.

"What difference does it make?" Lizzy asked. "If we could get anything, it'd have to be from here." She waved a hand vaguely in the direction of the village store.

"When was the last time you went to church?" Leanne asked.

Tommy and Lizzy laughed, not following at all. "You think we need to go confess our sins for wanting a nab a bottle?" Tommy said with a smirk.

"Sometimes, Tommy, you aren't all that smart. Confession...probably not. But what happens at communion?"

Leanne was right that Tommy was far from being a genius and the same could easily be said for Lizzy. It took a moment, but they seemed to reach the same conclusion at the same time, grins appearing on both their faces.

"The church!" they squealed in unison.

"But what about Harris?" Tommy asked.

"We'll see," Leanne replied, now feeling as though she were leading the group. "The church is open so we can go by, sit inside, and work it out from there. Must be worth a try."

***

"You go in first," Tommy suggested, looking at Leanne. "See if anyone is about." Leanne nodded her head at Jonah, signalling for him to follow, and made her way inside. They paused just inside the main doors, taking a moment for their eyes to adjust to the darkness. The church was ancient and had a distinctive odour, like polished wood and old books. The uncomfortable looking pews sat empty, the only light coming through the stained-glass windows and barely illuminating the space.

Leanne felt Jonah take a step closer. The place was eerily quiet but she told herself that it was supposed to be. After all, it's a sanctuary, a place to sit in silence and reflect or pray. "Tell them it's empty," she whispered to Jonah who was more than happy to dash back outside.

"Father Harris," Leanne called. No reply. Cautiously, she took a few steps down the aisle between the rows of pews. "Father Harris?" Still nothing.

"This place is well creepy!" Tommy announced as he stepped inside, his voice seeming even louder in the small space. His comment was met with a loud 'Shh!' from both girls.

"I don't think Harris is here," Leanne said. "There must be an office out back." The group made their way past the altar and found a closed door with Harris's name on it. Tommy reached for the handle, but Leanne stopped him. She knocked twice, straining to hear any movement coming from within. Nothing.

Leanne nodded and Tommy turned the knob, relieved to find it unlocked. He led the way inside, scanning the dull room for anything worth taking. It only took a moment before Lizzy pointed to a stack of wine boxes in the corner. "Probably just some cheap stuff they get from a wholesaler, but better than nothing," she said, grabbing a box of six bottles. "This enough?"

"Plenty," Leanne muttered. As happy as she was to have some drinks with her friends, the thought of them clearing more than six bottles of red made her feel sick. "Plus, we're not going to want to carry more than that around."

"We should go then," Tommy suggested. "Silly to hang around."

"Quite right," a voice said in the doorway to the office, startling Lizzy to the point she almost dropped the box. Harris stood blocking their only way out, but he showed little sign of anger. "So, want to explain what you think you're doing?"

The four remained silent, eyes fixed on their shoes. After an awkward moment of silence, Lizzy took a few steps and placed the box of wine bottles where she had found it. "We'll go now. Sorry, Father," she said.

"It's fine," Harris said with a sigh. "Believe it or not, I was young once too. But you shouldn't be stealing. Or drinking, really."

"We know," Lizzy said. "We'll head back to the fete now. And we'll stay out of trouble."

Father Harris stepped aside to let the group leave and they filed out, murmuring apologies. They'd made it halfway through the main area of the church when Harris heard Tommy say, "That was a close one. If he'd threatened to tell anyone, I might have had to offer your services Lizzy. But then he *is* a priest, so he'd much rather have a go on little Jonah here." Tommy laughed at his own joke, but the others just groaned, embarrassed by the volume at which Tommy spoke.

Harris felt something else entirely. Not embarrassment but anger. He was being ridiculed by this arrogant little prick and he'd had enough of turning the other cheek. Nothing good would come of Tommy, of that he was certain. Lizzy seemed like an airhead whose only aim in life was gaining followers online and clinging onto Tommy. The others seemed okay, saveable perhaps, but time would tell. After all the years spent here, guarding and protecting the church's secrets, Harris had finally had enough.

"Wait," he called after them. They were at the door by this point, Leanne at the back of the foursome.

"Yes?" she asked, turning to face the shadow of Father Harris at the far end of the church.

"That wasn't very welcoming of me," he explained. "I don't mean to be a killjoy. I know you shouldn't drink at your age, but we give wine to younger ones as part of communion. Can you keep a secret?"

All four of the youngsters were huddled in the main doorway now, listening to Father Harris as he took small steps towards them.

"If you promise not to tell our parents we tried to take the wine, we can keep a secret," Lizzy promised.

"I was planning on having a couple of glasses of wine myself in a moment. You can join me, if you'd like. I know you'll end up drinking somewhere today, so I'd feel better if I was there to supervise."

"Sounds shit," Tommy mumbled but Lizzy elbowed him quickly.

"Free wine, and we don't have to search around for drinks elsewhere. Could be worse," Leanne whispered.

"Does it not seem creepy to you?" Tommy replied, as quietly as he could manage. "He's either going to bang on about God all afternoon, or he's after something else."

"I'm sure he will talk about making the right choices and God and Jesus and all that stuff. But I think he just wants to make sure we're safe," Leanne said.

"I'm in," Lizzy said, loudly enough for Harris to hear, before scurrying down the aisle to meet him.

***

Despite Leanne suggesting otherwise, Father Harris had handed Jonah a small glass of red wine. The boy didn't like the taste but peer pressure from Tommy, who Jonah certainly looked up to, meant that he managed to finish it and take another. Leanne set out to be restrained, taking her responsibility for her thirteen-year-old brother quite seriously, but after the third glass of red she began to go with the flow.

Tommy and Lizzy, of course, were necking as much cheap Claret as they could get a hold of in case Father Harris put an end to their bizarre little gathering. Harris, however, wasn't exactly pacing himself either. He was still raging within about Tommy's constant jibes and needed the drink in order to go through with the dangerous plan he had concocted. While Tommy feared Harris would throw them out at some point, the vicar was desperate to keep his guests there.

They discussed religion, naturally, along with their plans for the future and Harris gave a little history as to why he was there. Conversation began to dry up and Lizzy, becoming tired from all the red wine, eventually suggested leaving. Harris could wait no longer.

"There is more to my job than you'd expect," he said, glancing at each of them. Nobody seemed interested in hearing about preparing sermons or checking in on the elderly. "Did you know this church has a secret room downstairs?"

"Like a torture room for little boys?" Tommy asked, finding himself even more hilarious than when he was sober.

"No Tommy," Father Harris replied, forcing patience into his voice. "It's a collection of artefacts the church keeps hidden. My role here is to guard them. To make sure nobody knows about them."

Lizzy started laughing. "Your job is to make sure nobody finds out about the secret room, so you tell us about it? You're not very good at your job, Father." Tommy started laughing along with her, but Leanne looked serious.

"What sort of artefacts?" she asked.

"All kinds of things. Evil things. Holy things. You'd be amazed."

"Bullshit," Tommy declared. "If there is even anything down there, it's probably old scrolls or coins or something."

"Why don't you come and take a look?" Harris suggested with a smirk.

***

The group watched as Father Harris dragged an old filing cabinet across the floor with a nasty squeak. It was just possible to make out the outline to a small door behind where the cabinet had been, but with no door handle. Harris pushed a part of the door gently and it opened a couple of inches. Grabbing the edge of the door, he pulled it the rest of the way and hit a switch.

Now he had everyone's attention and they gathered behind him, peering around to get a better look. The door didn't open into a room but a set of stairs going down. "What's down there really?" Lizzy asked.

"I've told you," Harris replied. "Old things. Come and see for yourself."

Lizzy looked at Tommy, her eyes questioning. "Nah," Tommy said. "Sounds boring." The fear in his voice was unmistakable, however.

"If you're scared, I understand," Father Harris said. "A lot of evil is contained in that room."

The statement had the desired effect. "I ain't scared of nothing," Tommy lied. "Show us the old crap if you must, then we'll be heading off."

Father Harris led the group down into a small basement. Small, yet packed with glass-fronted cabinets and bookshelves. "Jeez," Leanne said, looking around. "It's like that room at the Warrens' house with all the haunted stuff."

"Have a look around," Harris offered. "I'm going

to the loo. Anyone want another glass of wine while I'm up there?" Tommy gave a nod but nobody else answered, fascinated as they were by the displays.

Leanne heard Father Harris climbing the stairs back to his office, followed by what could have been the click of a lock. She pushed the thought from her mind as she looked about, running a hand across the spines of leather-bound titles on the bookshelf. There were books on all religions, some she had heard of, some far more obscure. There were books on the occult, on symbolism, witchcraft, and even books of spells.

Lizzy pointed at the bizarre items stored behind glass, seemingly normal things which were alleged to be either cursed or possessed. A few creepy dolls, a pack of Tarot cards, a Ouija board with what looked a lot like blood smeared across it, a black fedora, and a vial of something deep red all filled the cabinet in the centre of the room.

Leanne discovered a filing cabinet in the corner, one which looked surprisingly normal amongst the oddities, and pulled open the first drawer. Inside were newspaper clippings, medical reports, eyewitness accounts, and photographs from exorcisms the church had performed. Disturbing images of people bent into unnatural shapes, some clearly deceased, spewed from the pages. The images frightened her, and she shoved them back with haste.

Reluctantly, Leanne opened the second drawer to find a similar collection, minus the photographs, but much older. Details of religious persecution filled the files – witches being burned at stakes, homosexuals being tortured until they begged for forgiveness, non-Catholics imprisoned and executed for daring to question the might of the Vatican. The files were shocking in their detail and Leanne struggled to stop reading until her thoughts were disrupted by the sound of breaking glass.

"Tommy!" Lizzy shrieked. "Harris is going to be so pissed at you!"

"Oops," Tommy slurred, a smile plastered on his face. "Think I've had enough wine now. But at least we can get to the stuff…"

Lizzy watched as Tommy reached a hand through the broken pane and into the centre cabinet. "What do you reckon this is?" he asked, holding up the vial of dark liquid. "Looks like blood."

"That's gross. Put it back," Lizzy ordered but Tommy slipped the vial into his pocket.

"The hat is cool, though," he remarked, pulling the fedora through the gap and placing it on his head at an angle. "Pretty gangster, yeah?"

"Makes you look old," Lizzy said. "And where is Father Harris? He's been ages."

"I'll go check. Come on Jonah," Leanne said, climbing the stairs. Only halfway up, it became evident that the door was closed. Attempting to suppress the feeling of panic welling up within her, Leanne reached for the door and gave it a push. No movement. She knocked, calling out for Harris. Silence. *He's locked us down here!* she thought, not daring to speak it aloud for fear of frightening Jonah.

She looked to her younger brother, only to see that he fully understood the situation. He turned, running down to find Tommy, certain that the older boy would be able to help. "Tommy!" Jonah yelled. "We're locked in. The door won't open!"

Lizzy paled, looking to Leanne for confirmation. Tommy just laughed, ruffling Jonah's hair. "I'm sure the door just needs a bit more of a push. I'll see to it." Tommy took to the stairs, his drunkenness now evident as he ran his hands along the walls for support. They could hear him kicking at the door, banging on it, shouting for the vicar to open up. All to no avail. Coming down the stairs proved even more challenging than going up them and Tommy slipped from almost the top. He rolled over, hitting the floor at the bottom with enough force to daze him.

"Oh my god, are you okay?" Lizzy squealed, rushing to his side. With Leanne's help, they managed to get Tommy into a sitting position. "You're bleeding!" Lizzy yelled, a look of disgust on her face.

Next to Tommy's pocket, a thick, almost black stain was spreading. Instinctively, he pushed a hand into the pocket and felt the sharp stab of broken glass. "Not my blood," he said, sounding relieved. "That little bottle was in my pocket, must have smashed when I hit the floor."

"That's nasty," Lizzy said, scrunching her nose. "That could be anybody's blood." Before Tommy could reply, the room was plunged into darkness.

***

Leanne awakened to find herself laying in damp grass, moonlight trying desperately to peek through the grey clouds. Her first thought was of Jonah, and she tried to sit herself up, discovering she was gagged, her wrists and ankles bound. Her second thought was to wonder how she got there, how much time had passed, and who had put her in this situation. It was hard to make out much in the darkness of the rural setting, but she soon became certain she was in the graveyard attached to the church.

Using her tongue to push the rag from her mouth, she called out, "Jonah!", more concerned for his safety than her own. A sound of movement came from behind her and she rolled herself over. There, bound as she was, Leanne spotted three others. The most obvious thought was that Jonah, Lizzy, and Tommy were in the same predicament. As her eyes adjusted to the darkness, she soon realised that this wasn't the case. Jonah was there, Lizzy was there, but that was not Tommy. That was an older man, a man wearing black with a white collar…a vicar.

"It's about time you woke up," came a voice she did not recognise. Moving her head to the side she saw a figure, a silhouette really. The voice did not match but she knew instantly that it was Tommy, still wearing that ridiculous hat.

"Tommy?" she croaked. "What's happening? You sound weird."

"I'm afraid Tommy can't come to the phone right now, he's a little busy."

"What are you talking about? Untie me!"

"I think Father Harris has some explaining to do," 'Tommy' said, stepping closer. "Now, I'll get the gags off you all, as long as you promise not to scream."

Leanne looked at the faces of her friends, each now a mask of terror. *Has Tommy snapped? Is this just a prank? He's gone too far this time.* She watched as Tommy crouched in front of Lizzy and pulled the fabric from her mouth. As soon as she was able, the girl let out an ear-splitting scream. With inhuman speed, Tommy picked up a rock and thrust it into Lizzy's face. The first strike split her nose with a crunching sound and a whimper. By the tenth strike Lizzy didn't move at all.

"I said silence. Perhaps now you can see I meant it." Jonah began to sob and Leanne could feel tears welling up. Evidently this was no prank. "I can *hear* you crying. I said to be quiet…" Jonah managed to control his whimpering but the scent on the air suggested his bladder had released with fear.

"Better," Tommy said. "Now, Father Harris, would you like to tell our guests about your little collection? Surely you knew something like this was bound to happen when you locked them down there?" Tommy approached the vicar and yanked the gag away.

"I thought," began Harris, "that I'd lock them down there to frighten them. Tommy is a nasty little prick and I wanted to teach him a lesson. But no, I didn't think this would happen."

"Tommy certainly is wonderful, isn't he? He's still in here, somewhere. But not for long, I fear. What I'd like to know is why you even showed them the room? See, I think you're nothing but a fucking liar. Your job in this miserable world is protecting those items which makes me sure that you knew they wouldn't survive. But why? For a creature like me, it would just be sport. But for a man of the cloth to deliberately try to eliminate some poor, innocent children...well, I think you may be on the wrong side!"

"My motives are irrelevant now," Harris replied. "You know what I can do, the power I hold, my position in the church. It's time you went back."

Laughter filled the air as 'Tommy' wiped tears from his eyes. "What exactly do you think you can do? The only thing holding me in that musty room was the blood. *His* blood. Not quite so powerful when it's over some drunk kid's boxers, is it? Do you think your all-knowing god knew this would happen? That the blood of his only son would end up drying on some teenager's jeans in more than two-thousand years' time! What a hilarious fucking situation we find ourselves in."

"Just let us go," Leanne begged. "I don't know what's happening, but I just want to take my brother and go home."

'Tommy' smiled at Leanne, tipping his fedora. "How about I ignore the fact you spoke without permission and explain a little about what's happening? Would you like that?"

Leanne paused, trying to decide on the correct response. "I don't need to know anything. I'd rather just leave."

"I'm sure you fucking would! But you're involved now." 'Tommy' turned to Harris. "This one seems pretty innocent, you know. Pretty shitty of you to put her and the young one through this."

Harris didn't reply, just sitting with his eyes fixed on the creature before him. In the darkness, Leanne could make out the Father's lips moving quickly, almost silently, as he began to recite something in a language she did not understand.

"We *are* innocent," Leanne pleaded. "Whatever your issue with Father Harris is, you don't need us."

"Oh, perhaps you misunderstand me," 'Tommy' replied. "I don't care in the slightest if you're innocent or not. You'll be mine tonight. As will your brother, and the rest of this shitty village. My vengeance will spread from here, surrounding the earth, claiming souls for Lucifer himself."

Leanne glanced at Harris, his eyes still fixed, mouth working on what could only be a prayer. Until that moment, Leanne believed prayers were useless. But then she also wouldn't have believed her friend could be possessed by a demon, leading him to smash his girlfriend's face in. Leanne decided her only chance would be to keep the monster talking and let Harris continue his recital.

"So, what are you?" Leanne asked.

"It's not particularly relevant but I suppose your kind would call me a demon."

"And you've been trapped here? Harris trapped

you?"

"That pathetic creature?" 'Tommy' asked with a chuckle. "Not him. He's just a caretaker. He keeps certain *items* secure. But as you can see, he's not very good at it."

"But someone trapped you. Someone brought you here," Leanne pressed.

"The hat…" Father Harris said suddenly. "The evil lives within that bastard hat. It's turned up all over the world, the wearer taking a different guise each time. The church managed to get it after that debacle in London at the Castle Heights tower block."

"That's right Harris, tell her everything. That way I'll have even less reason to let her go."

"As if you would anyway," Harris replied, and Leanne's heart sank at the words. She took a look towards Jonah who remained still on the ground. He was staring ahead as he lay on his side, his chest moving with each breath, but he gave no other signs of life. *Is he in shock?* Leanne wondered.

"What now then?" Leanne asked, trying to distract the creature in the hope that Harris could find a way to end this.

"Well, as I said," 'Tommy' began, "I'm going to take your soul. And Jonah's. I don't want Harris's though. Filthy fucking thing, I'm sure. Fear helps the process, and it seems little Jonah may be as frightened as it's possible to be, so he'll be first."

"No!" screamed Leanne, yanking hard at her binds. "Leave him alone!" With all her might, Leanne tried to shuffle herself along the ground towards her brother. Hips bruised and shoulders sore, she moved painfully slowly as 'Tommy' stood over her in hysterics.

"Would you find it easier if I removed your restraints?" he offered with a smirk. He waved a hand theatrically and Leanne felt her wrists and ankles release. She eyed the monster suspiciously as she pulled herself onto her knees.

"And Jonah's?" she asked.

"Sure, why not? I'm in a good mood." The creature waved a hand once more, this time in the opposite direction, and Leanne heard a sickening crunch followed by a scream. Jonah rolled onto his back, four jets of blood spraying from the end of each limb. "Oops," Tommy said. "My bad. Did the waving thingy the wrong way. Righty tighty, lefty loosey. Sorry about that."

Leanne lunged for what used to be Tommy, her rage animalistic. All she could think of was to pull him to the ground and pummel him with a rock. She came within a few inches of his legs before his shoe connected with her jaw, landing with such force she was thrown halfway across the cemetery.

Bloody, battered and bruised, Leanne tried to stand, making it as far as getting to her knees. She knew Jonah was almost certainly dead and she felt nothing but contempt for Father Harris for placing them in this situation. She wanted to run, to take advantage of the distance between herself and the demon. But what of Jonah? What if he could still be saved?

'Tommy' seemed busy with Harris, gloating

about his plans for world domination, so Leanne began a painful crawl towards her brother. She had no idea what powers this monster possessed but did her best to creep along, knowing she couldn't live with herself if she abandoned the boy. She came within six feet of Jonah before she could make out anything more than a shadow on the ground. He was completely still and the faint light of the moon was just enough for Leanne to see his eyes were open. Open, yet glazed over. There was no gentle rise and fall of his chest.

Holding in a wail of sorrow, Leanne began crawling backwards, trying to put enough space between herself and the monster before scrambling to her feet and running. The darkness was thick, and she did her best to block out the creature's monologue as he lectured Harris on how powerful a demon he really was. A cracking sound made Leanne's heart skip as she realised she had knelt on a twig. She chanced a glance at the monster, but he was still preoccupied with the vicar.

Deciding that was her moment, she slowly rose to her feet. She took careful steps towards the edge of the churchyard under the cloak of darkness. *Is it too dark for him to see me?* she wondered. The question soon became redundant as the sky was lit up with fireworks. A series of multi-coloured bursts illuminated the frightened girl and she froze as 'Tommy' turned his head towards her. Their eyes met and she ran.

The demon moved his hands about in the air for a moment and Leanne felt her feet leave the ground.

Her legs continued to work as though she were running, even as she was pulled back into the cemetery. She screamed, as loudly as she could, but even Harris struggled to hear her over the fireworks.

"Time's up," the creature said, and as the final explosion of light lit up the sky, Leanne's spine cracked, folding her in half as she floated above the ancient graves. A few more horrific snaps and Leanne's arms and legs wrapped themselves around her broken body. "Ta, da," 'Tommy' said, letting the girl's body drop to the ground. "Just us now…" Harris hadn't stopped reciting the Latin prayers, despite them seeming to be next to useless. The demon showed no sign of caring what the vicar was mumbling. "Well, that was dramatic…" it said, glancing down at what was left of Leanne.

"I'm getting a bit bored now," 'Tommy' said with a sigh. "You'd probably have more luck with those prayers if you worked on your Latin. Pronunciation is everything, you know."

Seemingly undeterred, Harris kept up his mumbling, refusing to look away or react to anything the demon said.

"ENOUGH!" the creature roared with sufficient force that Harris paused for a moment. His bravado was slipping and something akin to fear finally showed on his face. "I've toyed with you long enough, *Father*."

"So kill me already," Harris said. "I'm ready to take my place in Paradise."

'Tommy' howled with genuine laughter. "Paradise?" he spat. "You really think that's where you'll go? After what you did? I don't think a priest who deliberately puts innocent children in harm's way, who releases a fucking demon, is going *up*. Lucifer can have your soul if he wants it; it's certainly not something I'd want to consume."

"Demons lie," Harris stated casually. "Where my soul ends up is not your decision anyway. So make your move – I'm ready."

'Tommy' launched himself at the vicar, raising Harris's head and slamming it against a broken headstone, once, twice, three times. The man was out cold but still breathing and the monster stood over him deep in thought. The world was his for the taking but he still needed to be careful.

***

Shortly before ten, a flash of lightning signified the beginning of a storm. The heavy clap of thunder followed only seconds after, and the ground was saturated with rain within minutes. The downpour, wherever it came from, was heavier than anyone had experienced for years.

Just in time, Harris thought, surveying the cemetery. Four fresh graves had been dug for four poor teenagers. He knew their disappearance would take some explaining but the kids had done nothing but complain about the boring village. Why would anyone be *that* surprised if they'd run off together on some teenage adventure? *Perhaps another glass of wine?* he mused.

Stepping inside the church, Harris grabbed a

small towel from the bathroom and dried his face. He slipped his shoes off, poured himself a large glass of communion wine, and got comfortable in the office chair. He caught a glimpse of his reflection in the glass frame of a print on the wall. *The hat suits me,* he thought with a smirk.

A Story on Baker Street

Jack Joseph

Louisa had enjoyed her day at the fete far more than she had expected. She was almost feeling guilty for underselling it so much to her friend Mel, who had joined her on a visit for the weekend. Come to think of it, Louisa had undersold the entire village. It was very pretty, no doubt. It was like a picture book come to life, but that was it. Nothing ever happened there. It was, for someone who had spent most of their life in one city or another, really bloody dull. She'd been living there nearly two years now, an elderly aunt on her mother's side had passed away and left Louisa her house. Seeing as she had been 'in between homes' at the time, it felt like fate had thrown her a life-line and she had grabbed it with both hands. "Never look a gift horse in the mouth," her mother had said to her. Why you would look any horse in its mouth was beyond Louisa. Unless you were a horse dentist, in which case there would be a lot of looking in all kinds of horses' mouths. Most likely ponies and donkeys too. But, regardless, she was happy to look into a mouth if it put a roof over her head. It was a very nice cottage too, a small front garden and a nicely spaced back garden.

She had moved in as soon as she could and found work at first at the museum, which was an odd place, then onto The Paradise Inn doing their books. She'd studied accountancy yet had never taken it up until she happened to be at the bar one evening when a flustered Darren 'Nev' Neville, the Inn's manager, mentioned the source of his despair was trying to get the monthly accounts in order. She offered to help and once Nev and Nick Eden, the owner, had seen what she could do they requested she continue the role in a more formal position. She accepted the job and it had resulted in her taking on the same responsibility for several other of the village's businesses. Not that there was a great deal of business to be had, but it paid her way, providing enough income to live comfortably.

"Hello, Ms. Hooper," David White smiled at them. He was always very dapper in his appearance and dripping with charm. Louisa imagined many a woman had fallen into his arms and then into his bed.

"Hi, David," she smiled back.

"And who may this be?" David's eyes glistened as they turned to Mel.

"This is my closest friend, Mel."

"Delighted to meet you," he bowed slightly.

"And I you," grinned Mel.

"Are you in the village for long?"

"Perhaps," said Mel coyly.

"Perhaps, we shall meet again," he said, and with another winning smile he ventured into the crowd.

"Who is that?"

"That's David White. Helped organise the fete and is pretty much involved in all the village's activities. I'd say he's probably only second to Nick when it comes to influence. I think he used to run a consultancy firm or something." Louisa looked at her friend and chuckled. "Close your mouth you'll catch flies."

"He's a silver fucking fox. No, he's *the* silver fox. Christ, I might move here." Mel checked her appearance. "Do I look all right?"

"Mel, he's probably old enough to be your bloody grandfather."

"Well, he can sing me to sleep any time he likes."

"For Christ's sake," said Louisa and they both laughed out loud. A few of the villagers glanced in their direction but walked on with smiles of their own.

They spent the best part of the day at the fete and left just after the Morris March began, heading back to Louisa's home on Baker Street. Mel had commented that it would have been cool if her house number had been 221b, but there were only a dozen cottages in total there. Still, it would be pretty awesome, and she had made a mental note to see if she could change the name of her cottage. She'd ask Nick next time she saw him.

Her home had a slight chill blowing through it, which was strange as she was certain she hadn't left a window open. She flicked the lights on as she walked through the hall and into the living room, which is where they found their guest. A man dressed in denim, both shirt and jeans. It was funny, the first thing that went through her head wasn't *who the hell is that?* It was *you should never go double denim!*

"I was wondering when you'd get back," the

man's words drifted out of his mouth and floated ominously in the air. He had found himself a comfortable place to sit in her aunt's old armchair. He'd shifted it to the centre of the room. He was clean shaven, his hair dark and tightly cropped. His eyes were empty, cold and blue.

"Who's this?" gasped Mel, unable to hide her shock, but unaware he was an intruder.

"No idea," said Louisa. "He sure likes denim though."

"You may not know me, but I know who you are, Louisa Hooper. I know who you are," said Denim, his face revealing no emotion.

"That's nice, now get out," Louisa said firmly.

"I can't do that, not yet," Denim said and that's when they noticed the gun in his right hand. Small, grey and spiteful.

Mel and Louisa took a short, sharp intake of breath at the same time.

"Sit," he said. They did.

"What do you want?" Louisa tried to keep her voice calm and level. For the most part, she succeeded.

Denim leaned back in the chair. "There was a man," he said. "He had a balloon. Loved this balloon, it was his favourite. He took it out with him one day. At first, he went to a café, ordered a pie. A beef pie, even though the woman who ran the place recommended the chicken pie, for that was their speciality, he went for beef, because beef pie is what he desired. It was a good pie. He had an egg too as eggs were on special offer. The egg was okay. He left a reasonable tip as the service and atmosphere had been more than acceptable. As he was leaving, the owner complimented his balloon. 'That's a nice balloon, lovely shade of green,' she said. He smiled at her and told her it wasn't a green balloon, it was yellow. 'My mistake,' said the owner, 'I thought it was green.'

'It isn't green,' he repeated, 'it's a yellow balloon,' and off he went. The next place he went to was the supermarket. He bought some macaroni cheese, he wasn't hungry, he'd only just eaten, but he was planning ahead for dinner and macaroni appealed to him. He also bought some bottled water, he didn't trust the stuff that came out of the taps. At the check-out, the assistant noticed his balloon.

'That's a nice balloon,' the assistant had said, 'cool shade of green.'

'It's not green, came the reply, it's yellow.'

'Oh, my mistake,' said the assistant, 'it looks like green to me.'

'It's not green, it's yellow,' asserted the man and he carried on his way. As he walked along the street a little girl pointed the balloon out to her mother.

'Look at the pretty green balloon, Mummy,' she squealed. The man stopped, smiled politely and corrected her.

'It looks green to me,' said the girl's mother.

'It's not green, it's yellow,' the man assured them, and he walked on. As he stood at a pedestrian crossing, waiting for the green man to signal it was safe to go, an elderly lady peered up at his balloon through her glasses.

'What a beautiful green balloon,' she said with a smile.

The man smiled back. 'It's not green,' he told her, 'it's yellow.'

'Oh, my,' said the lady, 'it looks green to me.'

'It's yellow,' the man reiterated.

'Maybe I need new glasses,' the lady chuckled.

'Quite,' replied the man as the green man appeared and he crossed safely. Throughout his journey he had to correct person after person that his balloon was not green, not of any shade, for it was yellow. But it wasn't that people didn't know their greens from their yellows that annoyed him. Do you know what irked him most?"

The two women looked at each other blankly, unsure if they were more confused than scared.

"Nobody," continued Denim, "not one single person complimented him on his big red nose, his curly purple hair, his oversized orange shoes, his undersized orange suit, the matching bowler hat, the water spraying sunflower in his lapel or his immaculately painted face. They were all focused on the balloon."

Denim took a deep breath and waited for his story to land. It never did. After a lengthy and awkward silence, Denim realised that the two women before him did not understand the tale. He sniffed the air in annoyance.

"What do you want?" said Louisa, finally.

"Eden," said Denim, his voice strained.

"Eden?" said Mel, confused.

"Nicholas Eden," Denim said.

"Nick...what do you want with Nick?" Louisa said.

"Why didn't you say that straight away, what was that bloody story?" Mel couldn't hold the words in.

"I knew you didn't understand. Idiots!" snarled Denim.

"Are you serious, that story was fucking insane!" Mel shook her head, flabbergasted.

Denim responded by turning the barrel of the gun directly at her.

"Wait...wait...please," said Louisa, quickly trying to calm things. "You want Nick, yes?"

"Yes," said Denim, his eyes fixed on Mel. "Call him, tell him to come here. Alone. If he doesn't come, you die. If he comes but has company, you die."

"Okay...I'll call him...okay?"

Denim nodded and she slowly removed her mobile phone from her bag. She typed in her passcode and found Nick on her contact list. She pressed call.

"Warn him and I shoot your friend," Denim said calmly.

Nick answered after only a few rings. She told him she had found the documents he had asked for, asked if he could pick them up now as she was going away for a few days. She apologised at having to pull him away from the festivities and ended the call.

"Well?" Denim leaned forward.

"He's on his way," said Louisa.

"I guess I'm not the only storyteller here tonight," smiled Denim.

Louisa couldn't offer a reply that wouldn't result in her murder, so she nodded.

"You don't want to mess with me," Denim's calm voice couldn't disguise the first hint of venom slipping through.

"I understand," Louisa said.

***

They sat together, quietly, for ten minutes though it felt like far longer. The silence was broken by a gentle knock on the front door. Nobody moved. Mel and Louisa looked at Denim who slowly stood and signalled for them to do likewise, which they did.

"Grab your car keys," said Denim.

The front door opened and Nick was greeted not by Louisa, but by the muzzle of a gun. At the other end of the gun stood a man clad in denim. Between them stood the very frightened looking Louisa and her friend, Mel.

"Evening," said Nick without a trace of shock or fear. "And who might you be?"

"Retribution," Denim hissed between clenched teeth. He pushed the women out the door, Nick helped to steady both as Denim stepped out behind them.

"Is double denim back in?" Nick looked the man up and down.

"Get in the car, we are going for a drive." Denim

steadied the gun on Nick.

"How lovely," beamed Nick as if they were off for a relaxing jaunt along a coastal road. Louisa didn't move, the car keys jangling from her left hand.

"It'll be okay, Lou'," said Nick gently. "Let's all get in the car."

***

It was a tight fit in Louisa's Fiat 500. She'd had the car for more years than she could remember, it had always been reliable. It wasn't, however, very accommodating when it came to four passengers. For two, it was great. Enough room and a nice drive. Three, not too shabby, the third could lay across the back seat if they pleased, but four, that was a tad too much. They had all squeezed in, however. Nick had been tasked with driving, Louisa and Mel had manoeuvred their way into the back seat and Denim had taken the front passenger seat, reminding them all he was not to be messed with. His gun stayed pointed at Nick.

"Where to?" Nick sighed.

"Head to Hartbridge Town," said Denim. Nick frowned, turned the key in the ignition and fired the engine into life. "You got a problem?"

"You're holding us hostage at gunpoint and you're asking if I have a problem? Hmm, let me think," Nick said.

"Don't get funny with me, old man," snapped Denim. "Just drive."

They drove for around six or seven minutes with nobody uttering a word. Nick remained calm, Mel was shaking, obviously very scared, but Louisa couldn't really decide how she, herself, was feeling. She had a mixture of emotions, fear, anger, frustration and an underlying sense of hope. She had passed on a hidden message to Nick during their phone call. When in danger, he had told her, mention you have documents in need of collection. She had done just that, yet Nick had arrived alone. He was calm though, as Nick always appeared to be, so maybe he had a plan. She liked the man, he was a good sort. She couldn't figure out his age, he could have been anywhere between early sixties to mid-nineties. Sometimes, he seemed to be frail, yet at others he was full of zest and youthful energy. Not that age mattered, he was kind and generous and, most of all, he was here when she needed him most.

"That's the famous Hartbridge Henge, huh?" said Denim as they passed the ancient stone landmark.

"The Chittering," said Nick, not moving his eyes from the road.

"The what?" sneered Denim.

"It's called *The Chittering*," Nick asserted.

"Is it, now?" laughed Denim. "Well, you need to look at more books. They all call it Hartbridge Henge. I guess you hate Hartbridge Town too?"

"It's an overblown village," said Nick.

"And Chittering," mocked Denim, "is an overblown hamlet."

Nick's left hand suddenly grabbed the barrel of the gun and pushed it upwards. The car veered to the left as Denim fought back. Louisa reached for his face and pulled his head toward her. Mel screamed. There was an ear cracking BANG as the gun went off, tearing a hole in the Fiat's roof. The car swerved as the struggle continued, lurching up and then over the verge on the side of the road. It wobbled like a jelly then pitched down, twisted then toppled into a roll. Louisa struck her head and the world faded to black.

***

Nick opened his eyes and the world was upside down. Denim was gone, the two women were breathing… unconscious, but breathing. He put his right hand on the roof and unclipped his seatbelt which sent him dropping, harder than he expected, onto his shoulder. He struggled into a more comfortable position so he could push open the door and climb out.

"Still with us then?" Denim sat on a grass mound, gun in hand.

"Disappointed?" smiled Nick.

"I was told you had to die, not how." Denim sounded quite serene.

"Do you do everything you're told?" Nick brushed dirt from his shirt with his hands.

"Depends."

"On?"

"On who's doing the telling."

"And who told you I had to die?"

Before Denim could answer, Louisa pushed her door open and tumbled out of the car coughing.

"Argh, fuck," she groaned.

"What were you told to do?" Nick called Denim's attention back.

Denim gave his answer some thought, then stood up. "I was told you had to die. I was told to kill you in Hartbridge. Having seen your face whenever the name of that town…"

"It's a village."

"…whenever that *town* is mentioned, I can see why. You hate that place. I tell you, my employer has a wicked sense of humour. Quite fitting when I think about it."

"Who is this employer of yours?" Nick stayed in place. Still. Calm.

"You won't believe me," Denim shrugged.

"Try me."

"The devil."

"The devil told you to kill me?"

"Yup. Well, he paid me to kill you. Paid very well too," he beamed.

"The devil?" Nick said, doubtfully.

"I don't care if you don't believe in him." Denim steadied his feet. "Let me tell you a story."

Louisa grimaced, she was already in enough pain without having to endure Denim's story again.

"There was this man, he had a balloon…"

A burning car came crashing down the verge and ploughed into Denim, flattening him with a crunch, he disappeared beneath it as it charged on down the hill. Louisa screamed.

The burning car veered sideways then tipped over onto its roof, where it slid for a few more feet before coming to a stop, bright orange flames licked at the sky, marking its resting place. Denim lay twisted and broken in its wake.

Louisa shakily got to her feet. Nick helped her.

"You'll be okay," he said.

"What...happened?" Louisa wheezed, pointing weakly at the burning wreck.

"I'll never know, he had only got to the part with the balloon," said Nick.

Louisa looked at him, then realising he was joking, smiled. "You know what I mean."

Nick shrugged. "Not quite sure."

"Was that an act of God?"

"I doubt it," said Nick. Denim groaned and Nick put a reassuring hand on Louisa's shoulder.

"He's alive?" Louisa couldn't stop the shivers.

"Go and check on your friend. I'll see to him," Nick spoke quietly, his voice instilling Louisa with security.

She took a breath and went to the car. Nick walked down to Denim.

"That looks sore." Nick bent down beside the crumpled Denim-clad man. Blood was spattered across him. His limbs pointed awkwardly in various directions, none of which were usually possible. A bone stuck out from his left side, skin had been torn from his face and his breathing whistled wheezily. He wasn't long for life.

"Now," said Nick, "if you could describe this

man who hired you, I'd be most grateful."

"The...devil," Denim struggled to speak, the pain engulfing his body immense.

"Describe him."

Nick listened intently, and patiently, as Denim slowly described what his employer looked like. It mattered not, he didn't feel he was betraying any confidence. His employer was, after all, the Lord of Darkness, The King of Hell. This old man posed no threat to Satan. When he had finished talking, Denim was surprised not to see fear in the old man's face, but amusement.

"That's not the devil," said Nick. "But you *are* going to hell." Nick placed a hand over Denim's face and pressed down, covering his nose and mouth. There was no struggle and it was mere seconds before Denim was dead. Nick looked up at the night sky, a storm was near, he could feel it. He looked down at the burning car that had prevented the assassin causing any further pain and rubbed his chin. It had turned into quite an extraordinary evening and that was saying something considering the things he had seen in his long life. The night wasn't over yet, still a couple of things to do. First of which was making sure the ladies were okay.

***

Rain rattle-tattled against the house windows incessantly. It was a torrential downpour outside, like the gods had switched on their showers and turned them up as far as they could go. The sky was pitch black, when the fierce streaks of lightning weren't ripping across it with heart stopping booms. David White quite enjoyed a storm, though he couldn't remember having experienced one like this before. He sipped his half empty glass of wine and leaned back into his comfortable sofa. He checked his phone, no calls.

"Expecting to hear from someone?"

The voice startled him and he almost spilt some of his wine on his nice shirt. He turned to look at his uninvited guest.

"I should have knocked, I know." Nick stood in the doorway, dripping with rainwater. "Sorry about dripping all over your floor, it's a little rainy out."

"Nick," David said, smiling and regaining his calm. "What brings you here?"

"Long story," said Nick. A bright flash of lightning and a boom of thunder shook the house, the lights flickered. "I'll try and break it down for you, though."

"Okay," said David, beginning to feel uneasy.

"This evening I encountered a man clad in double denim – not sure if that's a fashion faux pas or not, I have no real issues with it, but it does make you wonder, doesn't it?"

"I wouldn't go double denim, myself." David enthused his smile with charm. "But I rarely wear denim at all."

"That's an aside, really. Doesn't have any relevance on the main point of the story."

"Which is?"

"He was an assassin, paid to kill me. Can you

believe it?" Nick raised an eyebrow.

"Good heavens," David placed his wine onto a pristine glass coffee table and stood. "Are you okay?"

"I am. Can't say as much for the denim fellow, he's dead. Ploughed down by a runaway car that was on fire."

David's jaw dropped in an unspoken question.

"I know, I'm still trying to figure that bit out and I know everything about this village from The Chittering to Hawthorn Lane..."

Hawthorn Lane, mouthed David, there was no such place in Sweet Little Chittering.

"Me not knowing something is new and rather thrilling," continued Nick. "Anyway, back to the denim assassin, he's dead and I am not."

"Thank God you're alive. This all sounds insane."

"It does, doesn't it?" Nick took a couple of steps forward. "Do you know what else sounds insane?"

David shook his head to indicate he did not.

"He claimed the devil paid him to kill me."

"Clearly he had mental health issues."

"Indeed. But I wondered to myself, who would want me dead? Who would gain from my demise? So, I asked him to describe this devil to me."

David stood quietly.

"And he described you, David."

"Me? Dear Lord," laughed David. "The man sounds like he was a fair few cards short of a deck. I mean, I am most assuredly *not* the devil."

"You're a greedy bastard, David, always have

been," said Nick, a glint in his eyes. "But I know you're not the devil."

David was rooted to the spot.

"Because *I* am the devil."

Directly above them vicious forked lightning ripped across the sky in a flash of bright white and the accompanying thunder once again shook the house with a BOOM!

The lights went out.

***

Moments later, Nick stood outside allowing the rain to run down his face. He breathed in - he loved a storm, and he loved this village. He'd been told of it many, many years ago by a ruthless arsehole of a man called Oliver Hughes. The only time Hughes came close to being likeable was whenever he spoke of his home, a quiet, out of the way, almost off the map village. It had made Nick curious and a great amount of time later, he decided to find out for himself. He liked it so much he decided to stay. As intense as his dislike of Hughes was, he had to agree with the man on one thing; Sweet Little Chittering, there was no place like it.

Dream Cottage

Richard Rowntree

Moving from Hartbridge had long been the plan for Anthony and Melissa. They fantasized about the rural lifestyle – at least what it appeared to offer them on the surface. An easy commute into town for work, and the countryside on their doorstep. They could dispense with at least one of the gas guzzling automobiles – and more and more, Anthony could work from home – idyllic views of the expanse of seasonally coloured fields creating a spectacular backdrop for his mundane computer screen-staring existence. A short walk to the local pub and shops; peaceful Sunday hikes to the Henge or the old windmill and, should it ever happen for them, a welcoming and cutesy village school – but that was all in the future. Their dreams.

And so, when the estate agent had offered up Dream Cottage in the initial marketing email, it had intrigued them simply with its name – was it fate? Melissa had certainly latched on to that notion in her subconscious and had never really managed to shake the prospect.

It only took one viewing to sell them both – a chocolate box flint structure, the corners of which were rustic and ancient oak trunks supporting the rickety roof. Probably not something a surveyor would have passed had they needed a mortgage – but now, in their early forties, and having both worked full time since graduating, they were in a position whereby, given the untimely deaths of Anthony's parents (and the subsequent rather large inheritance), they were able to buy the property outright using cash. The estate agent had probably been able to retire himself off the back of that deal – after all, the cottage had been on the market for nearly three years. He hadn't mentioned the history of the cottage to the eager Melissa, and the sensibly reluctant Anthony – and with good reason.

They'd been residents of the village for almost three years now – and things hadn't exactly panned out how they would have liked. Not long after moving into the cottage, Anthony had realized that actually he didn't enjoy rural living at all. The smell of pig manure in the fields wafted daily into his nostrils which were already sensitive to the exceedingly high levels of pollen that had accosted him since the relocation. It was especially bad in the early mornings, when the dew lay thick on it and then the warm sun evaporated the moisture. He had lost his desire to walk to and from the shops – it now seemed like such a chore to get out and carry back his purchases – and what a waste it was when they had the Audi just sitting on the driveway doing nothing. He ferried Melissa to and from the train station, morning and evening, for her commute, and that was about it.

And so, given his job only really took up a couple of hours of his time each day, he had reverted to online grocery shopping with delivery – much to the chagrin of the local community, who encouraged an insular economic system. Cockroft, the butcher, had been particularly vociferous at the last parish council meeting (attendance was virtually mandatory) about how his business was being destroyed by newcomers and their "fancy" online retail habits. As treasurer of the fete organization committee, Anthony had uncomfortably shifted in his seat during the conversation, which he felt was directed toward him. Thereafter, a ridiculous discussion had escalated into a theatrical disagreement about the age of the village, during which Julian had tried to engage Anthony – but Anthony's lethargy toward such pedantry was matched only by his disdain for the education levels of these small-minded buffoons. He had resisted the temptation to stoke the fire by clarifying that the definition of a village, and the current population, didn't even align, as he knew this was also a major bone of contention amongst the establishment.

Melissa had also lost her appetite for long, post Sunday lunch walks. After their third round of IVF treatment had failed, she hadn't seemed (to Anthony, at least) to have much desire to do anything. She worked increasingly long hours in town and became more and more distant. She often complained to her husband of the creaks and groans that came from the supporting timbers of the cottage whilst she was trying to get to sleep and spent less time there than ever before. Anthony and she had grown apart – and for both of them, the dream of Dream Cottage was deteriorating.

The couple were awakened, as always, around

5am by the grating sound of the amorous cockerel who had taken residence in a nearby hedgerow. It had been a source of laughter on the first morning in their new home – a perfect counterpoint to the noisy hustle and bustle of the traffic outside their old place in town - but now, on their 998th morning (Anthony had a numeric brain, being an accountant), it couldn't have been more annoying if it had tried. Anthony opened his bloodshot eyes – his breath still heavy with the smell of vodka from last night - and he swung his legs over the edge of the bed, his feet falling into his pre-positioned slippers as always. He arched his back, and the cracking sounds from his vertebrae instantly eased his tension. He stood, went to the kitchen, and pushed the start button on his gourmet coffee machine (which he always loaded with a capsule and water before he went to bed). He looked out the wide, short window at the early morning mist hovering above the lawn, inhaled two lungs full of the pig shit stench, and then mused over Ella's plan for the day.

Melissa had just managed to get back to sleep when she was awoken with a start by a single gunshot. The cock-a-doodle-do wouldn't be bothering either of them again. She sat bolt upright in bed, before rushing to the kitchen. Anthony was standing in the doorway, back lit by the low sunrise, the small rifle his father had owned sitting across his shoulders. At once horrified and aroused by his masculinity, she struggled to comprehend what Anthony had done. This wasn't him – he was a boring, pussycat of a man, hollow and lacking in passion and that was the main reason she'd been socializing with colleagues more often after work. But now, although unhinged, he had never looked more attractive to her.

The sound of their vintage telephone ringing broke the tension before any words – Melissa turned over her shoulder, then back to Anthony, who sauntered in like Lady Chatterley's Lover and casually stood the rifle against the wood burning stove. She threw him a puzzled look before going and answering. He sipped from his flat white and she disappeared off down the hallway.

For some months now, Anthony had felt claustrophobic within his home. It was a literal emotion – he had been obsessively measuring the rooms, and they were shrinking. Albeit a small amount, the walls were physically closing in on him. Over the course of the first month, it had been small – his home office had started at 308.7cm by 293.2cm. His second measurement, a week later, had been almost 2mm off in both directions. Subsidence? Shrinkage of the timbers with the change in seasonal humidity levels? Something like that for sure. He wasn't too bothered – he'd only been measuring up for a new desk anyway. But now it was more than a centimeter off on both walls. He wished he'd measured the ceiling height too, because that felt to him like it was even further in. He'd only wanted the new desk to cheer himself up – a comfort purchase – something to take his mind off the text messages he'd seen on Melissa's phone from a "Joe". He was sure he must have misunderstood – they'd been together so long and been through so much that he was sure there was no way she was seeing someone else. The messages had been suggestive without being explicit or confirming anything. As was his way, he'd decided not to confront her about it – what would be the point? She was highly unlikely to tell the truth – she had it too good, there's no way she'd want to give up the lifestyle she had, Ella had told him.

When Melissa returned from the hallway, she had a pale look on her face. Her fear and bewilderment at the cockerel massacre had been hijacked, replaced by something altogether more sombre. "My sister's dead."

Anthony turned his head slowly and robotically toward Melissa's newsflash. He seemed unconcerned and took another sip of his coffee. "I need to go – can you take me to the station? I'm going to throw some clothes in a bag." She was in shock. "Can you let Nicholas know I won't be able to help today?"

For the first time, Melissa now also felt the walls closing in around her and didn't really pay any mind to the fact that Anthony wasn't responding to her queries. She busied herself in a disorganized rushing around to pack things for her imminent departure. There was a ringing in her head – she had been close to her sister (too close in Ella's opinion) – and the information wasn't computing. She stood over the bed, holdall half full, and suddenly burst into tears. The kind of sobbing that you can't abate no matter what breathing techniques you try. Until the blow to her skull knocked her unconsciousness.

***

When he'd agreed to take over as treasurer, Anthony suspected it would be an easy enough role. Certainly nothing like the scale of what he did for a living – no tax calculations, payroll to organize, overtime to calculate for staff. And although, much like Dream Cottage, it had seemed simple on the surface, there was something much more insidious occurring in the village's ledgers. Old Eden had been the first to approach him in hushed tones. "The contributions made by the Paradise Inn need to reflect the overall level of control I have over the festivities." Then it had been Aaron – "We generally finance the web advertising of the fete through income from the stalls, but then we cross-link that with the Inn, and advertise David's rental home in France, which eases some of the tensions in the village." Judy then asked if she could pay less for her pitch this year, given she had a lower income than the more established traders. And Harris had suggested that St Benedict's should receive a larger portion of the profits and then rinse the money through their books as they were a religious organization and subsequently were able to pay less tax – but of course they would also need to fabricate the donation envelopes so that they could reclaim the maximum amount of tax aid on the money. Small scale fraud. But then again, he probably wouldn't get found out. Pressures from all sides. Ones Anthony had to adhere to, so as to not rock the boat.

The voice had begun in the basement. Anthony was a regular visitor to the moist, black abyss beneath Dream Cottage – the central heating system required thrice daily fuelling with seasoned logs, harvested from the local copse beyond the windmill. The sawmill owner's boy would bring them weekly on the back of his open topped van. There was no electricity in the basement, but a paraffin oil lamp lived at the top of the stairs and would accompany Anthony every time he submerged himself into the darkness. It had been arduous during the winters – this past one especially. But, in a strange way, comforting. Anthony had realized, particularly since finding Joe's messages, that he actually embraced the darkness. Down there, he knew there was nothing. And he mused on the idea that his own soul was similar. There were no children with whom he could share love. There was, in all probability, no wife with whom he could now connect. No parents. No neighbours. He was alone. Until Ella had whispered to him on the second of February. The day before he measured up for that new desk.

As Melissa's head thumped hard on each step on the way down to the basement, it reverberated through the flint walls of Dream Cottage. She had been awkward to move – Ella had warned Anthony that this would be the case – but he had assumed it would be easier than this. As he swung her legs around, he had knocked the paraffin lantern, which had smashed, leaving broken shards of glass in the darkness. He returned to the surface nursing a nasty impalement to the sole of his right foot as a result and cursed his own stupidity. As he locked the door behind him, he paused a moment to remember the first time he and Melissa had met. It was a nightclub, dark and moist, and they had been in their early twenties... below ground – how fitting. *She* had approached *him* – he'd never really considered that before – but of course she had, that brazen bitch. He should have known then that she would be the one to hurt him – sexually aggressive, yes, that was it, it was his fault for not noticing.

By the time he reached the office, the distortion to the fabric of Dream Cottage had made it almost impossible to even get in. The ceiling was now less than six feet and the footprint barely larger than that, squared. His LED clock informed him that it was now past one. If he was to avoid suspicion, Ella told him, he would have to get moving. The shrinkage to the remainder of the house was less dramatic and afforded Anthony the chance to shower and change his clothes before he departed. He carefully removed a shard of thick, curved glass from his sole, and then dressed it with a bandage from the first aid kit in the kitchen and set off.

***

The Paradise Inn was only running a skeleton staff by the time Anthony arrived – mostly because everyone was watching the pompous asshole who owned it prattle on over at the green. Joe was pretty much everything Anthony had feared he would be – and what Ella had described. Tall, fair haired, relatively muscular. He would be difficult to take down for sure – but Ella had assured him it would be possible, with proper planning, of course. Everything was in the planning. And Anthony knew that, with everything in his life. Failing to plan is planning to fail.

The public bar at the Paradise Inn was dark and hazy, even during the day. The bar top unpleasantly sticky. Joe checked his phone to see if he had received any more messages – Melissa was almost twenty minutes late and this place wasn't his vibe at all. When he heard the door open behind him, he turned to see but had no idea who Anthony was (or at least, he had no idea what he looked like). The ruse had been an easy sell – Joe was the heroic type, you see, so when Anthony asked if he could possibly help with a young lady who'd sprained her ankle in the car park, there was no hesitation. Anthony's limp from the glass in his foot also gave him a sympathetic air, which Joe couldn't not help. The smashing together of the Morris Dancers' sticks had given the perfect cover to the breaking of Joe's legs with the cricket bat – Ella had made that suggestion – and his cries were drowned out by the bells of the ruggles. True folk horror. Gagging him had been easy enough – his mouth was wide open, after all. The Audi wasn't the ideal abduction vehicle, but the trunk was spacious enough to get him into, with a little light beating to the protruding head.

Ella had a raspy tone to her voice – not at all quiet – which had made Anthony question whether or not Melissa had ever heard them. It was unlikely, given that most of the conversations took place when she was out (which, of late, was most of the time) and in the privacy and seclusion of the basement. Anthony didn't remember being scared of the voice – it had been a gradual increase in conversations rather than sudden jump scares – and they had started not long after his sleeping medication had first been delivered by the online pharmacy. The lack of sleep before that had exhausted Anthony to the point where he wasn't entirely sure what was real and what was imagined (although he didn't share such information with anyone). Since the pills, the line had been blurred further between what was waking and what was slumber. He was sleepwalking through life, guided by the voice of a girl he had never met, who only existed in the back of his mind.

The distance from the driveway to the front door was the one thing about Dream Cottage that seemed to be expanding. Maybe Anthony was just feeling the exertions of the day but dragging Joe up that slight incline was exhausting. The front door swung open with a kick which made Anthony wince (smaller shards were still embedded in his sole), but Joe stopped struggling after another blow to the face – this time with a large wooden rolling pin (the nearest and most convenient thing to hand at the time). Tucked up in the basement with Melissa, what a sweet couple they made. In their very own Dream Cottage. Both awoke following a brief wafting of smelling salts from Anthony and they were now bound, back-to-back, in front of the furnace that heated the cottage. Broken glass still littered the floor, and paraffin stung their nostrils. The combination of heat and moisture made them sweat profusely, the salty sting in their wounds the least of their concerns.

Anthony wasn't expecting to win anything in the raffle – after all, he'd struck gold with finding Ella to guide him – but Ian had been persuasive and encouraged him to part with enough money to purchase five tickets. A free pie every Monday for the next year from the bakery wasn't something he'd readily be able to take advantage of though. A shame, as he planned meals out with enough enthusiasm and precision that it would have been one less thing for him to worry about. Enough profit had been made off the raffle to fund the tea and biscuit requirements of the organizing committee for another year and Anthony had kept up appearances by attending the fete twice across the day so that nobody would assume anything untoward was going on with *him* (little did he realise that his concerns were the last thing on pretty much everyone in the village's minds that day). Melissa hadn't engaged enough with most of them for her to be missed and Joe was an outsider anyway. As the bizarre sight of the Morris Dancers made their way through the High Street, Anthony followed behind the parade, trundling back to Dream Cottage with a slight limp, for the final part of *his* nightmare - *Ella's* dream.

The fireworks were to be at nine and Anthony wanted to see those before the *coup de gras*. He always enjoyed fireworks, there was something about watching them that lent a childlike awe to his psyche, almost dreamlike. Ella had never seen fireworks, but Anthony had described them in vivid detail. They sounded to her like a wonderful experience, and she would be able to watch them with her new love, before she claimed his soul for all eternity.

Joe's eyes were heavily swollen and bruised – his nose had been bent beyond recognition and it still leaked blood. His lips were swollen and split. Melissa's ears rang from the head blows, and her concussion had caused her to vomit down herself. Both were utterly perplexed by their situation. Work colleagues with the occasional banter-filled text message between them, now suddenly drawn into a situation neither of them could see themselves getting out of alive. Their confusion had worked its way out – why did she want to meet him today? She didn't. So why did she text him? She didn't. Well, somebody text him from her phone. It must have been Anthony. But why? That was the part they couldn't figure out. They'd had a few hours to do so by now as well – and despite struggling (which actually led to very sore rope burns), they were no closer to being free. Clearly, Anthony had gone mad, and they were going to die. He must have misinterpreted their correspondence. *Oh fuck* – if only they could let him know.

***

The fireworks were disappointing to Anthony – a similar climax to those he had experienced all too often – lots of buildup, and not a very satisfying end product. Ella was also less than enthralled. As he squeezed his frame in through the now almost comically small doorframe to Dream Cottage from the garden, he passed a wall-hung picture of Melissa and himself on holiday, the glass broken, a large split from the corner down, separating the couple. They had been on honeymoon in the Seychelles; dream-like; bright, sunny, idyllic - just the two of them, no work, no pressures, no Instagram lifestyle to keep up with back then. Just happiness, and the joy of being two people together in a moment. He mused on it for a moment, and then remembered her in the basement with her new partner (or so he suspected). The very idea had eaten away at him, cajoled in large parts by Ella and her suggestions on the subject. He crouched as he descended the basement steps, rifle in hand. Outside, the air was thickening, ready for the storm to come.

Joe's headshot had been at such close range that there was almost nothing left of him above the lower jaw. Just desserts for that home wrecking piece of shit, Ella had said. Melissa's sobbing was as uncontrollable as it had been this morning, but this time it grated on Anthony, like that fucking cockerel had. So she had to go. A single shot, the last bullet in the rifle, had put an abrupt end to her incessant wailing. She got what she deserved. She wouldn't cause any more problems for Anthony, Ella had said. The room had been shifting constantly throughout the shootings and when Anthony turned to leave, he realized that it was going to be an impossibility. The doorway was now little more than two feet by one, the staircase perilously close to the back wall, and the rainfall had saturated the land outside to the extent that it was now trickling in between the ancient oak beams as the rain pelted down outside.

Anthony was trapped, and he began to panic. He looked around – the walls were now visibly closing in on him. He saw Melissa – that dark nightclub, the text messages. He saw Joe's carcass – his bodily fluids still leaking all over Melissa. That motherfucker, Ella said. The water flowed now like a tap left on in a public bathroom. Anthony tried to move his feet, to get above the rising water line of the basement floor without success but there was no way out. His feet were entangled with his quarry, unable to escape his actions. The thunder struck loud again outside, and again. The water line in the basement now reached his neck and he struggled to breathe – his feet trapped in the quagmire of wreckage Ella had convinced him to leave behind – and all he could hear as he drew his last lungful of dark, bloody rainwater was Ella asking him if he was happy now. To rest, to dream with her, forever.

Rare Editions at Mysterious Magpie Books

Tristan Sargent

Inside the shop, the books peacefully slumbered. Elderly leather-bound volumes and middle-aged hardbacks stood upon the shelves in calm rows; brash young paperbacks waited nearer the door, hoping not to be noticed. Every now and again, one would be taken, dragged away to be read on a beach or a lawn where the summer sunshine would quickly fade its covers and hasten the cracking of its spine.

Today the sun did its worst, shining brightly out of a blue sky, but the bookshop remained a gloomy haven, cool and quiet except for the occasional sound of a page being turned.

The door was pushed open, and the bell above it tried to go 'ting-a-ling', but only managed 'dunk-a-lunk'. Then, the door was closed slowly and carefully by the person who had entered, and the peace was not badly broken.

The customer stood for a moment and looked around him. In the corner, behind a wooden counter and a thick pair of spectacles, a young woman sat reading. She looked at him over the top of her book for a second, before returning her attention to the page. On the book's cover, the title was visible in large lettering: *Bambi's Revenge*.

That seemed odd to Jack. He'd never heard of such a book, and the title was improbable. He'd have to speak to the woman in a moment, but just now she seemed so engrossed in the book that he felt it would be a shame to interrupt her.

She'd probably finish her chapter soon, and then put the book down. He was happy to wait; he was in a bookshop after all, and in no kind of hurry. He would browse.

On the first shelf that he inspected there was a handwritten label which said 'Trashy Romances'. This seemed withering if not unfair. Forty or fifty books with titles like *Love Lies Panting* and *Darcy's Naughtier Exploits* sat in a uniform row, each spine topped with the same flowery publisher's logo.

The shelf below was labelled 'Trashy Horror', and below that was 'Trashy Sci-Fi'. A nonfiction section included a shelf labelled 'Ghastly Childhoods', and another label proclaimed to prospective customers: 'Liked Ghastly Childhoods? You'll *love* Survivors of Crime'.

Jack quickly looked again at the young woman. She did not look back at him.

Next, he found the children's books: long, reassuring rows of Puffins and Piccolos, Lions, Knights, and Red Foxes. One title caught Jack's eye, and he quickly reached out and took it from the shelf.

He gazed at the cover. *Hobb's Hunt*, by Eloise Gallagher. "A thrilling supernatural adventure!" claimed an overenthusiastic ribbon of text just under the title.

Below that, two children were shown cowering from a huge black dog, its muzzle split wide to reveal fangs like ivory sickle-blades. In the background a dark figure watched, accompanied by a second gigantic hound which seemed to crouch obediently.

Jack carefully opened the book and was surprised to discover that it seemed to have been signed by the author. The previous owner had autographed it too, inscribing on the inside cover "This book belongs to Judy A. Ashleigh (Class 3)".

There was a gentle 'clap' sound, as of a book being closed sharply. Jack looked round and saw that the young woman had placed her book on the counter and was now looking directly at him.

"After anything in particular?" she asked in a calm voice. Her face was calm too, with the possibility of a smile.

Jack walked to the counter. "Actually, you're holding a book for me. I bought it online this morning."

The young woman blinked once, as if trying to work out what he was talking about, but then it seemed to come to her. "Oh yes," she said "Mr Warde. One moment please."

Then she stood and with a swish of her floral pattern dress she disappeared into a back room. *That dress*, Jack thought as he watched her go, *was far too old-fashioned to really suit her*.

There was a framed picture on the wall behind the counter. It showed a lady and an assembled group of crows. She was either giving them cookery lessons, or teaching them geometry, drawing a circle in the dirt with a long stick. It was also possible, Jack supposed, that she might be some sort of witch carrying out some sort of rite.

The young woman returned, holding a rectangular object in a brown paper bag. This time she smiled, politely if not warmly.

"One of our rarest books," she said.

"I didn't know that edition existed," Jack said, enthusiastically. "I'd never even heard of the publisher."

"Almost nobody has," said the young woman. "Jackson & Namaroff were a tiny operation, run by a couple of folklore enthusiasts. Almost everything they published is rare or collectible now. I have their *Book of Gorgons* somewhere."

She placed the book upon the counter, pushed it towards Jack, and sat down again. She watched him expectantly.

Jack realised he was still holding the other book he'd taken from the shelf. He held it up as if confessing that he'd been trying to hide it, which he hadn't.

"I'll have this as well," he said. The young woman looked disappointed when she saw the book. "It is for sale, isn't it?"

She laughed in a way that he found himself liking. "Absolutely," she said, "it's just, that's my old copy. I was secretly hoping that nobody would ever buy it."

Jack put the book down. "I'll live without it," he said, kindly.

"It's for sale," she said, shaking her head. "We can't hang on to everything from childhood." She took the book and checked the price inside.

"Besides," she added, without looking up, "you looked very excited when you found it."

"It's signed," Jack said. Judy A. Ashleigh nodded and closed the book.

"I knew the author. She was my English teacher."

"Really?"

Judy nodded. "Quite a dull woman actually, perhaps that's why she made her book so eventful. Have you read it?"

"Of course. Did you ever see the TV serial?"

Judy shook her head in a brisk manner that suggested she might not really approve of books being adapted for television.

"My mother knew one of the cast members, though," she said. "It was filmed quite near here, I understand."

"Which cast member?"

"She used to take him for walks. He played the main hound." Judy nodded at the book, and the terrifying beast depicted there.

Her manner was cool, but Jack saw there was humour in her eyes, and he laughed. Judy seemed to like that, so she continued.

"Samson's lick was much worse than his bite, apparently. Mrs Gallagher didn't like his performance though, said he wasn't frightening enough. Mum told me that later he lost out on the role of the Hound of the Baskervilles because he kept rolling over during the audition, wanting Sherlock Holmes to tickle his tummy."

Judy raised one hand, and it looked as if she was about to remove her glasses, but then she seemed to think better of it, and lowered her hand to rest it upon the counter.

Looking directly at him she opened her mouth and inhaled, but whatever she had been about to say, the thought retreated in the moment. Then she blinked, shook her head and shrugged as if embarrassed and said, "You can have that book, you've paid quite a lot for the other one already."

"Thank you so much," said Jack and smiled the lop-sided smile he saved for these occasions. Judy smiled back and gestured at the paper bag on the counter, as if suggesting that he check his purchase.

Jack opened the paper bag, and carefully took out the book. It was a handsome, dark blue volume. He opened it and began to flick through. Each story in the collection had its own full-page illustration, he stopped to inspect one.

Abruptly, his brow furrowed hard.

"Is this a joke?"

The young woman looked strikingly innocent in that moment.

"It's supernatural fiction, as advertised."

Jack closed the book sharply and looked again at the spine. His face contorted in confusion and disbelief.

"...though I've often thought," Judy continued, enthusiastically, "horror stories are rather similar to jokes when you think about it..."

Her voice trailed away and her shoulders slumped a little when she realised Jack wasn't listening.

"What is this?" he asked, and Judy could hear a slightly unpleasant tone creeping into a voice that had seemed so pleasant before.

She sighed. "It's what it says it is on the cover, and on the listing on our website. You bought it in full knowledge of what it was, Mr. Warde."

"This *is* a joke," Jack said, trying to understand what he was looking at.

The book's spine declared the contents quite accurately, now he looked at it. He was confused. Since when had such a book existed?

"*The Complete Goat Stories of Mr James*? What is this?" he demanded.

Judy visibly deflated in her exasperation. "It's a very rare collection of supernatural stories about goats by Mr. Montgomery Radford James. What did you think you'd bought?"

Jack's face contorted in several ways, all of them highly expressive. Judy seemed to know them of old.

"If you're going to get excited," she said calmly but firmly, "please put your purchase down. You can say what you like to me, but don't hurt the book."

Jack recovered himself and looked again at the volume in his hands. He shook his head as if to clear it, but the title remained. Remembering the respect due to an old book, he placed it carefully on the counter.

"But…" he said, "'Goat Stories'?"

Judy shrugged lightly in a way that Jack found as

vexing as it was appealing under the circumstances. "Mr James was a local vet. He lived in Chittering in the thirties, quite a respected member of the community until he went nuts."

"Was that something to do with goats, by any chance?"

"Yes, actually. He developed a sort of mania about them. It made things quite awkward for him professionally speaking, but he did write some very good short fiction as a result. He was a fascinating man."

There was a short silence.

"I think," said Jack, "I might have to ask for a refund."

"If you wish," said Judy. "Give yourself a minute to think about it though. It's a very rare book, that's why it's so expensive. This may be your only chance to ever own a copy."

Jack reached down and opened the book again. A frontispiece showed a man sitting in a high-backed armchair, reading an old book. He was quite oblivious to the extraordinarily large and ominous goat that was looming up behind him.

"Anyway," said Judy, interrupting his contemplation, "it's rather interesting that you should ask if it's a joke."

Jack looked up at her.

"Is it?"

"Well, there's an essential similarity between stories that frighten and stories that amuse, don't you think? They're both dependent on punchlines, for example."

This time he had heard what she'd said and he seemed to agree, so Judy continued.

"In a similar way," she said, "I think horror stories and love stories have a certain amount in common."

"Which explains…?" Jack asked, pointing out the intimately adjacent shelves of Trashy Romance and Trashy Horror.

"Well, yes. What I mean, though, is that the masters of these genres always knew when to hold back and let the reader fill in the emotions for themselves."

"M.R. James for example."

"Yes, him," she conceded, brushing the name away. "And our esteemed Mr James too. I really think you'll like his stories. They'll make you look at goats in a completely new way."

Judy lifted her hand and paused, once again considering whether to remove her spectacles. Then, with sudden resolve, she took them off and placed them upon the counter. She looked directly into Jack's eyes.

"Have you decided?" she asked.

Jack looked into her eyes and decided that he'd been cynically outmanoeuvred, but he didn't mind.

"I expect it would be a lot of unnecessary work to reverse the payment, wouldn't it?"

Judy shone with pleasure at his decision. Jack found this very charming even though he knew that her happiness probably stemmed from having sold an expensive book to somebody who hadn't wanted it. Ah well. She had a lovely smile, after all.

"If you do get hold of any rare editions of actual M.R. James ghost stories, please get in touch with me though. I collect them, you see."

Judy processed this, quietly, and then nodded. "Sure."

Then she looked a little awkward, as if uncertain whether to return to her book, or try to think of something else to say.

"So…" she ventured, "…are you going to go to the fete?"

"I'm here for the books," he said. Then he looked around as if noticing his surroundings for the first time. "Incidentally," he said, "I love your shop".

Judy straightened in her chair. As she looked at him, she started to nervously play with her glasses as they lay on the counter, one hand folding and unfolding the temples.

"Go on…" she said.

What else was there to say? "It's a wonderful bookshop."

Judy actually bit her lip in disappointment for a full second before straightening her face again, obviously hoping to appear unmoved. Then she cleared her throat and spoke, a little hesitantly.

"It's just that," she said, in a calm voice, "I don't think anybody around here really appreciates my shop, and it belonged to my parents. I work hard at keeping it, you know, sort of in their memory." She looked at him expectantly.

Jack looked around, hoping for a chair. Judy pointed out a kick-stool a few feet away next to a set of shelves that were labelled "Esoteric, Mystical & Weirdy-Weirdy".

Jack kicked the stool over to the counter and sat down on it.

"All right," he said, "Well, first of all – I love the labelling."

Judy blinked and was unmoved.

"But… there's also the sound."

Judy cocked her head very slightly.

"Proper silence," he explained, "not that rough silence that batters your ears and deafens you. It's not the sound of a library, either. You only get it in small, enclosed spaces filled with books as soundproofing. It's the softest kind of silence."

Judy seemed delighted and sat back a little, obviously wanting to hear more.

"Some places, there's that unhappy smell of books that have been allowed to get damp, almost mouldy but not quite."

Judy nodded. "The rank smell of unquiet literature," she said.

"But not here. The smell in here…"

"The *scent,*" she corrected him.

"Yes, the *scent* of books – the fragrance? The fragrance of books!"

"Just wood pulp and glue," Judy countered.

"When I was a boy, I read something a character said in a book and I agreed with them. They said they thought that books smelled like spices from far-off lands."

"I read that book at school," exclaimed Judy. "When I read it, I remember being amazed, because

I thought…"

"…you thought you were the only person in the world who'd ever held a book up, smelled its leaves and thought it was beautiful?"

Judy sighed a little sigh, looked around at her books and then back at Jack. "Yeah," she said, happy and sad all in one moment.

Jack let the moment breathe, until Judy strangled it.

"That's all very beautifully put," she said, "but it's true of any well-kept bookshop. What's special about mine?"

"Well, we've only just met; I'd have to get to know the shop a bit better. My first impression: I'd like to see more."

Judy's mood seemed to have taken a sudden, melancholy turn, and she said nothing. Then something occurred to Jack.

"It's the only shop I've ever been in that had a copy of this," he said, and held up his newly acquired copy of *Hobb's Hunt*. "I thought it was extinct."

"We pride ourselves on our rare editions," said Judy. "We have plenty of books that you won't find anywhere else."

"We?"

Judy looked uncomfortable. "Me, Mum and Dad. They're still here in spirit." She looked quite dejected.

Jack had an idea.

"Look, why don't you give me a tour. Show me some rare editions, perhaps I'll find another expensive book to buy."

She brightened again. Jack hoped it was the prospect of showing off her books rather than selling him another peculiar tome that excited her.

"My name's Judy," she said.

"I know," said Jack, and held up her old book, opening it to show her name on the inside cover. "I'm Jack."

"I know," said Judy, and held up a printed-out sales docket that showed his full name, address and the last four digits of his credit card number.

"Well, I'm pleased to meet you, Judy. Show me round."

"Are you sure? It's a lovely day, the fete awaits you."

Jack shrugged casually. "I didn't come here for the fete."

"You should at least wander around it before you go. It's usually amazing," she said with a conspicuously un-amazed look on her face. "There'll be a tombola."

"A tombola, really?" exclaimed Jack. "All the vices of a gambling den and an off-licence combined on a single open-air table."

Judy didn't seem to find that as funny as he'd hoped. "I like tombolas," she said.

"Will there be one of those paddling pools with little wooden swans that you have to catch with a hook on a stick?"

"I don't know," said Judy, "there might be. Mrs Gallagher might be there."

"Really? I'm surprised she's still alive."

"She's not."

"Ah," said Jack but didn't argue. "Well, it's not like I needed her to sign my copy of her book anyway, is it?"

Judy shook her head and now Jack was fairly sure she'd been joking.

"Anyway, it's a lovely day," she said. "You don't want to be stuck in here."

"Aren't you going?"

"No. I've been asked to do a book stall a couple of times, but I've always declined. For me village fetes are rather like road accidents – quite interesting when viewed through a pane of glass, but not something I'd want to be directly involved in."

"All right then," said Jack, with finality. "Neither of us is going to the fete. Show me some books."

Judy looked at her watch and then stood. She strode to the door and reversed the sign to tell the world that Mysterious Magpie Books was now closed. She turned back to Jack and looked across the shop at him.

"Our Esoteric section is very good, actually," she said, brightening.

Jack looked around at the shelves he'd noticed earlier and she came to stand beside him.

"What would be your pick?" he asked.

"We've got a wonderfully expensive first edition of *The Sentinels* by Harrison Zytem. He was an authority on stone circles and wrote a bit about Hartbridge Henge. Have you been there?"

"I haven't."

"It's worth going if you like giant stones that don't move or do anything. Professor Zytem liked them. He had some interesting ideas about the power of stones to influence the flow of time."

Judy pointed at another shelf. "Over there we've got a couple of signed Dennis Wheatleys. Those belonged to Mr Winnerden, the shop's original owner. Nobody wants to buy them."

"I thought Wheatley was very popular."

"Last century, yes. Now you can't sell his books for love or money."

"But you've kept those two?"

"Well, I can't sell them for love or money. Though to be fair I've only tried selling them for money. I can't just bin them, though; they've got some interesting scribbles on the endpapers."

"Scribbles?" asked Jack.

"Yes, well, you often find that with the more contemplative or academic book owner. I've got Aleister Crowley's personal copy of *Pride & Prejudice* here somewhere. He wrote some very interesting speculations in the margins about Elizabeth Bennett."

Jack didn't want to seem mocking, so he hid his smile.

"We've got a..." she began, but stopped, squinted at the shelves, and then sighed in exasperation. Jack guessed the reason and quickly retrieved her glasses from the counter. He handed them to her.

"Thank you," she said, staring at him in a way that made him suspect his face was just a blur to her at that moment. She put her glasses back on, but now seemed like she wanted to avoid eye contact.

"So, down here there's a very good book on local folklore that Mrs Gallagher once recommended to me. Actually, I've a feeling that this was her old copy." Judy paused and looked at Jack. "Whenever somebody old dies in the village," she said, apparently feeling obliged to explain, "their books always end up in here."

She found the book on a lower shelf and crouched to reach it. Then she stood again, holding a dark green volume in her hands.

"This will interest you, there's a picture in here…"

She found the page she was looking for and carefully passed the open book to Jack. A full colour plate depicted a large, maned creature somewhere between a hound and a wolf, rearing up and frightening a young couple who seemed to be walking innocently down a country lane. What immediately struck Jack, though, was how much it resembled the cover of *Hobb's Hunt*.

"Was this the source for that cover painting?" he asked, fascinated.

"It must have been," Judy agreed. "Especially as the story to which it relates has a lot in common with Mrs Gallagher's book. Ghost-dogs serving the will of wicked magicians and so on. She drew a lot of her ideas from folklore."

"There are plenty of legends of ghostly black dogs around the country," said Jack, trying to contribute.

"There are," agreed Judy. "They're usually thought to be a leftover cultural memory of Norse mythology brought here by Viking settlers. They believed in a sort of devil-wolf named Fenrir."

Jack reverently handed the book back to Judy and she crouched again to replace it on the shelf. She carried on talking as she did.

"There's a rather old book here on fly fishing that's supposed to be rare, but nobody wants it anymore and we've got a first edition of '*Practical Wasp Keeping*'."

"Wasp keeping?" asked Jack.

Judy stood again and turned to him. "I got the book from the widow of a man who was found stung to death in his own orchard. It's funny, when you think about it; most old books must have at least one death in their history, mustn't they?"

Judy led him a little further, then pointed out a narrow unit of shelving that ran from floor to ceiling. Every shelf was tightly lined with glossy black-spined paperbacks.

"This here," she said, "is the ominous monolith of Penguin Classics around which locals occasionally gather in mystification, before hurling animal bones in the air."

"Are you not fond of your local customers?"

Judy stared at him. When she spoke, it was in a whisper.

"One of them came in here one day," she said, clearly relaying something dreadful, "and asked me if I had a copy of *Fifty Shades of Grey*."

Jack's eyes widened in horror. "Well, that's just

uncalled for."

"Well, exactly," said Judy. "Exactly. So I banished him. I said 'anyway, Father Harris, it's Sunday morning, shouldn't you be in Church?'"

Judy seemed happy at Jack's reaction.

"True story," she added. "Come and look at this."

She strode toward a shelf on the far wall, near to the door, but paused long enough to point out the slender yellow spine of a book on a high shelf. "That's a copy of Mr James's first book, *Goat Stories of a Veterinarian*." Then she continued across the floor.

"Actually," said Jack, abruptly trying to change the subject, "you mentioned somebody called Mr Winnerden?"

Judy was about to point out something else, but she stopped in her tracks and turned slowly with her arm still raised, like a ballerina in a musical box. Then she noticed that her arm was still in the air and lowered it awkwardly, briefly pressing an index finger to the bridge of her spectacles as she did.

"Mr Winnerden. The shop was originally his. When Mum and Dad took it on it had been boarded up for a few years. It just lay empty after Winnerden disappeared."

"Disappeared?"

"Yes, just... 'disappeared'" Judy said, shrugging as if it was an everyday event. "People like to say things like 'mysterious circumstances', but it wasn't that mysterious. He just went one day, along with his car, his cigar collection and his budgerigar."

"Hmm," said Jack. "That must have been a bit shocking for a small community like this?"

"Well, it upset all the local publicans and wine merchants, I would think. Dad always said Mr Winnerden had just gone off to become a tramp on the shores of Loch Ness."

Jack seemed fascinated. "What do you think happened?"

"I like to think he went to Loch Ness," she said, simply. "It's so much nicer than speculating about unmarked graves and things. Anyway, people do just disappear sometimes, don't they? It's normal."

"Is it?"

Judy shrugged. "Anyway, look, here's Kafka's forgotten novel *Der Gefangene*, sadly never translated into English."

"So, did the shop still have all of Mr Winnerden's original stock when your parents took it on?" Jack persisted.

Judy pressed her lips together in a way that implied she didn't like the subject. "Yes," she said. "Lots of books upstairs in the flat, too."

Jack looked upwards as if the contents of the flat would somehow be visible through the ceiling.

"Are they still up there?"

Judy's eyes narrowed for a moment and she looked like she wanted to change the subject, but had decided that it was probably going to be futile.

Jack remembered himself. "I'm sorry, is that a bad subject?"

The look of suspicion vanished from Judy's eyes. "Oh no," she said. "Just, I don't really like going up there. I sneaked up there when I was little and scared myself. I thought I saw something in one of the rooms. After that, Mum and Dad always kept it locked."

"It's haunted?"

Judy gave him a look. "*Everywhere* is haunted, Mr Warde."

"Jack, please."

Judy inhaled through her nose and looked uncomfortable. "All right," she said, as if deciding something, and she walked back to the counter and sat back down. Jack watched.

"Come on," she said. "I don't tell stories standing up."

When Jack was back on the kick-stool, Judy began. "I was very young," she murmured. "I don't really remember what I saw. I just know that it was like an old man, but sort of like a… well, like a smell, too. Like tobacco fog and a piss-soaked armchair."

"You think it was Mr Winnerden?"

"I think it was my imagination," she said and removed her glasses again. Jack could see the tiniest of trembles in her hand as she did and he could hear the slightest of ragged edges to the sigh that she gave before clearing her throat.

"I went back up there when I inherited the shop. I don't think my parents really ran this place to earn money; they just liked having a bookshop. I wanted to keep it going, but I couldn't afford it."

Jack nodded.

"So, I was going to clear out all the stock, sell it

off in bulk. Then, I unlocked the flat and looked up there and that changed things." She looked into the distance. "All sorts of things," she added, quietly.

"There were valuable books up there?"

One side of Judy's mouth curved into a conspiratorial smile and she nodded slowly. "Oh yes," she said, in a low voice.

"I spent a day exploring the cupboards and boxes and found piles and piles of old books – all of them much more intriguing than anything downstairs. It was a gold mine. I didn't have to make money on the shop, I could just auction off choice volumes from Mr Winnerden's personal collection."

Judy paused and hugged herself.

"They were all objects of desire," she said. "Rare things hidden from the world. All sorts of strange people wanted to get hold of them."

"Strange people?" asked Jack. Judy ignored the question.

"In one room I found an impressive cabinet, very grand and very locked. So, I broke into it."

Jack was entirely focused on Judy now and it made her feel odd.

"What did you find?" he asked intensely.

"The first book I pulled out was this great, black slab, layered in dust. I sat there and opened that book and started reading. I was fascinated. I learned a lot that day."

"What was the book?"

Judy sat forward and encouraged him to lean forward too, as if they weren't already alone. She looked like she was on the verge of telling him the book's name, her eyes glittering with excitement.

She sat back. "Not all of the books are for sale," she said. "But it turns out that Mr. Winnerden liked to call himself something of an 'amateur occultist'. I found his notebooks, his 'grimoires'" – Judy widened her eyes when she said that word – "I found all of his lithographs, including that one" – and she pointed at a picture of a wolf hanging near the esoteric shelves. "Fenrir again," she said.

"I found this too," she added, and lifted a slender gold chain from under the neckline of her dress. "Not normally one for jewellery, but it suited me."

She tidied the chain back into place, out of view. "I also found all of his correspondence. He knew some famous people--a lot of those letters were worth a fortune at auction."

"And that's how you got into selling rare books?"

Judy nodded. "From that day I entered into the arcane field of Rare Editions. These days I'm rather well-established."

Jack had listened to all of this, apparently fascinated. "Do people ever try to get hold of these books by less honourable means?" he asked.

"Oh no," she said. "Except once. Two customers wanted my only copy of *Doctor Who and the Dead Planet* and ended up having a fistfight in the street. Grown men as well."

Judy rose from her chair. "Anyway," she said, "there we are. Now, I'm a dealer in rare books. I have quite a reputation, you know."

Jack nodded. "I'd heard, actually."

Judy wandered to another shelf and removed a very old-looking book. She held it up with as much care as if it were made of glass.

"This is *Madness & Matrimony*," she beamed, "Jane Austen's disastrously-received sequel to *Pride & Prejudice*."

She'd lost Jack at 'matrimony' and she noticed with irritation that he was now looking at her rather than the book.

"Judy," he said.

"Jack?"

She stared back at him, and carefully returned the book to its place on the shelf. "Go on," she said.

"Judy, would you go to the fete with me?"

Judy bit her lip to stop herself smiling and adopted an airy manner. "Don't see why not," she said. "Do you want to go now?"

"Whenever you like."

Judy nodded slightly more than she needed to. "All right," she said.

***

Judy claimed the lane was a short cut to the village green, but it was obviously no such thing. It did seem that they didn't run the risk of walking past other people, though, which Jack suspected was the point.

When they arrived, there was a crowd gathering at one end of the green. "Looks like something's about to happen," said Jack brightly.

Judy snorted delicately. "Nick Eden's about to

make noises with his face," she said. "It's his hobby."

"Shall we go and listen to him anyway?" he suggested.

Judy looked uncomfortable, but she agreed and sidled beside him to the fringes of the crowd.

Moments after they'd joined the throng, an older man appeared and began a speech that Jack found entertaining. It began with some confusion over a microphone and a nasty screech of feedback that made Judy grimace.

"I won't waffle on for too long..." said the man, prompting Judy to breathe the word "liar" in the direction of Jack's hearing. There followed some self-congratulatory waffle, some spiteful personal observations about people not in attendance, and some blather about the age of the village. The crowd seemed to like it though, laughing throughout. Jack wondered if he should laugh along with them in case they realised he was an Outsider. Judy seemed happy though, rolling her eyes at the laughter or glaring at a nearby child for some reason.

When Nick finished saying things, a group of green-waistcoated Morris Dancers processed onto the green and took their positions. Soon they were doing Morris Dancer things; Jack wasn't an expert and so to him it did look rather like some men prancing about with sticks.

Jack whispered an uncharitable observation to Judy. "Shh," she said. "They work hard at this, don't be mean."

"Hoi!" said the prancing men in unison and clacked their sticks together.

Jack looked at Judy, very seriously. "Hoi," he said.

Judy tried not to snigger. When she'd regained her all-important composure, she tugged Jack's sleeve to get his attention. She jerked her head to suggest an escape route.

As they moved away, somebody recognised Judy. "Hello Laura!" said the man. "Didn't expect to see you here."

Before Judy could reply, the man noticed Jack. "Oh," he said. "Hello," he added, and then smiled again at Judy, with something between surprise and approval.

When he'd moved on through the crowd, they finished their escape. Jack gave Judy a funny look. "Laura?" he asked.

Judy pretended not to have heard. "Oh look," she said, "there's a tombola!"

"Why did he call you Laura?"

Judy looked bored. "*Laura Ashleigh*. Lots of them call me that. Provincial wit."

"Oh," said Jack. "That's a bit lame."

"They don't read much. Anyway--tombola!"

Jack bought ten tickets at the tombola and gave five of them to Judy. Judy had no luck, but Jack won a very grand-looking old bottle of wine that sat on the table between a litre of *Victory Gin* and a half-bottle of *Black Pony* scotch. The bottle had obviously sat in somebody's drinks cabinet for a long time and that somebody, Jack suspected, was probably now deceased. It was still sealed, though, and it looked very expensive.

He turned and presented it to Judy. She accepted, rather self-consciously, and a couple of older ladies clapped and commented on Jack's chivalry.

Judy had an idea. She took Jack's hand and led him away down the row of stalls in search of something. He didn't argue.

She reached her destination, stopped abruptly, and gestured at something. Jack looked and saw a paddling pool full of little wooden waterfowl. A three-year-old was busy trying to hook one out with a stick. Judy paid the lady and was handed two sticks with hooks.

Later, they sat on a bench and talked about how much harder Hook-A-Duck had seemed when they were children.

"Somehow this goes on until nine in the evening," mused Judy. "Then they have fireworks."

"Exciting?"

Judy moved her hands in front of her, spreading her fingers suddenly to mime explosions. "Pshhhfttt!" she said and then added: "Fizzle."

"Underwhelming, then."

"Just whelming. I think the thunderstorm will be more impressive."

"Thunderstorm?"

"Can't you feel it? Definitely a thunderstorm on the way. Here by ten-o'-clock, I should think."

Jack narrowed his eyes at her. "Are you a witch?"

"I'm a country girl."

"Does that mean you're a witch?"

"It means I can feel when a thunderstorm's coming."

She looked up at the blue sky and played idly with her necklace. Jack looked at her.

"Are you happy living here, Judy?"

She looked round at him, innocently. "Yes," she said, confused at the question.

"Only, you don't seem to like the people here very much."

"Oh," said Judy. "They're all right. Mostly they leave me alone."

"Just you and your books?"

"Nobody else," she said, shaking her head. "Well," she added, "I've got a dog."

Jack said nothing. Judy noticed and assumed he was a cat person.

"Did you have any plans for dinner?" she asked and quickly added, "I mean, you paid for the wine, I should share it."

***

Judy lived in a cottage on Hobble Lane not far from her shop. The village was quiet as they walked back, with most people still at the fete.

Inside the cottage, Judy told Jack to sit himself down while she disappeared upstairs. He inspected the bookshelves in the living room, until he found something promising tucked at the back, almost hidden. He took it, looked at it, smiled broadly and pocketed it.

When Judy came downstairs, she'd changed her dress to something less floral and had lost her glasses. Jack was willing to bet that she'd put in contact lenses; she was far too self-conscious about those glasses, he thought.

Much later, after dinner and when the wine was properly chilled, they stood in Judy's garden and watched the fireworks arc into the sky. They streaked upward, bursting against the dark blue firmament like condoms filled with fluorescent paint thrown against a toilet wall. Finally, some tiny glowing bits descended apologetically, as if to say "well, we tried."

A thought came to Jack. "You said you had a dog?"

Judy nodded, still gazing into the sky. "He's around. Ooh, look," she said, excitedly pointing at a cluster of stars.

"Those are Hecate's Pigtails. You can make a wish on them, you know. It was the first spell my mother ever taught me."

"So you *are* a witch?"

Judy tutted. "*Obviously* I'm a witch."

"Not that obvious. It's not like you have a black cat."

"Jacobean propagandist stereotyping," she spat. "Anyway, I'm allergic."

They went inside and sat on the sofa together. After a little while, there was a sudden flash outside, and Judy counted the seconds until the thunder arrived. It sounded like the sky was cracking open.

Jack looked at the clock. It was nearly ten.

"Do you really know magic?" he asked her.

"Enough," she said, cautiously.

"Can you show me?"

"No," she said, but he asked her again.

"All right," she said, sighing as if what he'd asked would inevitably ruin her day. "Give me your hand."

He held out his hand, she took it and studied his palm carefully. Then she turned it over and examined the back. She seemed unhappy with what she saw, though not surprised.

"This line here," she said, pointing to a pale patch of skin, "tells me that you took your wedding ring off earlier today, probably before you entered the shop." She dropped his hand and stared hard at him.

Jack protested, with the look of perfect innocence that Judy knew only came from practice. She said she believed him but stood and retrieved the wine bottle. "I'd better put this in the fridge," she said, avoiding eye contact.

He followed her to the kitchen, hoping to get past this moment and be back in her good graces.

"I've worked it out," he said.

"What's that?" she asked, without turning.

"Why your shop is special; what I can find there that I can't find anywhere else."

She turned and looked at him blankly, waiting.

He walked toward her and she straightened up, tense as if ready to repel him.

"You're something of a rare edition yourself,

you know," he said. "Only one copy, priceless, would be much sought-after if the world knew about her."

Judy blushed ferociously and turned away.

"Oh..." she said, "please don't say that. It just makes this harder than it needs to be."

When she turned back, he was right next to her. She gasped in surprise but didn't retreat.

"I'm not comfortable," she said.

"Not comfortable with what?" he asked and moved very slightly closer.

"Tension," she said, and nervously went to press the bridge of her glasses, only to realise they weren't there.

"What?" he said.

"It's what horror stories and love stories have in common, the tension."

He shook his head, not understanding or else not caring.

"Well," she said and swallowed. "Those moments..." She looked at the corner of the room, to avoid looking at him.

"Those moments just before a kiss, they're just like the moment in a horror film just before something dreadful happens, aren't they? Filled with apprehension at what's about to happen."

"I didn't come here for a lecture, *Laura*."

She closed her eyes and with one hand she started to play with her necklace. The chain had a tiny charm attached to it, gold and silver and in the shape of some animal or other. She held this between thumb and finger and whispered something

Jack couldn't make out.

"Judy," he said, but her eyes stayed shut.

There came a sound at the door, a deep, insistent scraping. When she heard the sound, Judy opened her eyes and gently let out the breath she'd been holding.

"I have to let the dog in," she said, and sidestepped away, making for the back door. As she turned the key, she also flicked the kitchen light off. Light reached them from the living room doorway, so they were not completely in darkness. "He doesn't like bright lights," she said.

Judy's voice was sad. "I've had a lovely day, really. I like you, honestly. I could almost believe that you like me too."

"I do like you," he said. "I let you rip me off over that sodding book." Judy could tell from his voice that he was getting angry and she flinched when she saw him begin to move toward her again.

"But, if you really liked me, you wouldn't have lied to me. You wouldn't have stolen my book."

"What are you talking about?"

"Jack," she said. "You kept asking about Winnerden's old books. I think you're more interested in them than you are in me."

The scraping sound came once again at the door.

"I don't know what you're talking about, love," Jack said and clenched both of his fists.

Judy pushed the handle down and the door slowly opened inwards.

Outside, the rain was now torrential, and Jack could feel the dampness of the air flooding into the kitchen. Then, a great, dark shape slid into the room and settled itself on its haunches next to Judy. Jack felt every muscle in his body tense, he took a step back and then another.

Seated, the shape reached almost to Judy's shoulders as she stood there. "He's very loyal," she said, her voice as calm now as it had been when Jack had first met her. "He's not like other dogs. I can't take him for walks, obviously. In fact, he can't go out in daylight at all."

The hound was so still it might have been carved from solid jet.

"He always comes when I call, though, if it's night-time."

Jack took another step toward the exit and Judy noticed. "Put my book on the table," she said.

With a trembling hand, Jack did as he was told, removing the book from his pocket. Judy quickly took it back.

"Mr Winnerden's last notebook," she said. "Mostly nonsense, but he got the important spells right. So, you thought now you'd got this book, you'd take me for whatever else you could? Were you stealing this for yourself, or is somebody paying you?"

"Judy…" Jack began, but she cut him off.

"Thank you for today," she said. "Honestly, but I think you should just disappear now. Go on."

The hound hissed very slightly and Jack fled.

Judy listened to the slamming of her front door and noticed the wine bottle standing on the kitchen table. She carefully filled her glass halfway and then put the bottle in the fridge.

She stood in the near-dark for a moment, then sniffed and touched a hand briefly to her eye.

She counted to ten.

"Go!" she said to the huge black shape and it flew out through the back door in pursuit, without so much as a whisper. She returned to the living room.

Judy sat and listened to the rain. It was such a shame, she thought. She'd had such a nice day. He'd had such a nice smile.

These were lovely memories, she decided. She would just have to forget about the disappointments. She sipped her wine.

Then she noticed her copy of *Hobb's Hunt*, sitting on the table where Jack had placed it earlier in the evening.

Smiling, she took it and gazed at the cover.

Gingerbread Lane and its Vicious Cycle

MJ Dixon

"I think it's 'Circle'," Tabitha said,

Bradley looked up from his pacing, phone pressed to his ear, confusion on his face.

"You said 'Cycle', but the phrase is 'Vicious Circle'." There she stood, Tabitha Gloria Wellington, amongst dozens of boxes containing their belongings, piled up around them in a rotting wreck of a house.

"But you knew what I meant, right?" he asked. Tabitha didn't answer as she removed the brass sconces from the box and peeled back the soft wrapping around them to investigate.

It was though, he thought, *a Vicious 'Cycle'*. As he thought it, he darted a venomous glance at his wife, but she was paying no attention.

He wasn't wrong, about the cyclical nature of his phone calls, that is. He would call the estate agent, they would tell him to contact his solicitor, who would tell him to talk to the bank, who would pass him on to his insurance company who would tell him to talk to the estate agent. It was indeed a 'cycle' of phone calls and Bradley Montgomery Wellington was on his third agonising lap as he tried to figure out who was responsible for his problem. His problem being that they had just moved into their new home, to find a house that looked like it had been decorated for a horror movie. It seemed insane, yet how this had happened also seemed very simple.

Earlier that year certain 'occurrences' had made living in the hustle and bustle of the city somewhat undesirable. After complaining daily, and nightly, about how people were going about their business and growing ever more frustrated with the 'hideous' tower block that obscured the view from their fancy city town house, Tabitha had come to the conclusion that she wanted a change of pace, to live somewhere quieter, that she wanted a taste of country life. It was a fact that what Tabitha wanted she got, and so, with that, they packed up their things, and left their large, fancy, central town house and the unsightly view of Castle Heights behind them.

During this move, Bradley had made a couple of key errors, ones that most certainly would not have occurred without a demanding wife breathing down his neck. Taking to the internet, Bradley had found the perfect place; in a little town called Chittering, on a street called Gingerbread Lane. The pictures were gorgeous and with every click Tabitha grew more married to the idea. As they sat sipping a 2017 Château Belair-Monange rouge and imaging their new blissful existence in a small town with wonderful country air, one thing led to another, and before Bradley knew it he was making calls and signing contracts and they would soon be on their way to a brand new life.

However, in his infinite wisdom, combined with some country-wide occurrences, Bradley

Montgomery Wellington had decided not to view the house. He'd seen everything he needed to see on that website, what could he possibly have missed?

What would be the point in a viewing? The thought echoed through time, right to this moment, to him standing in this old, water damaged house, with its peeling wallpaper, a literal hole in the ceiling, cracked floorboards, moss growing on the bathroom surfaces and his wife, Tabitha, becoming increasingly annoyed as their ideal country living lifestyle slipped away.

Bradley had spent his time since they arrived on the phone, but it appeared that everyone involved now wanted to pass the buck. They all blamed each other for the mishap and none of them seemed to be able, or willing, to reach the seller about the house's now unfortunate state. Each one blaming the other and sending him on a wild goose chase. As he began his fifth phone call to the estate agent, he was beginning to get the feeling that he might be in quite a lot of trouble.

"Well, Mr Wellington," the estate agent said, in a rather smug tone, "the problem is that without a viewing, it's very hard to…"

"Prove that we didn't know?" Bradley butted in. "Yes, you've said all this, but what about the website pictures?"

"Disclaimers all over it," the agent explained. "People have a right to make their property look desirable in pictures, Mr Wellington."

"DESIRABLE!?" he exclaimed. "This house

looks like Tim Burton designed it."

"I don't know who that is, maybe you could…"

"Speak to the insurer, yes, you said that last time." He knew what he was going to say. "Fine, but someone is going to pay for this. This is a clear case of false advertising."

He started to angrily punch the number for the insurance company again, and it went straight to 'hold'. He was settling in for the wait when Tabitha let out an almighty shriek, he lowered the phone as his wife raced toward a box, water trickling from the ceiling and directly into it. She grabbed at it, trying to pull it out of the way. "Oh no, the Havish-Blomshire drapes!" she cried. "They'll be ruined!" Her tone reminiscent of a mother running to her injured child, she swung her face around, a rodent like sneer met Bradley's startled face. "Don't just stand there, get something to catch this water."

Bradley shifted uncomfortably and looked around for something to catch the leak with. Nothing. "I'll try the kitchen." He darted from the room. As he moved through the house, the wet floorboards felt soft under his feet, like sponge. Stepping into the equally disastrous kitchen, he glanced around the rotting lino and broken tiles. Pulling open a cupboard door, it came away in his hand. He dropped the door and looked up to be met by empty shelves. Nothing.

"Well?" Tabitha squawked. It grabbed his attention; he turned his head toward her standing with her hand on her hip in the doorway. "My drapes are getting ruined up there."

He stood and looked at her. "I can't find anything down here."

"Well then *I'll* go and find something", she snapped. She turned back across the squeaking floorboards and he heard her clumping up the stairs. He wondered how on earth she managed to sneak up on him in a house that made so much noise with every movement, almost as if she did it on purpose to catch him out.

Bradley snatched his coat from the end of the bannister and moved to the door, at least he'd get a break for a while. Bradley tore through the town in his Land Rover. As the large gas guzzling vehicle spewed dust and smoke out around him, he slowly began to take in just how picturesque Chittering was. Maybe it was helped by the transition from the rotting, mouldy, damp, hell hole of the house, but either way, this was a really beautiful corner of the country.

Reaching down, he pulled his phone from his pocket, punched in the number of the insurance broker and let it ring. It went to voicemail. That was new. The nasal women on the other end quickly gave him an answer as to why.

"Thank you for calling Hyde Bank Insurance services. We are now closed. Please call back Monday to Friday between 9am and 5pm. Or Saturday between 9am and 12pm."

He pulled his phone away from his face and looked at the time. 12.02.

Of course, he thought. *A Saturday, everyone closed early on Saturdays, a day when most people move. Makes perfect sense.* He sighed, resisted the urge to swear, and hung up.

The car came to a stop at the top of the street, the street which seemed to be full of cars, so he surmised he must be in the right place. Spotting a 'space' next to a bike rack, he drove up and reversed in, completely ignoring the no parking sign right there on the pavement.

As he opened the door and stepped out, he could hear the noise of the nearby fete. He had seen posters in the neighbours' windows that morning when they first arrived. An annual event it seemed. The noise of folk music carried in the air over old, rigged, industrial size speakers. He could see plenty of people gathered in the distance.

He wandered to the back of the Rover, to check his distance from the bike rack. It was fine. *Plenty of space*, he thought. Then he saw it. A beautiful, shiny, red bicycle.

He stood admiring it for a moment. Its long, red, slender, metal body swooping up to the curve of two luscious steel hands that wore exquisite rubber handles, adorned with the beautiful accent of a silver brake. Its rounded ball tip pointing out toward him. He walked over and ran his finger across it, stopping at the small, shining bell placed at the base of the clasp. At the front of it, it had been finished with a silver badge. The head of a wolf, welded perfectly like a spoiler on a BMW. It was a true work of art.

This thing is incredible, he thought. Becoming conscious that he was paying too much attention, he looked around to see if anyone had noticed. No one was there. So, he stood for a moment, just taking it in and then, with a smile, he wandered off on his journey.

As he approached, he could see the festivities in full swing. The village green was lined with stalls and people talking and face painting and music and village folk dancing and children running around, in the beautiful sunlight. It was intoxicating. Exactly how he imagined small village life would be.

I could really get used to this. He smiled as he wandered towards the stalls.

Moving through the tables, he was instantly struck by how varied they seemed to be. Each one had its own unique flavour, a table selling raffle tickets, one for an animal shelter, a woman selling homemade cards. He came to a stall selling overpriced fudge, but to a man used to city living, this was a bargain. He purchased a bag, a measly amount for £17, but he would have paid much more at those winter stalls at Christmas. To him this was a frugal investment and as he slipped around the various little village stalls, displays and eateries, he chomped on the sugary goodness. For the first time in a long time, he felt like, maybe, he was really enjoying himself.

After a good hour or so of wandering, manoeuvring his way around the fete tables, he stopped and watched as a kind looking old man clambered up onto the stage, and began a rousing speech, or so it sounded. Bradley never really took any of it in on any meaningful level, but it all sounded great, it all sounded just like the kind of community he would want to be involved in and the thoughts of the old rotten house and his angry wife gradually drifted from his mind. He smiled at a couple of elderly ladies as he began to feel like he fitted right in, in his new hometown.

After a beautiful display of Morris dancing, Bradley bought some more fudge and continued his walk through the maze of tables. The sun dipped behind the clouds for a moment and a chill ran up his arms and down his spine. Maybe it was time to head back, he'd been out a long while.

As he arrived back at his car, he noticed very quickly the parking ticket sitting on his windshield. He stormed toward it and plucked it off.

"What the bloody hell is this?" he shouted at no one. "So much for small town hospitality!" he continued, as he looked around to see if he had an audience. There was no one around. He opened the door, threw the ticket inside and climbed into the car. "How can they give someone a ticket for parking in a legitimate space?" he mumbled to himself, as he started the car. "I'll be straight onto the local council Monday m…" He reversed into something, it made the car jump and he heard the sound of scraping metal. He stopped and looked in his rear-view mirror, he couldn't see any cars behind him. He frowned, climbing out.

As he wandered around the back of the Land Rover, he saw the murder scene. That beautiful red bicycle, its wheels dented under the weight of his car. Its frame bent out of shape. "Oh god," he said. He was horrified, momentarily, about what he had done to such a beautiful thing. He caught himself. *Well,* he thought, *people shouldn't be leaving their nice stuff just lying around like this.*

He looked around for any witnesses, but he couldn't see anyone.

Still, he didn't want anyone pinning this on him. Not with the ticket putting him here with a time and a place.

He looked behind him. There was a wall, about five feet high, next to him. He darted around a second cautionary glance, grabbed the bike and yanked it from under the car. Some of its spokes were hanging loose as he hoisted it into the air. He dropped it behind the wall into the grass and then looked over at it.

The owner will just think it was stolen, he thought. *By the time they notice it was misplaced, it would be hard to tell what happened at all.* A masterful plan. Checking the coast was clear, Bradley climbed into his Land Rover and took off.

He had begun to make his way back, but he was a little turned around when he saw the museum. He had seen it on his way, but the path split and it looked familiar from both sides. Which way had he come? He vaguely remembered an incline, but they both felt like they were at the top of a slope. He guessed and headed down the street he was almost certain was correct.

As he drove a few metres, something caught his

eye. A shop. *A bucket*, he thought. The whole reason he had come out in the first place. He quickly pulled over.

He wandered up to it, its windows filled with various items. The stock seemed almost random, but something drew his eye - a bucket. It looked a little battered, like most other things in the window, but it was just what he needed. He was about to step inside when something else caught his eye.

A few feet away, on the corner of one of the lanes that ran behind the houses, a wheel popped out, followed by the frame of a bike, and there it was. That unmistakable red, pointing to that silver wolf.

Is that the bike, he thought, *from the fete?* It couldn't be, but he wasn't sure. *Had someone bought it?* he wondered. He started toward it. He saw the bike moving, almost recoiling as he made strides toward it. He stepped abruptly around the corner to find… Nothing. Nothing there at all.

"I could have sworn…" He wondered if he had just been seeing things.

He turned away and headed back to the car, his mind adrift, completely forgetting why he got out in the first place.

After some driving and misdirection, Bradley finally found his way back home. He had been gone a while; the sun was beginning to dim on the horizon as he stopped at the front door. He knew that he would be in trouble as he pushed the handle down and slipped inside.

The house was quiet and, without working

power, (another thing that the estate agent had failed to mention), the house was growing darker as the sun slipped down below the wall of the back garden. It was quiet as he closed the door behind him. *Maybe she went out*, he thought.

A noise came from upstairs, clumping and thudding on the floor, drawing his attention. He began to climb the stairs and as he did he could see movement in the bedroom. He approached it, opened the door and peered inside. Tabitha was there, she had one of the moving boxes open and she was stuffing clothes into her *Dolce & Gabbana* Sicily pink tote bag.

"What are you doing?" he asked.

She turned and looked at him, her stare full of anger. "Where the hell have you been?" she quizzed. "I've been here in this wreck all afternoon."

"I was… trying to find a bucket?" He realised that he was empty handed.

"It's a bit late for that, Bradley." She turned her attention back to her bag, stuffing more clothes in. "Did you sort out things with the insurance company?"

He moved his hand up to the back of his head, awkwardly scratching the back of his neck. Tabitha growled and zipped her bag up. Clutching her coat, she began to pull it on.

"Where are you going?"

"There's a guest house a few streets away. The Paradise something, I'm staying there until this whole mess is sorted." She picked up her bag and pushed past him. He tried to say something, but he couldn't think of what would stop her. There was also the fact that something else was on his mind. He finally managed to find some words.

"Tabitha." She paused. "Come on, Tabby Bear, just calm down a minute, there's no need for that. I'm sure we can sort something out."

She looked at him, her hand back on her hip.

"Look," he said, "why don't I make you a nice cup of blackcurrant and camomile tea and I'll fix up something for the night?"

She looked at him and dropped her bag on the landing.

"Fine," she said and turned, walking down the stairs.

After digging the kettle from one of the kitchen boxes, Bradley quickly brewed up a 'nice cup of blackcurrant and camomile tea' and handed it to his 'lovely' wife.

As he went out to the car, the amber streetlights were beginning to turn themselves on as the sun descended behind the horizon. He opened the boot, plucking a camping chair from the enormous boot of the Land Rover. As he closed the truck he spotted small flecks of red paint, embedded in the bumper. Pulling his sleeve down, he wiped them away as best he could and moved back inside. He stopped at the door, his hairs standing up on the back of his neck, as if someone were watching him. He peered around the quiet street, hanging under a veil of twilight, but couldn't see anyone.

Tabitha perched on the foldout chair as Bradley made for the stairs.

"Where are you going now?" she asked.

He leaned against the door. "To prepare our boudoir," his voice came out in what was supposed to a sensual tone but sounded more like an off-kilter impression of Lugosi. He turned and moved up the creaking steps.

Within a few short minutes, trawling through the boxes he could find, he had, with the help of a blow-up mattress and some of Tabitha's finest bed linen, made up a half decent place for them to sleep for the night. He stood looking proud of himself over his creation.

Glancing over his shoulder, he grabbed the curtain and was greeted by a flutter of moths as he pulled them open. Opening the window and shooing them out, he noticed the street outside. The night had crawled in now, yet the small town still held its charm. He stood hands on hips and smiled to himself. His smile slowly dropped as he saw it.

Right outside, there it was, the red bike. Perched on the other side of the pavement from their house. He looked at it, squinting through the reflections made by the shade-less lightbulb.

Is that...? He panicked inside. *Is that the same bike?* He looked at it. It looked in fine nick, not how he'd left the other one. *Maybe someone on the street had the same of kind? That must be it.*

The sudden sound of fireworks from outside

grabbed his attention and he glanced up, expecting to see an explosion of light, but to his surprise, nothing.

He turned his attention back to the bike. It was still there, looking right back at him. Bradley grabbed the curtains, and as if to block its view through the window, he drew them. He headed downstairs.

"It's all ready," he announced as Tabitha sipped on the last of her tea.

She placed the cup down and looked at him confused. She stood up as he gestured to the bedroom above. She gave him a dubious look, wandered past him and up the stairs. As she approached the bedroom door, she looked at him. He smiled and nodded as it creaked at her push.

Inside he had made a little, and not too shabby, set up. It almost looked homely; he'd picked the 'nicest' room in the house, and she looked at the little makeshift bed. Her pyjamas sat folded neatly at the foot.

"Well?" he said. "Not bad, eh?" She turned and smiled at him. "I mean, there's no reason why we shouldn't 'christen' our new abode." He wiggled his eyebrows.

"Well, Bradley," she shrugged. "You've outdone yourself." She leaned in, her lips pursed. He prepared for the kiss, but with a quick manoeuvre her soft lips touched his ear as she whispered, "But if you think you're getting any of this, you're an idiot" She leaned back and gave a quick and sarcastic, "Night, night," accompanied with the most aggressive smile he'd ever seen, as the door slammed right in his face.

He stopped for a moment, stunned. But not surprised. This wasn't the first time he'd be dismissed to the couch. Only this time, they didn't have one.

***

Bradley felt like he had only been asleep for moments when the sound of rain began to patter against the window. The thirty-year-old camping bed he'd drawn out of one the boxes wasn't in any way comfortable. He could just about handle balancing himself on the piece of cloth stretched over two pieces of metal, but the sound was becoming a bit much. What topped it off was the sudden presence of water, dripping onto his forehead. He sat up and grabbed the pull out, moving it away from the source of the drip.

He shivered, grabbing his arms. The room had become cold since he'd snoozed, and he stepped into the hallway to grab his coat. As he pulled it on over his full set of pyjamas, thunder echoed loudly across the room. Too loudly. He turned to see the front door was wide open. He walked toward it and grabbed the handle, looking out into the quiet street. The rain was really coming down now. Suddenly, lightning added itself to the mix, creating a fully-fledged storm right outside his door. He looked down at his feet, wet from the rain beginning to seep in.

On the wood across the hallway, something caught his eye. Tyre marks. In single file. His eye followed them, all the way to the foot of the stairs and then…

Tabitha lay quietly on the comfortable, blow-up bed. The top of her face covered with an eye mask, her ears adorned with fluffy muffs, she seemed blissfully unaware that there was even a storm as Bradley slipped into the bed next to her. She shifted slightly, refusing to come out of her sleep.

She groaned as his cold hand slid down her side. "Bradley, what did I tell you?" she mumbled. He continued pushing his hard body against her - she moved away from him across the bed. "I mean it," she said. "This is not the time and I'm not in the mood."

She felt his rubbery leg slide between her thighs. "I've told you Bradley, I'm too tired." She grabbed it and pushed it away, noticing how odd it felt. She reached out behind her and touched him. He felt cold, and smooth, and… metal?

Tabitha frowned. Pulling her mask away, she slid her earmuffs from her head and looked at the jagged lumpy blanket. Cautiously, she reached out, pulling the sheet away to come face to face with a shiny red bicycle.

Her screams bounced across the house, as Bradley pegged it up the stairs, following the bike tracks. "Tabitha!" he screamed as he smashed through the bedroom door. His face went white as he looked at the bed.

He saw his wife laying splayed out, her pyjamas in tatters, her head hung over the edge of the bed, looking right at him. Her sharp features now replaced with an indentation from the back wheel of a bicycle. The red bike sat on top of her, its wheel embedded in her face. Blood dripping from its rubber treads to the floor.

"Oh my god," Bradley exclaimed, the bike's handlebars twisted as if it were looking over its shoulder, right at him. "What...? What have you done to my wife?" His voice trembled.

The bike, obviously, said nothing. Then it moved, spinning its back wheel, as it burrowed deeper into Tabitha's face and sprayed the room and Bradley with face mush and blood and brain matter.

Shocked, he wiped the blood from his eyes. The bicycle crouched like a dog, ready to pounce. Bradley stepped back as the bicycle moved toward him. He stepped back again, but in the panic, his legs failed him and he fell to the floor. He hit the soft, cracked wood beneath him, but to his surprise, he kept going as it gave way to the full weight of his body. In a moment he went from feeling the scratch of broken wood against his hands and face to the dull thud of the floor as he crashed, spine first, onto the kitchen floor below. Then 'fudge'.

He could taste it, the fudge from the fete, like he'd just eaten it. The taste regurgitated in his mouth, his throat burned from the stomach acid, as it moved up his chest on the moment of impact. His mouth felt wet, but as he rubbed his hand across it, he checked. No blood. That was a good sign. He groaned as he lay there on his back for a moment, his head fast forwarding through events, from the fudge to the bike to the... *The bike!* His brain suddenly caught up with him. *The bike, it killed my wife, it's after me.*

He rolled to his side, trying to move, but his legs betrayed him. Reaching out, he grasped at the uneven kitchen floor. Then he stopped. A noise... from the hallway. Clump. Clump. Clump. The sound of rubber moving down the stairs, one at a time. Then two, for the two wheels. Clump, clump. Clump, clump. Bradley looked on in terror as the sound edged closer. He tried to get up, pushing through the extreme pain in his ribs and back.

As the bike appeared in the doorway, Bradley was nowhere to be seen. A dent was visible where he had landed, and then scuff marks dragging across the floor. The bicycle wheeled its way across the wreckage, tilting its handlebars back and forth as it scanned for the young toff. It twisted its wheels up and noticed the door missing from the cabinet on the wall.

Bradley, leaping from the bench and holding said cabinet door, brought it down hard on the metal frame. It splintered and broke as the bicycle twisted, 'looking' straight at him. Dropping the crumbling pieces of door in his hands, he looked around for something to defend himself with. He looked down at his coat and grabbed it as the bicycle moved toward him. In a swift move, he whipped it from his shoulder and over the handlebars.

It moved under the long coat, like a dog trying to shake off water from its fur. Bradley seized the moment and darted for the door. He grabbed it and pulled it hard. He was met with the noise of heavy rain and looked down for his shoes. They were sitting by the camping bed a few feet away, and he glanced back in time to see the bicycle careering into him. It knocked him hard, sending him into the air and through the open doorway.

He crashed down hard onto the cobbled road, water erupting around him. He had tried to brace himself, to avoid another abrupt knock to the skull. He sat up as quickly as he could. Lightning flashed through the sky, unveiling the shape of the bike moving in on him like a Baskerville hound. As the rain pattered down around him, running down his face, he cried out, "I'm sorry!"

The lightning flashed again, and the bicycle was up on its back wheel, as one would see a dark horse.

"What are you?" Bradley whimpered. It leapt upon him and, as he tried to force himself to his feet, the body of it became like a snake wrapping itself around him. He could feel the metal frame crushing the air from his lungs. Its wheels moved toward his face, spinning so fast he could feel the heat erupting from them as they desperately urged to pull the skin from his face. He couldn't breathe, he couldn't do anything.

Bradley reached out, grabbing the tires. They tore through the skin on the palms of his hands as he gripped tighter, eventually stopping them from moving. He screamed, summoning the last of his strength, and pulled as hard as he could. The wheels buckled and pulled away from the body, the chain flopped to the floor, and the bike's sleek, metal body flopped like a piece of rope.

He fell to the floor, wheels in hand, blood drenched and gasping for air. And in that moment, all he could do was laugh.

He was still laughing minutes later, as the light flashed across his face. Only this time it wasn't from the sky, it was the consistent light of a police car on the road in front of him. He looked up to see a very stern looking policeman standing over him.

"May I ask what you're doing out here sir?" he asked.

Bradley, a smile on his face, looked up at him. "Just out for a ride officer."

Another officer appeared from the doorway of his house and Bradley looked up at him. The officer's face was white as he shouted to his colleague. "Sir!" he called, "there's a lady in here, looks like she's had her face bashed in with a bicycle wheel! She's dead."

The officer turned back to Bradley, "You city folk, it's always the same." He shook his head. "Moving out here, causing trouble, then leave us to clean up the mess."

He wanted to explain, but all he could muster was a grimace. "I know what you mean, Officer," he said. "It's a Vicious Cycle."

The officer frowned, "I think it's 'Circle'."

Bryan vs the School Basement

Annie Knox

Lori spent her morning painstakingly assembling the hook-a-duck paddling pool, awkwardly fingering the business card hidden in her bra, and trying to decide which of her students to murder.

How she was going to kill them, she had planned. To get the *where* right she had carefully followed the instructions discovered on her doormat last week. Instructions in weird, twisted Latin which she had translated with help from Satanicbitchbabe98 on the *RiseAgainHornedBeast* chatroom. The letter had been written on a tea-stained piece of paper with, she suspected, a fountain pen dipped in red ink. The scribe merited a B+ for effort.

The basement beneath the school was a mysterious myriad of pipes and pathways. Various old doors blocked off various old rooms that no one had been in for decades. Keys for each room hung from the janitor's - pervy Pete's - belt, dangling over his crotch, brushing against his flies with every step he took.

Lori would not be going near that belt.

Instead, last night she had broken into the school.

Rumours of kids being tortured by teachers deep in the bowels of the basement loomed over the school like a cloud. As she had shone her torch down the hallways and listened to the squeaking of mice evading the light, Lori had frequently believed she could hear childlike crying, or the thudding of childlike footsteps in the distance. With each turn she had become more convinced that she would never find her way out - that the post-it notes she was leaving as a trail of breadcrumbs would get whisked away by a supernatural wind or plucked away by a ghostly hand.

The journey through the corridors, anxiously swatting spiderwebs out of her hair and wiping the ever-trickling dust from her glasses, had lasted a lifetime. Finally, she had found the deepest pit of them all - the ceiling had lowered, the walls had narrowed, and the end of the space had revealed itself to her in the form of a small wooden door, surprisingly sturdy and untainted by rot. It should have sat at the back end of the school, but judging by how long it had taken to find, she felt it was much further away - beyond the river, perhaps closer to Baker Street.

Having clumsily bashed in the lock with a hammer, she found the interior of the room pretty awful and she suffered an agonising moment of guilt over the thought that it would be the last thing a child would see. Then she had taken the guilt, crushed it away deep inside of herself, and gone about her business, occasionally peering down at her tea-bagged instructions and printed translation to make sure she had it right.

After hours of fussing about she had stopped, wiped her filthy hands on her cheap wool skirt, and peered up at the mouldy ceiling.

"I hope that's okay?" she had asked, before

realising how stupid she was being and looking down at the ground instead. "Oh, sorry."

No one had answered.

Now, it was nine-thirty in the morning, four hours after Lori had crawled into bed. She slouched over the garish paddling pool, dejectedly filling it with water from an old hosepipe that Pervy Pete had taken his sweet creepy time helping her unravel. He was lurking nearby with his broom, unashamedly leering at her.

Lori gazed into the water filling the pool. Her reflection gazed back. A reedy, weak character with bug eyes behind thick-rimmed glasses, gaunt cheeks and chapped lips. Wispy hair broke free from the plait she had tried to trap it in and curled around her oversized ears. A frumpy, hole-riddled cardigan swamped her body to mid-thigh, where swamping duties were taken over by an equally frumpy skirt.

She looked ugly.

"Lori!"

As if life couldn't get worse than planning to murder a child and wanting to drown yourself in a hook-a-duck pool.

She forced a smile onto her face that made her reflection look psychotic and turned around.

"Mrs Arkwright."

Barbara Arkwright sauntered towards Lori in a perfectly fitted business suit. Her blond hair was styled like she was about to step into a L'oreal advert instead of a day of Morris dancing. Her sharp eyes darted over Lori's appearance.

"You don't look well, my darling." She stopped

and peered into the pool, her glamorous reflection out of place next to Lori's. Lori was an alien in comparison to this perfect woman. "Can't you fill this pool up a little faster, my love? People are starting to arrive."

"The fete doesn't start until ten," Lori protested pathetically. "Pete said this is as much water as the hose can handle."

"Right." Barbara waved smartly at Pete. "Pete! Turn the hose up, will you?"

Pete snapped out of his leering to attention. "Yes, Mrs Arkwright!" He saluted, to top off Lori's internal fury. She wondered briefly if she could sacrifice him instead of a child and felt, instinctively, he wouldn't be enough.

"Maybe he didn't understand when you asked him," Barbara said helpfully. "Are you feeling alright, Lori? I can't allow you to go home today, not enough people."

"I'm just a little tired." Lori focused her gaze into the pool.

"You look awfully pale."

"I didn't sleep well."

"Your hair is a little... out of sorts."

"This is my natural hair, Mrs Arkwright. I didn't have time to blow-dry it." Largely because she had been setting up an altar underneath Barbara's beloved school, but she chose to omit that detail.

"That's a shame." Barbara dialled her megawatt smile up to a gigawatt smile. "I suppose laundry day also coincided with the village fete?"

"Sorry, Mrs Arkwright."

"We represent the school today, Lori, and we have standards."

Lori had a violent urge to snap the hose tight around Barbara's dainty neck. A scream built up in her throat, but she forced it down and nodded along. Barbara took a step closer.

"After your little...scandal, the last thing I want is for you to draw any negative attention towards the school. Understand?" The smile dialled back down to megawatt.

Lori gripped the hose until her knuckles went white.

"And you might want to be careful around the break room in future. Those biscuits are for the entire staff. Your particular brand of baggy clothing appears a little...less...baggy lately. We're role models for these children. We don't want them all gulping down packets of digestives and lounging around looking like slobs, do we?" The smile bumped up from megawatt to terawatt.

Lori bit the inside of her mouth until she could taste blood. Then she swallowed and spoke, the words coming out small and strained.

"No, we don't."

"Atta girl." Barbara held out a collection tin clasped within her perfectly manicured fingers. "Raffle ticket?"

***

Lori entered the loos, locked herself into a cubicle, sat determinedly on the toilet, and allowed herself to cry for fifteen minutes. The business card was digging into her nipple, so she pulled it out and let it sit in her hands, staring down at the tiny, life-changing piece of cardboard whilst bitter tears trickled down her cheeks.

It had been white when it had been given to her. She had shoved it into a pocket and not, initially, given it a huge amount of thought, occasionally pulling it out and frowning at the thing, wondering if the handsome, forgettable man who had given it to her could have been telling the truth about being able to save her.

It was only when, several weeks later, she had cut her wrists open one night in front of the TV (sobbing into her mid-week pint of ice cream), that she'd thought of the card again, and taken it from her coat with trembling hands. As her fingerprints had smeared sticky crimson over the white, a pattern on the card had emerged. An image intricately carved of an emotionless goat-headed man eating a baby. Her blood had soaked into the card, deepening the picture.

Several minutes later there had been a knock on the door.

He had been there. Knowledgeable, confident, otherworldly. Willing to save her, willing to help her, willing to give her a chance that no other person had been willing to give her before.

And here she was. Sobbing over his card in the loo.

***

Lori splashed water on her face and scurried back to the hook-a-duck before Barbara could clock that she had been gone.

It was a warm day. She felt flustered underneath her jumper but knew that once she got into the basement the chill would eat into her. As the sun crawled higher into the sky, families and their children started to ebb into the fete. Lori took tickets, watched people pretend to enjoy catching rubber ducks with small sticks, and occasionally handed out the odd box of chocolates. With each child that beamed up at her as they triumphantly clutched their yellow duck to their chest, she felt her heart sinking.

In the dead of night her plan had seemed simpler - faced with the reality of kidnapping a kid in the sunlight, she doubted that she could go through with it.

Someone was sure to see.

***

Two o'clock arrived. Nicolas Eden - the sort of man who would be the surprise killer in an episode of *Midsommar Murders* - came bounding through the green to read out his annual round of bullshit.

Lori squinted at the crowd around the podium. Nick beamed out at everyone, clasping his hands as if he was being presented with a delightful gift. The wrinkles in his face looked deeper every time that he climbed up in front of his microphone, his stature more hunched, his hair ever whiter and thinner. And yet year after year he was there, refusing to give up and die.

This village had a way of clinging to you, Lori thought - if you weren't lucky enough to have a university reach in and pluck you out, then you would never leave. You were doomed to wander the small, lifeless streets of the village whilst the pavement and the plants and the monotony of life slowly sucked your dreams and ambitions out of you. Every day Lori woke there she felt herself getting older. She felt the life bleeding out of her, like she was being slowly blended into a painting by an artist smearing her outline with his paintbrush.

Nick had been so entirely consumed by Sweet Little Chittering that he embodied the village; the way he moved, the way he spoke, the way he dressed and ate and probably even the way he pooped. When Lori watched him deliver his little speech every year, she hated him. Lori didn't see a man giving a speech, she saw the personification of the place she had come to think of as her own personal hell. And she saw it wearing offensively bright yellow corduroy trousers.

Nick cleared his throat and spoke into the mic.

"Hello, hello?"

The mic squealed painfully. Lori allowed herself a moment of petty joy.

"Oops, sorry, technophobe!" There was a small round of chittering as people pretended to find his old-man manner endearing. He faffed with the microphone. Lori absently felt the shape of the card in her bra, not noticing Barbara watching her seemingly rubbing and pinching at her own boob in disgust.

Something caught Lori's eye towards the tail end of the audience.

Bryan 'Badman' Broderick, her class clown. Nine years old, the youngest and most infuriating in the class. He had a habit of picking his nose and leaving the bogies hidden within his math book for her to find. His hair was permanently spiked up. When bored, he liked to throw paper planes at her butt. His whoopee cushion made frequent appearances in class, no matter how many times it was confiscated. He hated work. He loved embarrassing the girls by accusing them of farting at the top of his voice in the playground. His laugh had a way of drilling into her ears that made her wish for the sweet release of a busted ear drum. The other kids had love-hate relationships with him. His closest friends were the rag-tag boys on the school's football team. After every break they would come in sweaty, muddy, ready to disrupt any attempt at an education.

She hated him.

He was perfect.

Bryan was scowling furiously at his mother - Mrs Broderick, a sweet woman from whom it seemed unlikely such horrendous spawn could have been born. Mrs Broderick looked tired and upset as she scolded him for whatever horrible deed he had committed. Bryan stamped a foot. Mrs Broderick appeared to attempt to placate him. He stamped his foot again. She ducked down and put her finger to her lip, trying to tell him to be quiet.

The few stragglers around them were staring. Judy Ashleigh was watching with a disapproving eyebrow raised.

Bryan blew a dribbly raspberry at his mother. Even at a distance, Lori could hear that whiny voice screeching about unfairness, about Matt-can-do-what-he-wants-so-why-can't-I, about I-wish-Dad-was-here, you-hate-me, I-wish-you-weren't-my-mum. The final was delivered with a two-foot jump-stamp that seemed to crush Mrs Broderick's heart.

She put her hand over her eyes, waved at Bryan to go away, and turned to look at Nick, bravely pretending she couldn't see the people watching her. Bryan spent a moment looking enraged before charging away, little arms swinging back and forth in his righteous fury.

Nick was wrapping up - Lori knew his speech structure by heart. As he hedged his way into bigging up the raffle prizes, she slipped out from behind the paddling pool and started to sneak after Bryan whilst everyone was distracted.

Bryan charged until they rounded the final stall. Everyone clapped the end of the speech. His head jerked back to watch the villagers disperse. Lori ducked down. His eyes didn't come near her - they latched onto his mother, to whom Barbara was selling a raffle ticket. Without a backwards look, the two women headed towards the tombola stand.

The kid looked upset, eyes betrayed. No doubt

the little shit had been expecting her to come running after his highness, pleading for him to stay. As Mrs Broderick vanished from sight, Bryan's anger melted into a grumpy frown. He wandered away, kicking at the ground.

Lori hesitated, unsure. The card burnt against her fragile boob skin. She thought of the ugly room beneath the school. She thought about Bryan's whoopee cushion and how Mrs Broderick would feel when her son disappeared.

Somewhere behind her started up music that she knew was accompanying the Morris dancers, reminding her of where she was.

Lori thought of crying in the toilets, crying herself to sleep. The constant gnawing ache in her stomach and chest. The sense that she would die in the village but she wouldn't die old. The desperation to be a different person that hit her so hard at night she felt the physical urge to get out of bed, find a knife and rip off her own skin.

Her resolve hardened. She slipped off of the village green, into Hawthorne Lane. Bryan dragged his feet moodily, leaving small troughs in the dirt path. He paused by a nearby house and took a moment to fish into his nostril, produce an impressively big bogey, and apply it to the garden gate's handle.

Lori realised it was Barbara Arkwright's house and almost smiled. Bryan gave the house the middle finger, continued his amble down the road.

She tucked one hand into her tote bag, wiggled her fingers past the books and pens and the juice box and tickled at the hammer inside. Her breath quickened. If she could creep close, if she could get behind him without him noticing her…

Bryan suddenly plonked himself down on the curb with a huff. Lori tried to leap to the side, ran straight into a garden brick wall and toppled over it into the shrubbery on the other side, arm caught in her bag. She frantically wormed about in the soil, trying to get free from the homegrown lettuces.

"Miss Cooper?"

Bryan peeked over the wall, a bemused look on his face.

"Hi, Bryan!" She wiped her face, trying to hide the sudden tears.

"Why aren't you at the fete, Miss?"

"Why aren't you?" she tried to counteract.

"Why are you crying, Miss?" Of course.

"Because. I fell over. And hurt myself. But it's okay now." She floundered into a seated position. What felt like a potato dug into her butt cheek. A tomato vine stroked at her face. She shoved it away, maintaining an incredibly fake smile.

Bryan gave her a weird look.

"Did you hurt yourself on purpose again?" He blinked innocently at her. Lori blinked at him in shock.

"What do you mean?"

"Like at the start of the year. When you went to hospital. Mrs Arkwright was our teacher, and she said that you fell down the stairs, but my brother's *girlfriend's* friend was at the hospital, cause Mum says she took drugs and I'm not allowed to take drugs, and she saw you there and you had hurt yourself. She said you were sad."

He squinted at her expectantly. Lori's mouth opened and closed a few times. Bryan waited, then got bored of waiting.

"You shouldn't hurt yourself," he told her, like he was explaining two plus two to an idiot.

"It's not that straightforward." Lori shook her head. "You wouldn't understand."

He wrinkled his nose. "*I* think it is." He folded his arms stubbornly. "It *is* straightforward. It *is.*"

"Okay, Bryan." Lori was exhausted from talking to him already. "I get it now."

"So you won't hurt yourself again?"

"No."

"Good."

Bryan picked up a stick from the floor and swatted the air with it, engaging in a fencing match with an invisible enemy. Lori watched him from behind the wall, stumped as to how to move onto the next part of the plan.

"I don't want to go back to the stupid fair," Bryan announced to no-one. "Mum was mad at me. Just because I didn't want to listen to stupid Nick's stupid speech. I didn't even want to come in the first place, but she made me come and now she's mad at me."

"Nick's speech is stupid, isn't it?" Lori found herself agreeing. Bryan looked up at her in surprise. His face broke into a wide grin. Lori found herself smiling back.

"Do you want to see something cool?" She got

up, tugged her jumper into place. "I have a secret place with cool stuff in it. I can show you."

Bryan looked dubious.

"It won't take long." She tried to sound friendly. "It's at school. You'll be back at the fair before your mum realises you're gone."

A dark cloud crossed his face. "She told me to go away. She doesn't even care."

"Even better!" Lori beamed. "You won't get in trouble at all."

"I won't miss the raffle?"

"Why do you care about the raffle?"

He looked shifty. "'Cause I do."

"You won't miss it. This will take ten minutes. You'll like it, I promise."

Lori racked her brain for a way to convince him.

"Don't your friends call you Badman?" she teased. "You don't seem very Badman."

"I *am*!" Bryan was indignant. "I *am* Badman!"

"Imagine how much more Badman you'll be after you've been in the school basement. None of the other kids would be brave enough."

"It's in the basement?" He looked stunned. "Like, the *basement*?"

"Yep."

"I double-dared Danny to go down there once and he didn't 'cause he was scared, so we made him steal Mrs Arkwright's computer mouse."

"That was you?" Lori laughed for real, momentarily forgetting. "She was so angry."

Bryan mulled over his decision. "Danny wouldn't go in the basement. And Danny's brother is in the army."

"Imagine if you get to tell everyone you went in there. You would be a legend."

Lori watched him anxiously. He looked at the school across the field, glanced back in the direction of the fete.

His face set. The allure of infamy was too much to resist.

Bryan 'Badman' Broderick nodded and followed the woman planning to kill him towards the school.

***

As they crossed the field Bryan talked her ear off about a movie he had watched.

"And then the guy's head exploded, like *exploded*, and there was blood everywhere, and then, and then -"

Lori tuned him out, making sure no one was around. The sun was hot. She was sweating. The odd echo of music or laughter drifted across from the fete.

"...and then the other guy shot the *other* guy, but only in the arm, and then -"

Lori rolled her eyes to the sky.

"- got shot in the leg, but his ear fell off -"

"Aren't you nine?" Lori interjected, desperate for the synopsis to end. "Why are you watching this movie? Didn't your mum tell you off?"

"Mum doesn't know." Panic entered his voice. "So you can't tell!"

"I won't."

"Matthew let me watch it. He told Mum we were gonna revise but then we watched it with his headphones. He has his own laptop. He's really cool."

"Matthew is your brother?"

"Uh-huh. He's the best. But he's leaving to go to university, and Mum's sad and she takes it out on me all the time 'cause Matthew is way better than me at stuff, and she wants me to be more like him. He's really clever."

Lori glanced at Bryan, who was glaring at the ground, kicking his feet in and out of the muddy areas. He looked resigned, not upset. Like how 'you shouldn't hurt yourself' was a steadfast truth, him not being as good as his brother was also a fact.

Lori was so distracted that she failed to notice the figure following them.

"Why do you think you aren't clever?"

"'Cause! You shout at me all the time. *All* the teachers shout at me all the time. *Everyone* calls me stupid. Whenever I have to answer in class everyone laughs."

Lori led Bryan through the back gate onto the painted football / netball / basketball / every-ball-game-ever pitch. They crossed, their feet making slapping sounds against the hot tarmac, and moved into the playground.

The shadowy figure hugged the treeline and hopped over the side gate, incredibly graceful, very much out of sight.

"Is that why you're always so annoying?" Lori dug around in her bag as they walked through the empty playground. It was more like a graveyard than a school. Bryan felt it too, scampering to keep up.

She touched the head of the hammer, then decided it was easier to let Bryan wander to his death, rather than having to lug his body through the basement. She found the crowbar she had used to jimmy the door open the night before. Bryan watched, amazed as she pried it into the same dent, and - after a struggle - got the door open.

Lori found Bryan gazing up at her in newfound awe, his gap tooth showing.

"Woah! We're really breaking in!"

"Remember, it's a secret." She winked, half-enjoying how deliriously happy he looked.

"Cooooooool." He peered inside. "It's dark."

"Don't turn the lights on. We don't want anyone to come and get us before I can show you the basement."

Bryan nodded solemnly, her adult-reasoning very sensible to him. He trotted obediently after her through the Year 3 classroom.

Lori led him to the school entrance, where a grand grey-stone staircase ruined by a hideous purple-blue carpet led to the upper floors. Sat behind this staircase, tucked out of view, was the door to the basement.

Bryan stared at it in trepidation.

This door was the stuff of legends; painted a deceptively cheerful blue. He had heard that once a teacher had taken a kid down there and eaten his eyeballs for not listening. He had heard that there was a monster - like the minotaur - down there, waiting for someone to wander in by mistake. He had heard that once a girl called Betsy had gone down there on a dare, but she had never ever come back.

He looked up at Miss Cooper, who gave him a reassuring smile. She didn't seem scared, and she was a girl. So it must be fine, he reasoned. Matthew told him girls were scared of everything, so clearly there was nothing bad down there.

"Ready?" she asked him.

Somewhere in the school behind them, a door suddenly slammed shut. They flinched.

Now Miss Cooper looked scared.

"Maybe someone followed us," Bryan whispered, managing to be louder than normal. "We should go in before they come."

She didn't speak, eyes trained in the direction of the slam. Bryan pulled open the door decisively. He wanted to see the cool secret thing, and he wanted to go back to the fete and tell everyone that he had gone into the basement. Miss Cooper was right; he would be a legend. He would be the original *Badman*. Matthew was clever, but Bryan was the *cool* one, and nothing was cooler than doing someone everyone else is scared to do.

"Come on, Miss!" he urged. From the darkness of the first few steps, she looked less like a teacher. More like the lady he remembered coming back to school after a month in hospital, somebody too broken for him to throw spitballs at anymore. For a second, he wondered if he was making a mistake.

Then he thought that maybe when she showed him the cool thing, she would cheer up.

"Come on, Miss," he encouraged again, holding out his hand. After a second, Miss Cooper took it, stepped down into the basement, and closed the door.

***

They stood in blindness. Bryan could feel Lori's clammy hand shaking. A piercing white beam blinkered into life. Miss Cooper waved a torch around, pointed it down the steps, and led him downwards.

Something in the atmosphere made Bryan keep quiet. Once they hit the bottom of the stairs they passed through room after room of huge gulping pipes and linoleum floors. He wondered where they were in relation to the school above them - maybe underneath the assembly hall?

Miss Cooper silently opened the next door. Bryan's shoulders crept towards his ears nervously. The ground here was earth, and the walls were dirt. There were no more pipes or wires. It didn't feel like school anymore. It felt like someplace where he wasn't supposed to be. Someplace that wasn't supposed to exist.

Something in his gut told him that going down there would be what his mum would call '*a very bad idea,*' like when he had jumped off the garage roof. If she were here now, she would be telling him that this was clearly a '*very bad idea*', and be taking him back up the stairs, to the sun and the Morris dancers.

Miss Cooper turned back to look at him. She looked ill. Her pale skin was deathly white, the bags under her eyes deep and dark. Skeletal.

"Come on, Badman," she grinned. Her teeth glittered in her skull. "We're almost there."

"You promise? You said we would be ten minutes."

"I promise." She gestured for him to follow. He decided that he had come so far, it wasn't worth going back without seeing the cool thing. He stepped into the tunnel.

There were post-it notes dotted along the wall, every few metres.

"Are those yours?"

"Yes. It's so I don't forget the way."

They took a few more steps, silent.

"Miss?"

"Yes?"

"Why were you so sad?"

She faltered. "Why do you ask?"

"'Cause."

He listened to his footsteps echoing.

"Well…I…you won't understand, Bryan. You're a kid."

"I'm not dumb." He frowned at his feet, which he could just about see on the ground. "I'm stupid a lot, but I'm not *dumb*. Just 'cause I'm a *kid*, doesn't mean I don't get stuff. Just 'cause I'm not good at math doesn't mean I don't get *anything*. I'm not bad at stupid maths, but I could only do it when my dad would explain it. He said that I'm *really* clever, but sometimes people are clever in different ways, and teachers don't know how to teach different people."

"Your dad sounds like he was really nice." Miss sounded upset. He wondered if she was sad 'cause she knew his dad had died. When he had returned to school after it had happened, everyone had treated him weird. No matter how badly he behaved, no one wanted to tell him off.

"So, why were you so sad, Miss?"

She stopped. Bryan ran into her legs. "Are we there?"

Up ahead stood a thick wooden door with a mangled handle hanging loose by a screw.

"Maybe we should go back to the fete." Miss Cooper looked like she wanted to be sick. "Maybe we should go back, right now."

"What!?" Bryan folded his arms. "No *way*! I wanna see the thing!"

"We've been a long time. Much longer than I meant us to be. We need to go back right now."

"But... but..." He couldn't believe it! "But... it's right there!"

"I'm sorry. I'm sorry, Bryan. I'm sorry that I brought you here. We have to leave, okay?"

"But..." His protest died a swift death. Her fingers wrapped around his forearm, he was jerked away from the door - and then jerked back as Miss Cooper gasped.

Blocking their way out was a man, standing several metres back down the corridor, watching them.

Bryan's insides turned to mush. Without meaning to, he clutched a fistful of Miss Cooper's skirt. The figure stood utterly still in the dark, so still that they could have been a picture.

Miss Cooper's eyes were wet. Bryan started to cry in response. He knew something really bad was happening and wished more than he had ever wished for anything before that his brother or his mum or even his dad back from the dead were there with him.

"Get in the room," she whispered. "Quick, quick, get in now."

They hustled backwards to the door, Miss Cooper fumbling in her panic to get it open, Bryan's fist tight in the fold of her skirt. As Miss Cooper hauled the door shut behind them, Bryan was unable to tear his terrified eyes away, which is why he was the one to see that the figure started to walk towards them.

Bryan screamed. Miss Cooper shoved the door closed. They backed away into the room, Bryan now with both arms fully wrapped around her legs. "Who is that?" he squeaked in terror. "*Who is that?!*"

"Oh my God." Miss Cooper's shoulders heaved with the force of a sob. "Oh, my God. What have I done?" She sank down to her haunches, eyes red and wild.

BAM. Someone knocked, hard, on the door.

BAM. Bryan screamed.

BAM. Miss Cooper sobbed.

Quiet…

"W-W-Why are they kn-knocking?" Bryan whispered into her ear. "The d-door is broken."

"I don't know, I don't know." She buried her face into her hands. "This is my fault, I'm sorry Bryan."

"What did you do?" He tried his best to be brave, but he was too scared. His face screwed up and his voice wobbled. "What did you do, Miss?!"

She shook her head miserably, then suddenly scrabbled at her chest. Bryan watched in confusion. Lori reached into her bra, yelped in pain as she dug the card out, held it up.

Bryan saw that it was red, then burning orange. Smoke started to come off it. She threw it away as it started to sprout flames. Fire exploded into life, ripping along the floor until the two were encased in a circle of heat.

"What's happening?!" Bryan stared around at the room revealed to him. Someone had painted patterns along the walls and floor in different colours, bizarre patterns he couldn't understand.

"I don't want to do this!" Miss Cooper screamed. "I changed my mind! I DON'T WANT TO DO IT! LEAVE US ALONE!"

There was a great rumbling from the earth. Bryan plopped onto his butt as the ground jumped and dropped beneath him. Miss Cooper got onto her knees and tore off her cardigan, swatting uselessly at the fire. With her bare arms on show, Bryan saw the moment that both of her wrists violently tore themselves open, blood gushing down her arms and dripping to the ground.

"Oh my God...." Miss Cooper moaned.

"There's no need for that kind of language."

The door swung open. On the other side was the silhouette from the corridor; as he stepped into the light of the fire he was revealed to be an unremarkable-looking man. He smiled at the sweaty, panting, petrified people in front of him. His eyes were dead and emotionless. "Hello again, Lori. Hello, young man."

"You can't do this," Miss Cooper was anguished. "You fixed them," she held her bloody arms up to him.

"Calm down." His eyes locked onto Bryan, who felt the urge to wet himself, and valiantly held it in. "You won't bleed out for hours. Your attempt was a little weak handed, if I may say so."

He grinned, revealing a row of neat, identical, very white teeth. Despite the instinct to bury his face in his arms and pretend he was very far away, Bryan forced himself not to break eye contact. Matthew had taught him that if anyone was being mean to him, breaking eye contact first gave them control. *'Stay strong, little man,'* he had said, ruffling Bryan's hair. *'And if that kid tries to take your kitkat again, tell him I'll beat him up.'*

"I don't want to do this anymore." Miss Cooper tried to get the man's attention. "Let us go."

"I can't do that." He spoke to her but kept locked into Bryan. "You made a deal with us, Lori."

"Well..." her voice trembled. She looked at Bryan, and saw how he was shaking, trying so hard not to blink that he was looking a bit cross-eyed.

"Well, I'm backing out." Stronger. "You said I won't die for hours. You've already taken back the blood. We can leave."

"You're forgetting about one thing," he grinned. The skin on his face stretched far more than any human's should do, the corners of his lips meeting the corners of his eyes. "Interest."

Lori screamed as the gashes on her wrists tore open all the way to the crooks of her elbows, tendons and arteries stretching to the limit and ripping, blood bursting free. She shook her arms, and crimson drops sprinkled in the flickering fire.

"Miss!?" Bryan tried to look at Miss Cooper out of the corner of his eyes, but the vision stretch made his eyeballs want to fall out. "MISS!?"

"I don't want to die," Lori cried, defeated. "I made a mistake."

The demon's eyes widened. His lips stretched to his hairline. He was salivating. "We all make mistakes," he told them, never once blinking.

The ground started to truly shake. An ancient echo of a roar ground against their eardrums. Dirt exploded over Bryan from all sides. He tried to keep his eyes on the demon, but the wall to his left burst and clumps of soil hit his face as he ducked. He slammed into the floor as it rose to meet him. His chin thunked into his face, blood spurted from his mouth as his teeth bit into his tongue. Everything started to fall inwards. He felt himself tilting headfirst into the wide, gaping funnel of filth taking shape between himself and Miss Cooper.

Lori - flat on her stomach where she had fallen -

stared at her arms, torn so deeply that the skin was flayed out on either side of the bones of her wrists. Blood wept from the wounds into the ground around her.

A terrible hot air billowed from the earth, sending up clumps of damp soot as something older than anything snorted in the smell of her blood. Lori caught sight of Bryan across the room, staring into the abyss beginning to show itself to them. With a great roar, the room splintered further apart. Bryan wet himself.

Lori's organs trembled in her body.

Something was climbing up from the depths of the planet for her.

"What do we do?!" Bryan screamed. "MISS! WHAT DO WE DO?!"

"It's okay." She tried to smile at him. "It's coming for me."

Both of them slid helplessly towards the centre of the room as the crumbling basement became a whirlpool of mud.

Lori shouted at the demon, whose terrifying grin hadn't altered in the slightest: "Bryan lives! I changed my mind, you can have me!"

Slowly, his body shifted to Lori.

"We won't break our deal," he told her, voice somehow carrying over the sound of the world breaking apart. "He won't be taken, so long as you give yourself. But as to whether he lives… Do you think he will be able to survive the impact of the Great One rising to collect your debt? This place will collapse. He will be crushed."

"Give him something else!" Bryan scrambled backwards, crawling desperately, but the ground gave way beneath his palms and knees. "Give him something better!" He yelled again, one hand suddenly not having anything firm to land on. He sank to his shoulder into the dirt. The earth yanked him in towards the centre of the room. He screamed and panicked and thrashed, and then his other arm was sucked in, and one leg got tugged under, and he wiggled and struggled like an animal in a cage, but he was just going deeper. "Please!" He begged, losing hope. "Please! Please please please please ple-"

And then his mouth was full of dirt. He gagged as it went down his throat, and his nostrils filled, and his eyes, and he saw Miss Cooper, arms raw and skinless, watching him vanish and looking like she was waiting to die.

And then he was completely in the earth, his small body being crushed on all sides, and he couldn't breathe because mud was rushing to fill every cavity it could find, and he knew he was going to die and it wasn't fair, and all he could think about was Matthew patting his head and promising that one day he would take him to see that cool place in America with the faces on the mountains, and his mum's face when he had upset her at the fete, and how she was going to be so upset when he didn't come back and he felt so guilty that it was eating his stomach up, and he could feel the heartbeat of the monster coming to eat Miss Cooper vibrating in the Earth around him, from miles and miles and miles below...

Bryan 'Badman' Broderick tried a few final times to kick free. The last bits of air in his lungs ran out. His body screamed for him to escape, and he knew that he couldn't. He hoped, in the back of his mind, that Miss Cooper was okay.

***

Bryan 'Badman' Broderick coughed himself awake.

A figure leant over him, impossible to see in the darkness. He hacked and felt lumps of grit coming out of his mouth. When he sniffed he felt grit going up his nose. Grit scratched his sore puffy eyes as he blinked.

"Bryan?" a voice whispered urgently. "Bryan? Are you awake?"

He tried to say yes and erupted into coughing.

"We have to go." A pair of sticky hands gripped him around the shoulders and hauled him to his feet. Unsteady, he nearly fell, and grabbed the first thing he could, which turned out to be fabric.

"Mz cupph?" He hacked up what felt like his stomach. "Miss?"

"Come on." She was faceless and figureless above him. "This place is falling apart. Come on, quickly."

Bryan, not quite with it, pressed his face into what he was pretty sure was her skirt and tightened his grip. "M'kay," he told her.

Lori felt her way to the door and struggled to get

it open against the piles of muck around it. Neither spared the time to look back into the room, but if they had, all they would see would be rubble.

The corridor was pitch black. Lori blindly felt her way along, tracing the wall to the right with her hands, feeling her fingertips brushing the edges of the post-it notes from time to time. Her bag hung over her shoulder, but her phone inside was dead, her torch lost.

With Bryan trying to keep up, struggling to lift his feet high enough off the floor to walk, they made their way back through the labyrinth of tunnels. Neither cried, or spoke, or panicked. They just kept going, steady and in a state of shock, one step at a time. Further and further away from the secret room in the bowels of the basement.

After what felt like a lifetime, but was really maybe half an hour, Lori squinted and saw that there was light coming from the distance.

"I think we're nearly there," she whispered. The quietness of the tunnels wasn't scary - they were alone now, she knew that. Bryan mumbled something inaudible into the wool under his face. She continued to lead him back towards the light, a shepherd with her sheep.

They emerged into the cleanliness of the back end of the school basement, pale and covered in a mixture of mud and blood. Bryan peeled himself back from Lori, blinking hard, eyes watering to be exposed to brightness after so much darkness.

"Miss?" His voice was hoarse. "What happened to your arms?"

Underneath thick layers of muck and dried brown-copper blood, the skin of Lori's arms was marred only by thin, purple-white scars.

"What did you give him?" Bryan rubbed his eye and stared up at his teacher. She looked back at him and he didn't feel like he was talking to a teacher at all. There was a long beat where he knew that she was trying to decide if she should tell him.

"Come on," she said instead, decision made. "Let's get out of here."

Bryan, exhausted, accepted the omittance. He dutifully plodded after Miss Cooper, following her through Pervy Pete's domain and up the narrow stairs out of the basement. They emerged into the school reception, babies being born, taking their first steps into the world, breathing air for the first time.

Outside the sky was darkening. They gathered together and peered out into the playground, unsure and anxious about going back to life.

"I think we missed the raffle," Bryan observed.

"Sorry." Miss Cooper gazed at the sunset. "Why did you want to see it so badly?"

"I put Matthew's rat in there to scare Mrs Arkwright."

Lori started to laugh. Bryan let her go at it for a few moments before it became contagious. Then both of them were laughing like idiots, like nothing was wrong in the world.

"Shall we go?" Lori reached for the door handle.

"Wait!" Bryan stopped her. "I don't want my mum to find out."

"I'm not keen on her finding out either, no."

"So we won't tell anyone, right? It's a secret."

"Okay." Lori nodded, her glasses - one lens now cracked - bouncing on her nose. "It's a secret."

"Fine."

She waited for him to move.

"Did you really want me to get eaten?" Bryan asked with a straightforward, non-judgemental childish candidness, which made Lori, instead of giving him some blanket lie of a response, really think about what to say.

After a beat, she shook her head. "No. I just wanted to stop wanting to die. I didn't even really want to die. I just wanted to stop living. It doesn't make sense, does it? It sounds stupid. I thought I wanted to die. But actually, I wanted to have been born someone else. And if I gave him a child, they could make me better with the child's potentiality. I didn't want you to die, I just wanted to live, and I went manic trying to make it happen."

Bryan tried to process all of this. There were quite a lot of contradictory statements for his nine-year-old brain to muddle through. Eventually he thought he got it, or at least the gist of it.

"Once we go outside, nothing happened," Lori told him. "If you want to tell your friends you went into the basement, then you can tell them, but you can't tell them anything else. Okay?"

"Okay," Bryan looked at her sadly. "After this you're going to yell at me in class again, aren't you? We won't be friends or anything."

"I won't yell anymore," she promised. "In fact, I

don't think I will be a teacher for very much longer." She smiled suddenly, for real. "You *are* a Badman, Bryan. You're brave. Much braver than me. You just faced up against the scariest thing in the whole world. You're the *real* Badman. Bryan Badman Broderick. Even if we aren't friends, that's what I think of you."

Bryan pushed his shoulders back and swallowed down the sudden lump of emotion lodged in his throat. He nodded decisively.

"I'm going home to shower before I find Mum." He spoke with righteous authority, emboldened by his validation. "I need to wash where I peed myself."

And then he was swinging open the door, and striding out into the playground, determinedly not looking back, trying to ignore the fact that he felt very old for his age, and very sad to be leaving Miss Cooper on her own, and very sad that he would never really be able to talk to her about what had happened again. When people survive something intense and terrible together, no matter how much they dislike each other, they form a strange connection based on their shared trauma. Bryan felt both more strongly bound to a human, and more alone, than he had felt his whole nine years of life.

Lori watched the child she had planned to murder in the school basement stride away and she felt in her heart that she had made the right choice.

She knew that she had made the right choice all the way through showering off the crap and blood and terror, scalding hot water failing to warm her bones. She felt that she had made the right choice as she pulled on clean clothes, covering the scars on her arms.

When she arrived at the fete, and Barbara raced gleefully across the grounds to rip her a new one for abandoning the sacred hook-a-duck stall, Lori still knew that she had made the right choice and resigned on the spot.

She sipped on a cup of tea and thought of travelling, of buses, flights, countries, knowing that she would never be able to run away from what she had done, but willing to give it a go.

As the weak fireworks sputtered up towards the sky from the schoolyard, she spotted a clean Bryan seeking out his mother. Lori watched how he held her hand and tried to be brave. She cried a little watching Mrs Broderick breaking a chocolate bar in half and sharing it with her son.

She knew she had made the right choice, even as she put her hand over her stomach, aware of the new life inside of her. Feeling the coldness bleeding into her womb. Unable to forget the sensation of its formation, her entire body bathed in evil, plunged into ice as the demon had taken her hand and shaken it with his own, sealing the unbreakable deal in exchange for both her and Bryan's lives.

Lori felt her stomach, and watched the fireworks break the night, and listened to Bryan telling his mother how much he loved her.

At least she was finally getting herself out of Sweet Little Fucking Chittering.

History Comes to Life at the Museum

Teige Reid

His slippered feet made soft shushing sounds as he shuffled along the carpeted length of the darkened front hall of the Museum of Sweet Little Chittering. Though he would never see eighty again (not in this life, anyway), Albert Sutton had no fear of stumbling in the dark. Lights, or no lights, he could walk through this museum with certainty, navigating the irregular narrow corridors with a confidence born of decades of familiarity with the space. The shape and sense of each room, the character of every nook and cranny, were a part of him. There was not so much as a lifted corner of carpeting in this small building that he did not know.

He had walked the halls of this house for years before it had become a museum; he had watched over this place and its secret long before the first posts of the first crude building to stand here had been driven into the ground. He had kept the altar safe.

Sweet Little Chittering had been his charge and his prison for a cruelty of years.

He paused, wondering if that was indeed what a vast number of years was called. *If it wasn't*, he thought, *it should be*.

'It gives "murder of crows" a run for its money," he said aloud. "I should write that down: a cruelty of years, yes, I like it."

He smiled quietly to himself as he continued along the passage. It was some relief to him that he could manage a smile given the stakes he was facing tonight.

One hundred years had come and gone so quickly, again.

Albert heard the fireworks begin, shattering the silence like nearby gunfire. They signalled the close of the village fête and reminded him of how little time he had left. He could not see a clock, but he knew that the fireworks had started right on the button at 9:00 pm. Nick Eden was not the kind of man who would tolerate even the slightest deviation from the schedule. Albert smiled again as he recalled the Morris Dancer Parade that had passed by the museum, barely an hour ago. He had watched them from the small window of his attic office. Malcolm, the squire, had clearly been warned not to dally. The pace he had set for his dancers, as he led them along High Street, had been tragically comical. It had taken all the strength the poor man had to keep from breaking into a full run.

Nick wasn't even on the organizing committee. But, as history likes to remind us, the true movers and shakers of events often remain in the shadows, pulling the strings that control others. The man was a pain, and Albert personally found him exhausting, yet there was no doubt Nick was a tireless advocate for Sweet Little Chittering. Their recent prosperity was due solely to Nick's efforts to raise the profile of this little corner of God's green earth. His agenda was clearly to fill his Paradise Inn with visitors, and by extension his own pockets with cash, but to his credit the man did understand that his own success was more certain if the whole village was thriving. Over the last ten years or so, he had transformed the place. Nick may have benefited most, but the whole village had profited, and they all knew it. Which is why he had come out on top over that spat about the age of the town.

There was no doubt that people had lived in and around the area for far longer than the seven hundred and fifty years that Nick Eden insisted upon, the henge was proof of that, as was Albert himself. But there was evidence, of a sort, to support Nick's argument that the name *Sweet Little Chittering*, and therefore the village "proper" had first been used that many years ago, give, or take. Nick had become obsessed with the number, likely as a promotional contrivance that he thought would help draw outsiders to the village fête. Julian Thomas, for reasons that Albert couldn't fully understand, had staked his reputation, not to mention his council seat, on fighting the idea. Over the last year or so, as planning for the fête had ramped up, the argument had become bitter and divisive, and Julian had eventually lost out. He had become a bit of a local pariah as a result.

Julian had come to Albert many times, seeking his support, and it had pained Albert to turn him away. He considered the young man a friend; his only friend, truth be told. Albert had struggled with the problem and had likely handled it poorly. But in his defence, he had been preoccupied. A petty argument about a few hundred years – either way—was of little consequence in the grand scheme of things.

Albert had eternity to worry about.

He had told Julian to let Nick have his celebrations. That had been the last time Julian had spoken with him. Their estrangement hurt Albert, but he knew only too well that time dulled all wounds. In a few decades, Julian would be nothing more than a fond memory.

As he neared the front door, Albert reached out for the light switch on the wall to his right. He pulled his hand back, slowly drawing his fingers into a tight fist to still the telltale tremor.

Tonight, the lights would stay off.

Satisfied that the door was unlocked, Albert turned and shuffled back along the dark hallway. Unlocking the door was mere courtesy, but Albert felt that observing such niceties was important and set the correct tone.

This was a small museum, even by the standards by which such museums might be measured, but the walls and five modest display rooms – three down two up – faithfully mapped the town's history. Just how faithfully, Albert knew only too well.

He took his time as he walked by the paintings and photos of prize-winning cows, pigs, and chickens, and the portraits of local human notables which lined the main hall.

He passed the stairs and gently touched the glass frame that held the battle-charred green tunic worn at Waterloo by local man Oliver Hughes, of Hell

Corner. Hughes' grave was one of the "points of local pride and historical significance" that Nick loved to promote. Albert wondered if Nick would have been so enthusiastic had he known that Hughes was a brutal and unpleasant figure with a fondness for drinking, brawling, and urinating on the church steps, or as Hughes had called it, performing *baptpissms*.

Hughes had always had a temper, but when he had returned from the war he had been changed. Till the day he died, he would not go near a horse – a troublesome phobia for that era. With the benefit of time, and the enlightened understanding of mental illness that had come with it, Albert had no doubts that the man had suffered from PTSD.

Albert passed the four small glass cases that displayed the museum's collection of locally discovered Viking combs, tools, and jewelry. Each item on display was a piece to the puzzle that was Sweet Little Chittering, and very nearly every one of them had once belonged to him.

With a heavy heart he recalled the men and women he had known then, and since, and before. He had tried not becoming attached, living as a recluse – an eccentric loner – but it was impossible. They had many failings, but human beings were creatures possessed of an undeniable character and he found them endlessly enthralling. Generation after generation they never ceased to amaze and amuse and delight him. For all the pain and sadness that came from it, he never regretted getting to know them.

He paused under the oil painting of the Chittering, the henge that sat just outside of town and known officially as the Hartbridge Henge. The stone circle was considered the property of that neighbouring village, but Sweet Little Chittering had always been associated with it, in more than merely name. In the deep dark of this windowless hall, he could not see the painting but, as with everything in this place, he knew every facet of it intimately. It had been painted in 1623, by a remarkable man with an unremarkable name: John Smith. John had been a dynamic soul, curious and engaging and he had been a good friend.

Of all the depictions of that terrible place, many of which could be found within his collection, this painting was Albert's favourite. It had an almost photographic precision and clarity so unlike the somewhat ambiguous, dreamy quality typical of oil paintings. Even though it was dark, he closed his eyes to view the painting in his memory. He marvelled at the tone and the textures, and the clouds and trees, frozen in place and yet rendered with such perfect vitality that they seemed to move in an unfelt breeze. The painting was stunning, and many a visitor had commented that it was like looking through a window into the past. But it was not the painting's perfection that he loved so much; it was that Smith had painted a small group of people standing at the centre of the stone circle.

"Why will you not walk with us to the henge?"
"I have enough to occupy me here, John."
"It is but a short walk, you damned fool; I am

not asking you to follow me to the Americas!"

"Perhaps another time, I have much to do today."

"Damn your blood. Obstinate fool that you are. We will see you at the henge if I need to paint you there myself!"

Albert opened his eyes and reached into the darkness to touch the canvas. Even in the light, it was not possible to make out the faces of the group, but he had known them. John, his wife Elizabeth, her sister Ann, and himself. John and Elizabeth had made no secret that they had hoped he would marry Ann, and he might have been tempted had his heart not been spoken for.

This painting was as close as he could come to the henge, though it was barely three kilometres from where he stood. The people of Hartbridge held legal proprietorship, but it was Albert Sutton who held the deed to the obligation that came with it; a responsibility bought and paid for with the lives of his children and his own soul. A price that had cost him his humanity.

The henge had stood for centuries; he had known it when it was known as the *Hill of Whispers*. No one, not even he, knew who had erected the large stones that sat at the top of the hill, as far as he knew they had always been there. Over the years, it had been used as a place of worship, a site for sacrifices, secret meetings, and murder and was now frequented mostly by teenagers, who met there to drink and fuck.

Albert noticed that the fireworks had stopped.

Time was short, and he had much to prepare before the storm hit. Though he knew how this night would end, the ordeal always frightened and saddened him; he would miss being Albert Sutton, just as he had missed all the lives he had led before. But for now, it was time for him to focus upon his first life, and ready himself for the consequences it had wrought.

"Nullam requiem malis," he sighed to the darkness, and continued down the hall, walking past the items that chronicled the history of this cursed village and the lives he had led.

***

Fuelled by a potent mix of humiliation and alcohol, Julian Thomas strode along the strangely empty High Street with the erect certainty of a barrister walking home to get lunch from his mother.

He had been ridiculed, insulted, discredited, and reminded, over and over, that he was not a native son of Sweet Little Chittering. Through it all, he had refused to submit and remained unbroken by the ingrates and dullards that called this place home. He knew that he was right, just as he knew that Nicholas Eden, that blistering boil of a human being, knew it as well. Sarah, his wife, had begged him to just drop the fight, but she was more concerned for Julian and the strain this had put on his mental health than she was bothered by what had been done to the truth.

Sarah knew him better than anyone and

understood the demons that drove him, and had nearly succeeded in convincing him to abandon his anger. Nick Eden's smug attitude no longer bothered him, but there was one thing that Julian Thomas could not stomach, one thing that he could not overcome: Albert Sutton's betrayal.

The two had a relationship that went back more than twenty-five years. He had always thought of the man as something more than a mentor, more than just a friend. Julian would not go so far as to suggest that Albert had been like a father to him, or even an older brother – both of whom Julian had lost to a traffic accident only a few months before he had met Albert, but the man was as close as Julian could claim. Albert had been there when Julian's mother had died and he had been there when Julian had brought Sarah back to Sweet Little Chittering to get married after college; he may not have been family, but Julian loved the man.

And he had believed the feeling mutual.

That Albert had refused to support him in his argument with Eden had shaken Julian. There are precious few things in life that can be counted on, he knew this as well as anyone, but Julian had always thought that he could rely on Albert.

Julian fought back tears; he felt like such a fool. He had never really felt at home in this town, the place was odd, and the people more so, he had always felt as though there was something wrong here, and Sarah felt it too. She had summed up the strange, country quirkiness that ruled the place after spending less than a week here:

"This village's motto should be: Sweet Little Chittering, home of the scared," Sarah laughed.

"What, why?"

"Everyone acts like they are haunted or something; always looking over their shoulder."

From the moment Julian had met him, Albert had made this place bearable; he had made it feel like a home. Albert was why Julian and Sarah had decided to stay in this godforsaken place.

As he neared the museum, Julian tried to channel his emotions and keep them focused on his anger and on Albert's betrayal, but instead he found himself on the verge of crying. Tear-filled eyes would not serve to express the proper state of things; he wanted Albert to encounter the full measure of the outrage he had been living with; he wanted the man to understand the depth of his treachery. But angry though he was, Julian was having a hard time keeping the sadness at bay. And being drunk wasn't helping.

Julian wasn't much of a drinker. He was good for a couple of social pints from time to time, but he had never been the type to power through half a dozen cans and the better part of a bottle of Ardbeg. He was not looking forward to waking up in the morning. It had been years since he had been badly hungover, and this one was going to be a beast.

That was tomorrow's problem – right now he had a bone to pick with Albert. He closed his eyes tight, and breathed deeply, trying to clear the fog.

When he opened his eyes, he wasn't alone. His older, and very dead, brother, Oliver, was standing on the path in front of him.

Julian pressed the palms of his hands against his temples and shut his eyes.

"Not now," he said, working to control his breathing. "Not. Now."

He opened his eyes, but his brother was still there.

"Fuck off! Fuck off!"

Julian picked up a stone from the street and hurled it viciously at the spectre.

"Not! NOW!"

Oliver reached out, as though to hold Julian, his face a torrent of emotion.

"I SAID NOT NOW!" Julian roared, almost becoming unhinged as the full weight of his anger towards Albert swelled within him.

With a pained look, Oliver faded away.

Julian looked around for signs that anyone had heard or seen him. He was alone. The last thing he needed was for Nick Eden to hear about him drunk and ranting on the High Street.

Julian had taken his meds, but the drinking must have muddled things. He couldn't remember any specific warnings, but he doubted that any doctor had ever suggested that a patient "take two of these, before bed, with as much booze as you can stomach."

If he was seeing Oliver, he was in more trouble than just being drunk. He had not seen his brother for a few years, and he had begun to hope that the hallucinations of his brother's bloodied body were finally a thing of the past.

He felt as though everything was falling apart. He kicked at a discarded can, sending it angrily skittering across the road. With a grunted "fuck me" he followed it and crossed the street to the museum.

In the middle of the road, he stopped. His brother was standing in front of the museum door, both hands held up, his head shaking, as if in warning.

"These visions of your brother, Oliver, when do you have them?" Dr. Harkness asked gently.

"When I'm sad, or scared, or when I feel alone," Julian whispered.

"Does it scare you, when you see him?"

"No. I'm not scared of him."

"When did you first see him? Was it right after the accident?"

"No, they started when we moved to Sweet Little Chittering."

"Ah," mumbled Dr. Harkness, nodding, "change." She tilted her head, taking note of the body language of this troubled young boy. He had been through a terrible trauma, of that there was no question, and these visions he was having were an important part of his healing. There was a lot for this child to unpack, survivor guilt was never easy.

"Oliver was very good to you, wasn't he?"

"He looked after me."

There it was. She needed to remove his reliance upon Oliver, but it wasn't enough to simply take the visions away, that would cause more problems than it solved. She needed to give the boy an understanding of what Oliver was, not a ghost but a part of himself, a reflection of his own conscience.

She needed to help the boy understand that these visions were not a haunting but manifestations of his own feelings.

"Does Oliver ever speak to you?"

"No. His mouth moves, sometimes, but I can't hear the words."

"What do you think he is trying to tell you?"

Julian stared at Oliver, this time the meaning behind his appearance was simple. Julian's subconscious might as well have hung a sign over the museum door: GO HOME, JULIAN, YOU'RE DRUNK.

Home, he thought as he looked past Oliver to the museum. When his mother had first moved them here, she had said, "I have a feeling about this place, Julian, it's like something wants us to be here. I'd never even heard about it till I stopped at the inn for lunch. But I know that we are meant to be here."

Sweet Little Chittering had never felt that way for him, though meeting Albert had done more than help. The times he had spent in the museum with Albert, talking to him, learning from him, had transformed the village from a place where his mother and he "could make a new start" to a place he could try to think of as home.

That legacy further undercut the anger he was trying to cultivate, and he very nearly spun on his heel and fled back to his house. But that same legacy also compounded hurt and shame that had come with Albert's dismissive attitude towards him.

Going home and arguing with the rest of that

bottle of whisky instead of Albert was easily the right choice, but tonight was not a time for making the best of choices.

Julian stalked towards the door, and the apparition dissolved into the night. Gripping the handle, Julian stopped when realized it was unlocked. Albert never left the door unlocked, even when he was home.

"Seriously, it's like you're a completely different person," he snarled, pulling the door open and stepping into the hallway.

He drunkenly fumbled for the lights for a few moments but quickly gave up, opting instead for the light on his phone only to discover that had forgotten to charge it, and it was dead. But he knew which room Albert would be in.

Julian placed his left hand on the wall and began to pick his way as silently as he could through the darkness to the door that led to the largest of the museum's rooms, the one with the armchairs for reading and the stone fireplace. Albert never lit the fire, citing a problem with the chimney, and had used a small electric fire to heat the room instead. But that room and fireplace had always been special to Julian, and he fought to keep away the memories of nights spent sitting beside it, unlit and cold though it was, and listening to Albert reading Tolkien and the *Iliad*, *Gulliver's Travels*, *Robinson Crusoe*, *Treasure Island*, and so many more.

As he thought back on those magical evenings, his hand found the doorknob and he slowly opened the door.

***

As the last of the applause for the fireworks faded, Sarah Thomas left the fête and began to move along High Street, heading towards the museum. She was in a near panic over worry for Julian. She knew that her reputation in the town was that of a poor man's Lady Macbeth; the conniving wife pulling her husband's strings. There was nothing to be done about it, if there was one thing that she understood about small towns it was that they were fuelled by gossip. And gossip never cared about truth.

The few interactions she'd had at the fête, asking for Julian's whereabouts, would no doubt spark new rumours, and her concern over Julian being drunk would be misinterpreted as a fear of scandal. In truth, she was frightened that Julian might have harmed himself. Julian was a gentle and kind soul, but fragile, and haunted – not literally, of course, though he did "see" his dead brother when things were bad. His demons were volatile; he could quickly become broken, and all too easily plunged into darkness. She had been able to steady him, and he her to be fair, but she had felt that he was losing ground for some time now.

He had been doing so well, up until he became obsessed with this nonsense about the seven hundred and fifty years. He had not had an episode for years. But she had seen the signs, as old, troubling, behaviours had re-emerged. He had always struggled with a feeling that he was the reason his father and brother had died. It was irrational but unshakable. Several times over the last two weeks he had woken her by calling out his brother's name in his sleep, crying "I'm sorry, I'm sorry, I'm sorry." She had tried talking to him about it, but he could not remember having had any nightmares.

He had also started muttering and talking to himself more than usual; it was a habit of his, especially when he was writing and working through passages by talking them out. But she didn't think he was even aware that he was doing it.

She had debated mentioning all this to his doctor but had kept silent, hoping that things would get better. Then, this evening, she had come home to discover that he had been drinking, heavily. Fear that she had waited too long sped her steps as she raced along High Street.

The street was empty, and quiet, and the air felt unnaturally heavy and still. Even her footfalls seemed dull, and the normally sharp slap of her runners off the concrete sounded muted and distant. She slowed her pace. It was as though the world had stopped. She couldn't even hear the fête being packed up – and there was no sign of the notoriously boisterous and drunken post-fair revels that perennially rivalled the fireworks for explosive volume.

She stopped dead, frozen in place by shock. A translucent figure stood in the middle of the road.

She was looking at Julian's forever-to-be-sixteen-years-old brother, Oliver.

There was no moment of doubt, no questioning, this was no hallucination. Julian had not been imagining him. Oliver was real.

She had only ever seen photos of Oliver, the usual familial mixture of candid shots from birthdays and football matches alongside formal class photos from school. What was standing in front of her now looked nothing like the pictures.

Julian said that when he saw Oliver, he looked like he had come from the wreckage of the crash, bloodied, and injured. But he had never done justice to what that meant.

Julian had spoken of the blood-soaked white shirt and bloodied visage, but he had never mentioned the protruding bones in Oliver's right arm and left leg, nor the grotesquely distorted and twisted fingers, or collapsed collar bone, or the ruptured left eye, the broken jaw and torn and dangling left ear, or the crushed nose and broken teeth.

She covered her mouth with her hand to stifle a gagging cough, her mind drowning in thoughts of the horror of a terrified ten-year-old seeing this … thing.

Their eyes met, and she felt a devastating and helpless sadness emanating from Oliver.

Sarah went weak with terror; she was not upset by Oliver's ghostly, gore-soaked form; the dread that gripped her was born of what his appearance intimated.

Driven by fear, she sped through the spectre, gasping as though she had been splashed with freezing water, and ran as fast as she could to the museum.

***

"Albert," Julian slurred, "I need to talk to you …"

"Julian!? What the hell are you doing here?"

"There's no need to shout," Julian snapped, as he searched the wall for the light switch. "Why are you sitting in the dark?" he said, turning the lights on.

"Turn that off! Now!"

Albert's tone was so charged, so undeniable, that Julian dowsed the light before he had fully registered Albert's words. The darkness seemed even deeper now, after the retina-searing severity of the sudden light, and Julian closed and rubbed his eyes to ease them.

"Trust me, you should leave."

"Trust you? That's rich, Albert."

"You've been drinking."

"You think?"

"You smell like a distillery."

"What are you, my mother?"

"Go home."

"I'm angry. I want to talk."

"This isn't the time, Julian. Go home to Sarah. Sleep this off."

"Fuck that, Albert! I won't go home. I won't. I deserve an answer. You know I am right. I deserve an answer."

"This is about the seven hundred and fifty years?

Jesus Christ, Julian, it's just an excuse for a party, what is your problem?"

"You lied – to me – that's my problem."

"Go. Home," Albert said evenly. "Please, before it's too late."

"Too late? It's already too late. You heard the fireworks; the idiots are done celebrating. It's all over bar the public puking. Happy 750th to Sweet Little Chittering. But it's bullshit and you know it, Albert." The words began to flood out of him, spurred on by anger, alcohol, and the relief at finding Albert unhurt. "This town sent representatives to Simon de Montfort's Great Parliament in 1265, which means that the town must have already had an established reputation by that time – the kind of reputation that can only come with time. It's even in that book you made me read, by that professor, what's his name … Zytem! *The Sentinels*, the one about the henge."

"That book is more a local curiosity than reliable history."

"Fuck you, Albert. That's bullshit. That fragment of parchment, the one that they found in Lowestoft, Dr. Rash says it's at least as old, if not older, than *The Chronicle of Aethelweard.* Dr. Fucking Rash, Albert, you can deny me or Zytem all you want but you can't ignore her. You know you can't. This goddamn town can't be only seven hundred and fifty years old! Why won't you admit it? Tell me the truth!" There was a pause. "I need to sit down," Julian slurred. "I feel … sick."

"Then sit."

"It's fucking dark! I can't see the chair."

"It's in the middle of the room, right in front of me."

"Fuck, Albert, I can't see you either."

"It's right in front of you, just a few steps," said Albert.

Julian felt his way into the darkness, sweeping the floor with his feet like a soldier moving through a minefield or a parent crossing a child's Lego-strewn bedroom, till he found the small stool. The dark, emotion, and the alcohol combined to make his sitting no mean accomplishment.

"There, I'm sitting," he said, breathlessly, once he was sure he was not going to fall off the small seat. "Why this stool? Where's the armchair?"

"The stool was not meant for you. I am begging you, Julian, go."

"Not till I get some answers."

"Then you should start asking the right questions."

"What the hell is that supposed to mean?"

"You say you are looking for the truth?"

"Yes."

"The truth is all around you, you have walked with it, studied it, talked about it, lived within it, but you have never seen it."

"*Riddles in the Dark* now? That's where we are, is it? Why are the lights out? How did you even know it was me opening the door?"

"The dead do not need light to conduct their business."

"The dead …?"

"Truth is a complicated concern, Julian," Albert said, sounding distant and cold.

"Not as complicated as lies."

"Truth is rarely as simple as we wish, and never as important as we want it to be."

"Not important? How can you, of all people, say that the truth is not important? You run the fucking museum!" Julian shouted, standing, and raising his arms in the air in frustration. His right hand struck against something hanging from the ceiling.

"What's this?" he snarled, and the anger evaporated almost immediately as his fingers closed around the rough fibres unmistakably in the shape of a rope noose. Shock and sudden understanding very nearly sobered him up. A single thought emerged from the morass of alcohol and emotion: you can't kick away an armchair.

"*The dead do not need light to conduct their business.*"

Julian's heart sank. He had been so engrossed in his own petty issues for so long that he had completely misinterpreted Albert's behaviour over the last year, or more. The man was hurting, alone, sad, and desperate.

Julian opened his mouth to speak but held his tongue when he heard a noise in the hall.

"We're both out of time," Albert said sadly.

"Who is it? Who's coming?" Julian asked.

Julian turned; he did not hear the door open and could see no one, but he felt, with terrible certainty, that they were not alone.

Julian squinted, trying to follow what he thought

was movement. To his struggling senses, challenged by booze and darkness, it seemed that a deeper shadow – a deeper night – was reaching out for him. Compared to this, the darkness in the rest of room had form, weight, and texture, but what was moving towards him infested his senses with the brutal and unrelenting emptiness of eternity. Julian tried to back away but could not move.

Freezing cold, fleshless, fingers caressed his cheek, almost tenderly.

"How wonderful to meet you, Julian."

The voice was a woman's, lyrical and soft, but without a trace of warmth. Julian gasped as unseen hands gripped his face, drew him closer as though to kiss him. He felt as though his face was being pressed against stone.

A shocking cold burned his mouth and a spine of iced pain drove into his skull.

The right hand released him and traced a path across his cheek and down his neck, moving at the intimate pace and pressure of a tender lover. The hand pressed against his chest. Julian tried to resist, to cry out, but he couldn't, his breath caught in this throat, coming in short, strangulated gasps; his lungs felt as though the air within them was freezing solid.

"I can feel his heart, Ceolwulf," she sighed. "It beats with love and with life, as yours once did."

"Release him, Leofe," Albert said, and though he could not see him, Julian knew that the man was crying.

"I have tried, in life and in death-in-life, to find a

way to get you to do what you must," she sneered.

"What I *must*? What you *want*, you mean. After all this time, Leofe, do you really believe that I will ever do what you ask?"

"So, you will refuse me what is mine, again?"

"I will, my love."

"LOVE! You dare call me LOVE!"

"I do dare, Leofe. And I always shall."

"You have doomed me to this form and yet you cannot even bear to look upon me!"

"That is not true."

"You keep these meetings confined to darkness!"

"It is easier to see you in the dark."

"What does... what does that mean?" her voice betrayed a moment of confusion, and Julian felt the pain lessen.

"In the light, you are indistinct, and fragile, barely a whisper. In the dark, you stand out. I keep the lights off so that I can see you clearly."

"I cannot tell if that is love, or cowardice."

"It is both. Now, please, let Julian go. He is not supposed to be here."

"Oh, but he is, Ceolwulf."

"What do you mean?"

"You will not give me what I need, but perhaps... another might, with the proper leverage, of course."

"Julian has nothing to do with the henge – nothing to do with my oath!"

"This may surprise you Ceolwulf, but not everything is about you. Julian is here to test the strength of another oath."

"What oath?"
"Light the fire."
"What oath!?"
"Light the fire, it is time."

Leofe's hand moved from Julian's chest and gripped him by the throat, forcing him to his knees. Julian clawed at his throat, desperate to break her grip, desperate to breathe, but his hands found no purchase; he was scrabbling at air. As he felt himself slipping into unconsciousness, he heard Sarah calling his name.

***

A low hanging full moon lit the path through the trees, paving the way from the Weeping Stone all the way to the distant henge with its pale and hoary light. The light revealed a solitary figure, moving along the trail, heading towards the stone.

Ceolwulf was frantic with worry. His wife and children had not been seen since the early morning. He had searched far and wide, but no one had seen or heard of them. Then a voice, almost like that of Leofe's, had called to him and told him to go to the Weeping Stone.

When he neared the clearing, he saw a noose hanging from a branch of a tree that stood behind the Weeping Stone. A figure was kneeling before the Weeping Stone, lighting a fire in the hollow in its base.

"Welcome, Ceolwulf."
"Leofe! Where have you been?"

"Preparing the way." Her voice sounded wrong, distant, not unlike herself but something was out of place. She looked different too. He could not put his finger on it, but something was not right.

"What way?"

"Lighting the fire so that they might be free."

The fire caught, tall tendrils of flame sent sparks skyward and cast swaying shadows across the ground. Transfixed, Ceolwulf watched the flames. This fire was not like any he had ever seen. He had always felt that fire was alive, a being of infinite hunger and savagery that sought to feed and ravage; a creature that could be used if contained, but this flame was something else. This fire burned with intent.

"This is the fire of the demon Xaphan," Leofe said, her tone reverential, and awed. *"The fire that was to burn heaven. We have been offered at a chance at a gift, my love. If we are bold enough to take it."*

"What gift?"

"Eternal life."

"What are you talking about?

"This stone is the seal upon a lock that keeps them imprisoned in the Hill of Whispers. But once every hundred years their prison weakens, sometimes enough for a spirit to bleed across the boundary, but not always, and never enough for them to break free."

"I know the legend: on the Night of Storms, evil bleeds from the Hill of Whispers and into the world."

"Yes, and tonight is the Night of Storms."

"Stories, only stories. Look at the sky, Leofe, feel the air. There will be no storm tonight. We should go, this is not a place to be at night."

"Only stories? Then why are you afraid to be here in the dark?" Leofe sneered. "Once this stone is no more, the standing stones at the Hill of Whispers will fall, and then those imprisoned on that cursed ground will be free, all of them, and not merely a spirit or two, but all of them and whole, body and soul."

"Who?"

"The Fallen Ones; they fought a war for freedom from tyranny, and they lost. They were cast out and they fell from the heavens. Those who fell here were sealed within the hill."

"Leofe, please, come away, you are scaring me."

"This fire needs a soul so that it might burn hell hot and melt this stone. Your soul, Ceolwulf."

Ceolwulf looked at her, horrified.

"I have committed to the ritual, Ceolwulf. I have prepared the way, as the voices of the hill have instructed me. I have prepared the Weeping Stone. Now you must do your part, or we shall all be lost to you forever."

"Lost to me? What have you done? Leofe, I do not understand."

"You must cry."

"What?"

"Have you never wondered why it was called the Weeping Stone? I have wet the stones with the blood of the innocent; now you must wash it with *the tears of the sorrowful."*

"The blood of the ... where are our children? Leofe, what have you done?" he cried.

Leofe rose from the stone, and moved towards him, her feet drifting two feet above the ground, a shadow against the night sky.

"I told you, I have prepared the way, now it is up to you. Finish the ritual. Before heaven douses the flame with rain."

Ceolwulf collapsed to the ground as terror took the strength from his legs. The thing that floated towards him was his wife yet was not his wife. He could make no sense of this.

"You are not Leofe, you are a demon!"

The figure reached out and he gasped as her dead-cold fingers caressed his cheek.

"My love, I am she. They have given me part of the gift. I have taken the darkness, now you must offer the light of your soul to balance it all out."

"You MURDERED our CHILDREN?!"

"It was necessary to bind you to this; all that remains is for you to complete the ritual. Cry upon the stone and then hang yourself. It is simple. Then you and me and our children will be together for all time," she said as she rose into the night, cruciform against the moon.

"I will not be a part of this."

"The ritual has begun; it must be finished! If not tonight, then in one hundred years! I have made you a part of this! You will never be free of this! You will do as I ask. Would you not die to protect me from harm? How is this different, my love? Am I not

worth the sacrifice?"

"I will never do as you ask. I swear to you. I will not be a part of this."

He stood, and tore away through the night, scrambling along the path.

***

"Julian!" Sarah called his name over and over as she felt her way through the dark hallway to the backroom. She found the handle and pulled the door open. Her eyes took in the scene in an instant: a fire blazed, in the fireplace that was never lit, tended by Albert. A noose hung from a beam in the ceiling, and Julian was on his knees, being choked by a wraith.

"Julian!" she cried, lunging towards him.

"You swore an oath to this man, did you not, Sarah?" Leofe said in a cruel whisper.

"An oath?"

"You made wedding vows?"

"I did," Sarah nodded.

"And do you love him?"

"Leofe, her tears are not my tears, this will not change things. This will not bring our children back," Albert pleaded.

"Silence! You know nothing. This is not about our children; they are lost to time. This is about ME! You have lived a life, many lives over and over and over, washed clean by the rain on the Night of Storms, made young again, the memory of you erased from the minds of these fools, while I have existed as less than nothing for centuries! The stone requires tears, the fire needs a soul. You will not return my life to me; you cannot return the lives of my children to me! But I can still free those in the hill. And then they will give me my vengeance on you."

"They are deceiving you still, Leofe, as they have always done."

"Enough husband. Your time in this is past. Sarah, were I to kill this man, this Julian, would you cry?"

Sarah nodded.

"And if I told you that there was a way to bring him back – would you?"

Sarah nodded again. With a blinding motion, Leofe produced a stone knife in her left hand and plunged it into Julian's heart.

Sarah screamed.

"Now Sarah," Leofe said, letting Julian's body drop to the floor. "Stand by the fire and let your tears fall on the stone."

"Don't, Sarah," Albert begged, reaching out to her. Leofe grabbed him by the hair and pulled him away from the fire. Sarah screamed again.

"DO IT!" Leofe screeched. Sarah moved towards the fireplace. Her tears fell, a complex mixture of sorrow and fear, and hissed on the heated stone of the fireplace.

"Now, Sarah. The noose. Give your soul to the fire."

Through tear blurred eyes, Sarah saw Oliver's ghost standing before her.

"My god," muttered Albert, cringing at the sight of Oliver's broken body.

"You should not be here!" cried Leofe.

Oliver looked at Sarah, and down at Julian's body, then touched his hand to his heart and dove headlong into the fire. The fire exploded as though someone had thrown petrol on it. The blast threw Sarah back and knocked her to the ground next to Julian's body. Weeping, she reached out and touched his face. Sarah looked towards the fire. The flames burned white and hot, and the stone of the fireplace glowed with a golden light.

"The fire was not for him!" Leofe screeched in a shrill voice ripe with panic and hatred.

The fire flashed again, and Oliver appeared, fighting to free himself from the flames. Clawed hands reached out from the fire and pulled him back in. The fire began to burn hotter and whiter.

"Hah!" cried Leofe. "An honest soul, a brave soul – willing to try but not strong ENOUGH! This can't be stopped now. Give your soul to the fire, Sarah!" Leofe screamed, pointing to the noose. "Save Julian!"

Sarah closed her eyes and covered her ears as Leofe's screams resonated painfully through the room. The fire roared and raged like an animal caught in a leg trap.

"What… what's happening?" Sarah whimpered, and then jumped as thunder tore through the sky, shaking the museum's foundations. A torrential rain began to fall. The flames in the fireplace hissed and sputtered as the rain poured in down the chimney.

"NO!" Leofe begged.

Sarah turned to look at her just as the wraith dissipated like smoke in a strong breeze.

"Well, this is... different," Albert said as he decayed from flesh to dust right in front of her.

Sarah's mind was a reeling mass of dismay, shock, and terror. Nothing made sense, but through the confusion one thought kept repeating over and over:

"Give your soul to the fire, Sarah. Save Julian."

She looked down at Julian's body and then at the fire. It was barely hanging on, the flames writhing like a nest of dying worms against the deluge that beat down upon it. Mechanically, moving as though without thought, she climbed up and placed the noose around her neck.

"Give your soul to the fire, Sarah. Save Julian."

She kicked the stool away.

The stone at the heart of the fireplace cracked and the flames roared back to life. In the distance, the stones of the henge began to fall, one by one.

Epilogue

Major Charlotte 'Charlie' Drake stretched her back and rubbed the nape of her neck. It had been a very long day and it didn't look like ending anytime soon. Light rain tapped gently on the canvas shelter above.

"Okay, let's start with you, Porter." She turned to look at her three colleagues; Lance Corporal Rebecca Cole, Lieutenant Arthur Mortimer, and John Porter, a civilian advisor assigned to her team at her own request. All of them had been selected because they were 'elite and discreet', and they had to be. The work they did was better kept from the public eye, believing in ghosts and ghouls was one thing, *knowing* they were real was another. People were safer not knowing what was truly happening in the darkest corners of their world. When the darkness seeped out, Drake and her team mopped it up.

Porter adjusted his spectacles. "Yet to identify the plants. They're like nothing I've come across before."

"Alien space pods?" Cole smiled weakly attempting to bring some levity to proceedings.

"Possibly," said Porter, completely missing the point. "We've secured some samples and incinerated the rest."

"It was like a scene from that Leonard Nimoy film," said Mortimer. "We all saw it."

"I preferred the original," said Cole.

"I'm not talking about the film, we all *saw* what

was in that blasted village," snapped Mortimer.

"I think Bex knows what you meant, Arthur. Let's keep our tempers, eh?" Drake spoke with more calm in her voice than she knew she had. "We're all very tired but losing our heads will not help us."

Mortimer raised an apologetic hand to Cole, who nodded and waved it away as she felt there was nothing to apologise for.

"Bex?" Drake turned her attention to Lance Corporal Cole.

"We recovered two crashed cars on the road to Hartbridge, one of which was burnt out. The stones at the henge have fallen. We found what looks like a human sacrifice…"

"Probably the Morris dancers," said Mortimer, "never trusted Morris dancers."

"The museum…the whole village…we're still gathering information, but it's a mess. It wasn't just a single event last night, we have evidence that suggests it was a…well, a shit storm," Cole finished.

Drake looked to Mortimer.

"I have a young boy who shot the man who killed his father. He's traumatised. He somehow grabbed an item from his father's killer's possessions and won't let it go. The freaky bit is, it's the front page of a newspaper. Today's paper. But the page is old. Years old and I've checked that paper, today's headline is very different," said Mortimer.

"What was the headline?" Porter leaned forward.

"It was about the murder of his father, but the actual headline today is about the storm and mysterious catastrophe at the village."

"It's not a mock-up?" Cole said.

"I know a mock-up when I see one, this was genuine," said Mortimer, slightly offended he even had to state it.

"What's the explanation then?" Drake said.

Mortimer shrugged; he had no explanation.

"Time travel?" suggested Porter.

"Why not? We have alien space pods," said Cole.

"After that tower block, I'm open to anything," said Mortimer. The tower block had been mind-blowing. It's what had brought the unit together. Clean up, cover up and work at stopping it happening again.

"Anything else?" Drake perched herself on the side of a desk.

"The cleaners from the inn refuse to co-operate without a lawyer. They have the foulest mouths I have ever encountered, but I think they may have something to do with those wrecked cars. The inn's owner is far too calm and helpful for my liking. I can't put my finger on it, but I don't like him. The wrong vibes. The priest too." Mortimer really disliked the priest.

"What about the priest?" Drake wondered.

"Dead eyes," said Mortimer. "That's no man of God. He and Eden, the inn owner, seem to be very close. Like old friends, but ones that hung around with Charles Manson for a bit of a laugh."

The group sat quietly for a minute, listening to the rain as they tried to soak in what had occurred in Sweet Little Chittering.

"Let's clean this all up as quickly as we can. How many villagers are left?" Drake said finally.

"A dozen or so," replied Mortimer.

"Does that make them a hamlet now, then?" Cole asked jokingly, but it didn't land well in the room.

"Okay," Drake took a breath. "Officially it was a gas mains explosion. Say the fumes affected the survivors. Get that kid into therapy, get the man he killed onto an autopsy table - find out where or *when* he's from. Put some pressure on those cleaners, find out what they are guilty of and keep eyes on everyone else, especially the inn owner and the priest. Somebody knows what happened, let's see if we can find them."

Mortimer, Cole and Porter nodded and got to their feet.

"And be careful," smiled Drake. "Please." Drake thought she'd seen the deepest depths of the dark, but she was quickly realising they had barely scratched the surface.

"Will do," said Porter.

"Let's get to work," Drake pushed herself upright. She knew it'd be a long time before any of them were going to see their beds and, even then, she very much doubted any of them would be able to sleep. She didn't sleep much anymore, not since Castle Heights, and when she did, she was plagued by nightmares. They all were. And those nightmares were real.

Also from Red Cape Publishing

Anthologies:

Elements of Horror Book One: Earth
Elements of Horror Book Two: Air
Elements of Horror Book Three: Fire
Elements of Horror Book Four: Water
A is for Aliens: A to Z of Horror Book One
B is for Beasts: A to Z of Horror Book Two
C is for Cannibals: A to Z of Horror Book Three
D is for Demons: A to Z of Horror Book Four
E is for Exorcism: A to Z of Horror Book Five
F is for Fear: A to Z of Horror Book Six
G is for Genies: A to Z of Horror Book Seven
H is for Hell: A to Z of Horror Book Eight
I is for Internet: A to Z of Horror Book Nine
J is for Jack-o'-Lantern: A to Z of Horror Book Ten
K is for Kidnap: A to Z of Horror Book Ten
It Came From The Darkness: A Charity Anthology
Castle Heights: 18 Storeys, 18 Stories

Short Story Collections:

Embrace the Darkness by P.J. Blakey-Novis
Tunnels by P.J. Blakey-Novis
The Artist by P.J. Blakey-Novis
Karma by P.J. Blakey-Novis
The Place Between Worlds by P.J. Blakey-Novis
Home by P.J. Blakey-Novis
Short Horror Stories by P.J. Blakey-Novis
Short Horror Stories Vol. 2 by P.J. Blakey-Novis
Keep It Inside & Other Weird Tales by Mark Anthony Smith
Something Said by Mark Anthony Smith
Everything's Annoying by J.C. Michael
Six! by Mark Cassell
Monsters in the Dark by Donovan 'Monster' Smith

Novelettes:
The Ivory Tower by Antoinette Corvo

Novellas:
Four by P.J. Blakey-Novis
Dirges in the Dark by Antoinette Corvo
The Cat That Caught The Canary by Antoinette Corvo
Bow-Legged Buccaneers from Outer Space by David Owain Hughes
Spiffing by Tim Mendees

Novels:
Madman Across the Water by Caroline Angel
The Curse Awakens by Caroline Angel
Less by Caroline Angel
Where Shadows Move by Caroline Angel
Origin of Evil by Caroline Angel
The Broken Doll by P.J. Blakey-Novis
The Broken Doll: Shattered Pieces by P.J. Blakey-Novis
The Vegas Rift by David F. Gray
South by Southwest Wales by David Owain Hughes
Appletown by Antoinette Corvo

Art Books:
Demons Never Die by David Paul Harris & P.J. Blakey-Novis

Children's Books:
Grace & Bobo: The Trip to the Future by Peter Blakey-Novis
My Sister's from the Moon by Peter Blakey-Novis
Elvis the Elephant by Peter Blakey-Novis
The Little Bat That Could by Gemma Paul
The Mummy Walks At Midnight by Gemma Paul
A Very Zombie Christmas by Gemma Paul